STEPS

FINDING THEIR MUSE - BOOK ONE

BEA PAIGE

GRITTY, ANGSTY, DANGEROUS ROMANCE

STEPS

To Sergei Polunin, for being my muse.
To Courtney and Janet for always believing in me.
Steps is dedication to you three especially.
Bea Paige xx

PROLOGUE

Ivan

STANDING in the dimly lit dance studio, bare chested, covered in a sheen of sweat I wonder if I'll ever be able to see myself differently from the broken man before me. Whether I'll see someone other than the man who no longer burns with passion, but with a very real hate for everyone and everything, including himself.

The low bass of the music vibrates through the shiny wooden floor and up through my bare feet. Dark bruises already flare over my chest and back, colouring my olive skin a shade darker.

I've already pushed myself too far, but it isn't enough. It never will be.

The memories of her...

I squeeze my eyes shut and let the music wash over me. I

push away everything but the sound of the music as it blasts out of the speakers and concentrate on the feel of the floor beneath my feet as I run across it. I ignore the blisters, the warm slickness of blood as the torn soles of my feet bleed. I ignore the scream of my muscles as they protest at the abuse.

I'm not even sure how long I've been in here torturing myself. An hour, two? More? All I know is that the physical pain from the exercise blocks the other kind. The kind that fucking haunts every waking moment of my life.

Today, would've been our eight-year anniversary.

Instead it's two years since she's been gone. This very room, where I bleed now, is where her heart bled out. A knife to her wrist.

I was too late to save her. I was too fucking late.

In the centre of the studio, I can still see the stain of her despair, a dark shadow pooling across the floor. No amount of scrubbing has been able to get it out.

So, this is all I can do. I add my blood to hers now and in some sick, twisted way, I feel close to her.

Even when I slam my body into the wall, I feel close to her.

Her pain and mine intermingled forever.

Another kind of dance to the one we used to share.

I can no longer use this room as it was originally intended. I will never dance again.

It's no longer my sanctuary but a place to come and torture myself. A place to remind me that I can never be happy again, not whilst there's breath still in my body.

The room is still beautiful, with high vaulted ceilings and windows set above the mahogany panels that make up three of the four walls. The fourth is covered in a run of mirrors, the soft wood of the barre running along its length. The same barre her delicate hand would move across, perfect white alabaster skin against the darkened wood.

Ten years ago, I had the grand hall of the manor converted into this dance studio for my wife.

Back then, we would dance here together. Prima ballerina and principal dancer, a match made in ballet heaven.

Until she took her life, that is.

Svetlana and I would make love on the bare wooden floor, our ballet shoes and clothes discarded like scattered petals across the vast hall. This room held our love once. Now it is filled with despair and twisted moments of pain.

I slam into the wall so hard that the wooden panel splits under the impact, a shard of wood embeds itself in my skin. But I don't stop. I can't.

This is my punishment.

This is where I come to remind myself why I must never dance again. Why I am not worthy of anything or anyone but the pain I choose to inflict on myself.

I crave pain now.

Svetlana is gone because of me. She would be alive today if I hadn't betrayed her.

Slamming my fist into the wall, making the dent I'd made with my body even wider, I scream until my lungs burn.

I drove my wife into the deepest pits of hell. I deserve every second of torture.

Turning my back on the hole I've made, I lean against the wall until my feet can no longer hold me up. Sliding to the floor, I collapse into a heap. Sweat drips from my chin, falling against my bare chest.

Even after all this time the tears don't come, just the empty hollow of loss and the swirling pit of grief. It takes me a long time to calm myself enough to do what I must.

Across the room from me, tied to a wooden chair with swathes of red silk is a woman. I'd almost forgotten about her.

Almost.

Her eyes are pressed shut, her scarlet lips parted on a rapid breath. Her chest is heaving with anticipation, with fear? Probably both.

That's why she's here after all. She wants domination. She needs to feel alive, just as much as I do.

And I'm going to fuck her until all thought leaves her mind.

This woman is another one of the many who've passed through these doors on my search to fill the void that sits like a chasm within my chest. My addiction to the sins of the flesh is what got me into this mess, and what keeps me from being free.

I see the pink slash of her pussy pressed against the hard wood of the chair. Her full breasts and tight nipples, as hard as marbles. She's been in this room with me before. She knows what to expect and her physical reaction to me tells me she is more than ready to be mine.

I both want her and despise her for what she represents.

My wife is dead because of my sins, because of my craving for something darker than her sweetness was able to give. It should've been enough, and it was for a while.

I loved her... but there was something I needed, and it was something she was unwilling to give. So, I sought it out elsewhere.

I'm a bastard. I know that, I've accepted that.

I can't fight the demon inside of me. No amount of physical

pain will ever quell the desire in my heart. After all, my wife's pain didn't stop me. So, I seek out my other release hoping that one day it will be enough.

I get up on unsteady legs, my cock painfully hard, and pull off my trousers. The silky material pools to the floor. Stepping out of them, my cock falls free, seemingly the only part of my body not covered in purple bruises.

"One word, that's all I need," I say, stalking towards the nameless woman on the other side of the room.

I watch as her cheeks flush. The pink of her tongue wets her bottom lip in anticipation. But I never kiss these women. That's too personal. There's too much emotion in a kiss.

I fuck them. I dominate them. I take everything they're able to give, and they all give it willingly.

Stopping before her, I slide my finger along the curve of her breast.

"Say it," I murmur.

A smile plays across the lips of this woman whose name I do not know. Even though she's been here before, I don't know anything about her life. But I do know every curve of her body, every moan and sigh. I know where she likes to be touched, licked, caressed. I know her limits, I know what makes her pussy twitch with pleasure. I know what scares her but thrills her at the same time. This nameless woman who comes alive beneath my hands is mine to play with.

I'm going to fuck her until I get the release I so crave, those few seconds where nothing but the potency of my orgasm fills every thought. Where neither my past nor my future is clear and only the present takes control. Where I find peace.

"Say it," I demand, grasping her chin and making her look at me. Heavy-lidded, deep blue eyes gaze back. There is fear in them, but excitement too. I can smell it.

Her mouth parts, she pulls against the constraints. A single word falls from her lips...

"Brisé..."

CHAPTER ONE

Rose

PLACING my hand against my pounding head, I groan loudly. The bottle of red wine I drank by myself last night probably wasn't the best idea I've ever had.

"Way to go, Rose, just what you need on the morning of your interview," I say to myself.

The digital clock next to my bed is flashing eight forty-five am. I have less than an hour to get ready and up to Browlace Manor, and given my car died its final death last week, I'm going to have to walk. That's a good mile on an unseasonably cold September morning. Thanks goodness it's Saturday tomorrow. I can sleep in without feeling guilty.

Ripping back my duvet cover I stumble from my bed, instantly regretting moving so quickly as a sharp spasm almost cripples me. I bite down on my lip, trying to override the arthritic pain in my hips and lower back with the sharp cut of my teeth. It doesn't work.

I stretch my hand out, resting it on the chest-of-drawers next to me and fight the overwhelming need to throw up. Being hungover and in pain isn't the best combination frankly.

Drawing in deep breaths I slowly straighten my back, ignoring the agony I feel and hating that my body has betrayed me yet again. Most days I feel as though I am ninety years old, not a woman of thirty.

Fuck this body of mine.

My eyes catch the pair of satin ballet shoes hanging from a hook on the back of my bedroom door, a constant reminder of my past. They are well worn, the platform dirty, the ribbons frayed. It has been over a year since I wore them last. A lifetime in the ballet world.

Even if I were fit, it's highly unlikely the company would take me back. Most ballet dancers retire in their mid-thirties having started their career around nineteen.

The cruel reality is, I'll never be able to dance again, professionally or otherwise.

Sighing, I haul myself upright with as much grace as an ex-ballet dancer with arthritis can muster. I refuse to call myself disabled, even though that's what my doctor had implied. He'd been so matter of fact about my condition. There was no breaking it to me gently. Even now, those words still sting.

"Your body is tired, Rose. I'm afraid your blood tests show a high rheumatoid factor. I'd advise against continuing to dance because this condition isn't going away. There are no drugs that can cure it, only ones that can help alleviate the pain and inflammation around your joints. You have an autoimmune disease.

Even if you weren't a ballet dancer, it would've happened anyway. As it is, the physical stress you've put your body under may well have contributed to it developing earlier. I'm sorry, if you ignore what I have to say you will be in a wheelchair with no hope of ever dancing again, even for pleasure."

At the time I'd refused to believe it was true, returning to the company without giving them the full picture. The doctor had been right of course. Six months after my diagnosis I had been asked to leave the company for 'my best interests' after messing up on stage when my knee had given way beneath me. Another six months on, here I am living in my family home in a quaint village in Cornwall, burning a hole in my inheritance.

Home? This place isn't my home. I feel sick waking up here most days. The memories embedded in the bricks and mortar haunting me daily. If I had a choice I would leave this place and never come back. The first thing I did was take down the photos of my parents and burn them when I returned. It was satisfying for all of ten minutes, but the memories I have, they can't be disintegrated so easily.

Dad had passed when I was a teenager, and my Mum two years ago of a sudden illness. I can't say I miss either of them very much, but right now that's a wound I'd rather not pick.

I haul arse into the shower, wash myself as quickly as my aching joints will allow and get dressed. Less than twenty minutes later I'm as presentable as I can be in a knee length, black skirt and red silk shirt. Pulling on a pair of boots and thick woollen overcoat, I head out in the dank Cornish air and make my way, hopefully, to a future that is probably about as exciting as working in the local library. Not that I have anything against libraries, on the contrary. It's just that the one in my village consists of a few dog-eared classics and a dozen or so Mills & Boon books for the racier villager. I've read all the books, three time over now. They really need to get a better collection.

"Morning, Rose. Going out somewhere nice?" Mrs Samson calls from the front step of her house. She's smoking a pipe, a strip of her grey hair yellowed from the nicotine.

"That's right," I respond, not willing to give her, or the rest of the village, any more gossip. Since I've returned home, my name has been on everyone's lips. The local girl turned star, turned cripple. The girl whose past *still* has the ability to ruin her future. All the whispered talk remains, even years after his death.

"Going somewhere nice?" she persists, interrupting my dark thoughts.

I stop at her gate, an ingrained politeness forcing me to respond.

"An interview, Mrs Samson."

She looks at me, her beady eyes narrowing with interest. "Interview you say?"

"That's right. I must be off, or I'll be late," I say quickly, pretending I don't hear her next question as I rush off down the lane and towards my destination.

It takes me another forty minutes to reach the sprawling grounds of Browlace Manor.

The cold air has already settled in my joints, making my body stiffen further. I know my condition enough to know that if I don't get into the warm soon then I will be in bed for a week straight. The ease and grace that I was once accustomed to is less and less apparent these days. I'm like the Tin Man from the

Wizard of Oz, in desperate need of lubrication to loosen my rigid muscles and ease my painful joints.

Frankly, if you'd told me at the start of my dancing career that by the age of thirty I'd be crippled and about to willingly spend the rest of my life as an assistant to some wealthy aristocrat, I would've laughed. As it is, I'm desperate for this job. Desperate enough to yank myself out of the depths of depression that has plagued me every day since I returned home. It still hangs over me like a dark cloud threatening to unleash its wrath but, for today at least, it's under control enough so that I can make it through this interview. *Happy pills*, as my mother used to say, taking the edge off. I hate that phrase. These pills don't make me happy, they make me *even*. Just.

Stepping up to the main entrance, I ring the doorbell. From inside I can hear the sound of footsteps against a stone floor. A few seconds later the door swings open and an attractive woman in her mid-seventies smiles warmly at me even as her hazel eyes assess me astutely. She doesn't ask me who I am or why I'm here, she simply waits. It's unnerving. Realising she isn't going to start the conversation anytime soon, I fill the strange silence.

"I'm here about the job. My name is Rosemary Gyvern. Rose for short," I ramble.

"Indeed," she says, cocking her eyebrow. "You'd better come in."

She moves aside, pulling the door wide as I step into the entrance hall. A cold blast of air lifts the dark tendrils of my hair against my cheek as she closes the door behind us.

"Mr Sachov isn't here to take the interview, but he has entrusted me to ensure the right person is hired for the job.

Please, follow me," she says, striding off towards a door at the other side of the hall.

"Oh, okay. That's perfectly fine, Mrs..." I start, realising she hasn't introduced herself.

"*Ms* Hadley. I am the housekeeper here at Browlace Manor. I have looked after the Sachov family for most of my adult life. I know all there is to know about these men and their... ways."

"Men?"

"Sorry?" she says, looking at me with confusion.

"You said men."

She shakes her head, plastering on a broad smile. "No, I didn't," she replies, and something about the way she looks at me prevents me from challenging her.

"I must've misheard..." I mumble, biting my tongue, my upbringing successfully curbing my insatiable need to know everything.

Nosy, that's what my mother had called me. Inquisitiveness was not appreciated in my family. Too many secrets to be kept hidden for that personality trait to be encouraged.

"I trust you've read the job description and you understand what is required of you?" she asks, barely turning to look at me.

I nod my head, even though I'm still trailing behind her and she can't see my response. Ms Hadley is surprisingly sprightly for someone her age. I feel suddenly inadequate with my achy and swollen joints.

"Yes, I've read the job description. Mr Sachov needs a personal assistant to help him manage his affairs."

"That's right," she says, stopping in front of a door on the other side of the hall.

I almost walk into her back, not expecting her to stop

moving so abruptly. I watch as she pulls out a set of iron keys. They chink heavily against one another. She pulls one free, puts it in the lock and turns. It strikes me as odd, that the door is locked. Who locks *internal* doors?

A sense of foreboding scatters over my skin.

"Ivan is very particular about the doors remaining locked when he's not home. We were broken into once and a lot of personal items were stolen. I abide by his rules. Everyone does," she says by way of explanation.

"Sure, rules are important," I respond, thinking her weirder by the minute.

Ms Hadley seems to like my response, because she looks over her shoulder at me and smiles brightly. It changes her face dramatically. From stern and aloof, to warm and welcoming. I relax a little.

"This way please," she says.

I follow her through the door and into a dimly lit corridor on the other side. At the far end is another door, and two on either side of the corridor. We enter the one on the right. I'm pretty sure I can hear a violin being played from behind the furthest door away, but Ms Hadley ushers me into the small office and shuts the door before I can be certain.

"You can hang your coat and bag on the hook over there, then take a seat. I have some questions to ask you," Ms Hadley says, pointing to a coat rack.

I do as she asks, pulling off my woollen coat and hanging it alongside my bag. My skirt has ridden up a little because it's so close fitting, and I have to pull it down to a more respectable length. I'm kind of glad Mr Sachov isn't the one to interview me, given he would have seen more than I'd bargained for.

Turning around, I find Ms Hadley watching me closely from her seat behind the oak desk. Her eyes trail up from my feet to my face. That same astute look reappearing in her eyes as she takes her measure of me. I feel my cheeks flush under her gaze. Why do I suddenly feel like I'm a broodmare being sized up for mating?

"Sit, please," she says, holding her hand out and pointing to the chair opposite her.

I take a seat and fold my hands in my lap, crossing my legs at the ankles. I may be a disabled ex-dancer, but today, it seems, I can still just about manage to be graceful despite my long walk in the cold. Years of good posture from dancing is still ingrained in me despite my medical condition that tries daily to twist my body into something less than perfect.

Ms Hadley takes it all in, her eyebrows rising minutely. She seems a little... surprised that I'm sitting like a lady, or perhaps it's something else entirely, I'm not sure. Whatever the reason, my palms become sweaty, and it isn't because of the heat from the open fire.

"What makes you think you'd be a good personal assistant to Ivan... Mr Sachov," she corrects herself.

I lock eyes with her, glad to be back to safer territory. I'm here for an interview, I can answer these questions. Being scrutinised like she's looking into my very soul, I'm not so keen on. I should be used to it. As a ballet dancer my technique, my ability to dance effortlessly was studied continuously when I was in the Royal Ballet. I could be utterly exhausted and in pain, but if I didn't dance with perfection every single time, then there was always someone ready to take my spot. It's a wonder my *disability* wasn't spotted sooner. I guess I'm an expert at hiding. There's a kind of irony in that given my past.

"Miss Gyvern. I asked you a question," Ms Hadley says tersely, successfully drawing me out of more dark memories that threaten to break free.

"Yes, sorry..." I mumble, trying to bide some time.

"What attributes do you have that would make you suitable for this job?" she asks once again. The question is phrased slightly differently but the answer I have is still the same.

I straighten in my seat and look her in the eye. Bethany at the recruitment agency said that maintaining eye contact in an interview is extremely important. So even though I want to look away from her gaze, I don't.

"I'm very organised. I have good interpersonal skills. I'm a great timekeeper. I can type fifty words per minute, I understand confidentiality is extremely important and I will remain professional with all personal matters that might arise. I work hard, and am available to start as soon as possible," I reel off without taking a breath.

These are all the things my recruitment officer at the agency suggested I say. The truth is it's all lies, well, except maybe keeping things confidential. I know what it's like being on the receiving end of gossip, I certainly wouldn't dream of sharing any personal matters with anyone. Not that I have anyone to share anything with. My cat, Bud, doesn't count. Uncrossing my ankles and lifting my leg to place it over the other, I wait for the next question.

Ms Hadley purses her lips. Her eyebrows pinch together, and she sniffs loudly. I almost ask if she'd like a tissue, but then realise her reaction isn't from a cold, but from distaste.

"Did I say something wrong?" I blurt out, unable to help myself.

Ms Hadley stands abruptly and holds her hand out for me to shake.

"Thank you for coming," she says sharply.

I get to my feet, shock and disappointment propelling me upwards. I don't reach for her hand, instead I cross my arms over my chest defensively.

"That's it? I've come all this way to answer one question?" I can't help the sharpness in my voice. Despite the warmth of the fire, my joints are beginning to ache. Walking here had been a mistake, coming here at all an even bigger one it would seem. What a waste of time.

"You're not what we're looking for," she says. Her voice is level, without an ounce of sympathy in it.

"And you know that by the answer to *one* question?" I respond, blanching.

"Mr Sachov is very particular. Please, if you wouldn't mind..." She moves around the table and gathers my coat and bag from the rack.

"I don't believe this," I say, anger marking my words now.

She doesn't respond, merely passes my coat and bag to me. I snatch them from her, wincing as my fingers curl around the material. I don't need to look at my fingers to know the joints are swollen.

"What's wrong?" she asks abruptly, her eyes flicking from my face to my hands.

"I don't have to answer that, given the interview is already over," I snap, yanking on my jacket even though it hurts me to do so. I sling the strap of my bag over my shoulder and glare at her.

"You're in pain. Why is that?" she presses, stepping closer to me. I take a step back. Christ, this woman is creepy.

"That's none of your damn business."

She steps forward again and pulls at my hand, grasping it in hers. Her fingers run over the bulbous joints of my middle and fourth finger.

"You're sick," she says.

"I am *not* sick," I protest, snatching my hand back.

"What is wrong with you?"

I almost tell her to shove her questions up her arse, but then figure it makes no difference whether she knows the truth or not. Either way I haven't got the job.

"Rheumatoid arthritis..."

Her eyebrows inch closer to her hair line, whilst the cogs whirl in her head. I have zero clue what she's thinking or why she seems so interested in my health. All I want is to get out of this place as quickly as possible.

"But you seem so graceful," she mutters, almost to herself. The way she says graceful is just plain odd, as though it's a dirty word or something.

"You hold yourself like a dancer," she continues, her gaze roving over me once more.

"Ha! This body is incapable," I respond tightly. It's not a lie. I can't dance anymore. I won't ever dance properly again. But what the hell has dancing and my ability to move gracefully got to do with whether I get the job or not? This is all just weird.

"Well, if that's all?" I ask, turning on my feet and striding to the door. I pull it open, hissing through my teeth as another sharp pain lances through my finger joints and the small of my back.

"You start Monday, eight am sharp."

I stand still, one foot in the corridor, the other still in the room. Did she just offer me the job after all that? What the hell is happening here?

"Mr Sachov will return Wednesday. It's better you start before he arrives home. That way you can learn the ropes before he's back."

Turning to face Ms Hadley, I pull a face. "I don't understand. Have you just offered me the job, after turning me down just a moment ago?"

"Yes."

"Why?"

"Why doesn't matter. Do you want the job or not?" she asks.

I stare at her open mouthed, unsure what answer to give. Part of me wants to tell her to stuff the job up her scrawny backside. The other part needs the money.

"Well? Yes or no, Miss Gyvern?" She locks eyes with me a final time, the kind smile back again. This woman is completely nuts. I can only imagine what this Mr Sachov is going to be like if she's anything to go by.

"Yes," I say, finally.

"Good. I shall see you at eight am Monday morning." Her smile widens, and instead of making her look kinder and more approachable, it makes me shudder. I nod curtly then make my escape, the mournful sound of a violin being played following me out of the house.

CHAPTER TWO

Rose

AFTER A WEEKEND in bed watching Netflix and eating what's left of my pantry, I wake up at six am without the need for an alarm clock. Nerves, anxiety and a very real need to pee has me climbing out of bed. My knee joints are aching and my fingers throbbing, but rather than ignoring the pain, like I used to do, I stop and stretch out my limbs gently.

I know this could be a bad idea. That sometimes all my body needs is rest. That even stretching is potentially dangerous. But I can't be the Tin Man all the time, this is my way to keep my body lubricated. It's my way of saying fuck you to this condition I loathe.

Holding onto the chest-of-drawers to steady myself, I draw in a deep breath and raise my arms into first position. With my arms bent at the elbow, my palms facing me, the tips of my fingers a hands width apart and held opposite my navel I raise up onto the balls of my feet. Then, drawing in more deep breaths I prepare myself for the inevitable pain I know I will feel in my knees as I lower my heels to the ground then draw them together, turning my toes outwards. I pull in a sharp intake of breath as my knee joints groan under the pressure. Refusing to be defeated, I hold the position, the tenseness in my muscles slowly relaxing as I do.

"That's it, Rose, you can do this," I say softly.

For the last year I've been living with this pain. At first it was horrific, and I'd cry hopeless tears as I forced myself to work through it and dance. The damage I had done to myself in those first few months of denial almost crippled me. Now, I know better. When I relapse there's nothing to do but take the pills, rest, and hope that soon the inflammation will pass. I mean, the pain never really goes, but the levels of pain vary greatly day to day.

I've learnt to listen to my body far better now than I have ever done before. It's why I'm able to place my body in first position this morning, because I know, today, my body can take it.

I won't kid myself into thinking that I'll be dancing like I used too, but I can still maintain a little of my flexibility so long as I keep working with my body and not against it.

For a few minutes I work through each of the five positions slowly, allowing my body to form each pose as I stretch out my spine and loosen the tightness that has formed overnight from sleeping. Not only does it help me to keep as flexible as I can with this condition, but more than that, completing the basic ballet positions helps to ease my anxiety. It's a form of meditation, I suppose. Being without dance would kill me quicker than this physical pain ever will.

Eventually, my full bladder forces me to stop and I head into my en-suite to relieve myself. Then I step into the shower, the powerful jets of warm water helping to ease the lingering pain further. Today is a good day. I feel almost normal, at least as normal as I can be with the dull pain I live with constantly.

With a towel wrapped around my body and the smell of coconut shampoo in the air, I walk over to my wardrobe and survey my newly bought work attire. Ms Hadley hadn't mentioned what I should or shouldn't wear, but I figure smart over casual is a better guess. At least until she tells me otherwise, which I have no doubt she will, given her outspoken nature.

Grabbing a pair of smart black trousers, a cream silk shirt and flat shoes, I get dressed. A few minutes later my dark hair is dry, and my face made up with a dash of mascara and some clear lip gloss. One of the things I don't miss about dancing is having to cake my face in makeup. It took my skin ages to become blemish free after years of wearing thick layers of foundation and heavy powder. Now it's smooth and healthy looking. I even have a little natural colour in my cheeks. I suppose you could call it an English rose complexion but with my mother's dark hair and green eyes, a throwback to her Mediterranean heritage.

I brush my shoulder length hair, deciding to put it up in a bun rather than wear it down as it looks smarter that way, then head downstairs for a quick breakfast of tea and toast. At seven o'clock sharp I'm making my way up to Browlace Manor and towards my first day of work.

———————

"THIS WILL BE YOUR OFFICE," Ms Hadley says, unlocking the door to a huge room with two large desks facing each other from opposite sides of the space. The office would have been really dark given the wooden panels and maroon carpet had it not been for the floor to ceiling window allowing as much winter sunlight into the room.

"Will I get a key?" I ask, pointing to the one Ms Hadley is holding.

She nods towards the desk on the left-hand side of the window.

"In the top drawer you shall find three keys. One for this room, one for the corridor leading to this room and one for the front door. Everything else is locked unless Mr Sachov agrees you should have access. I'll leave that decision up to him."

"Sure, okay," I respond, not bothering to question the weird-ness of all the locked doors. Perhaps it's better that I don't know what's behind them.

"All the passwords you need to access the computer and Mr Sachov's files are in the notebook on your desk. I suggest you log on and familiarise yourself with the computer system," she says, pointing to my new desk.

"You're not staying?" I ask as Ms Hadley begins to back out of the door.

"No. I'm needed elsewhere. I shall come back in a couple of hours. I assume you've brought lunch?"

"Actually, no," I say, kicking myself at my stupidity.

Why hadn't I thought of bringing any food, it's not as if I'll be allowed to make myself a snack in their kitchen.

"Then I shall return at midday with something for both of us." Ms Hadley smiles kindly, throwing me off once again. I can't seem to figure her out.

"Thank you."

She nods her head and retreats, shutting the door behind her and leaving me to settle in.

Pulling off my coat and bag, I hang them on the coat rack then survey my new work space. The room is warm and though a little bare, it's beautiful. My desk is massive and made of solid, dark wood. It's surface shines as though recently polished and beneath the table are three deep drawers all of which are empty, bar the keys Ms Hadley mentioned. I pick them up, marvelling at the weight of the heavy iron.

Pulling out the leather chair, I take a seat and turn on the computer. The monitor lights up revealing the login screen. Grabbing the notebook on the desk, I flip it open and type in the password: La Bayadere.

La Bayadere?

My fingertips hover over the keyboard. How odd that the password would be an iconic 19th-century Russian ballet, and the first performance with my company back when I was part of the corps de ballet. Anxiety fizzes in my chest. Could Ms Hadley know about my past? And if so, why would she want to remind me of what I've lost?

Deciding it must be a coincidence, I type in the password and hit return. It takes less than half a minute to load before I'm presented with the desktop screen. It's empty apart from three folders. The first is labelled *House,* the second *Business* and the third *Personal.*

I double-click on the *House* folder and it opens to reveal a list of files all labelled alphabetically. I scan over them, there's *Grounds, Kitchen, Staff* and *Utilities.* Clearly these folders hold all the information about running Browlace Manor. I close it, then open the *Business* folder. Similar files appear, all pretty self-explanatory. It would appear Mr Sachov is a property developer. The files are all listed by names of developments. I open one excel spreadsheet linked to a property development in France and nearly keel over at the total money spent on the development; 3.5 million euros to be precise. Just how much money does Mr Sachov have? His business must be worth a fortune.

Swallowing, I close the spreadsheet and file, then click on the last folder labelled *Personal.* This folder has a few files within it. I click through them. There's a document with general information about Mr Sachov's measurements, shoe size and a list of Saville Row tailors. Another word document has a list of restaurants in all the main cities of the UK, and some in other countries. Every single restaurant listed has the name and contact numbers of the Maitre'D. There's also a document with a list of five-star hotels in London, Paris, Rome, New York and Moscow.

"Jesus, Mr Sachov has expensive tastes," I mutter, suddenly feeling woefully inadequate.

My hands drop to my lap and flex over my black polyester trousers. My outfit cost me less than thirty pounds. My silk top, found in a charity shop and though my trousers are new, they're from a cheap clothes store in town.

"What have I got myself into?" I say, continuing to have a conversation with myself.

Blowing out a shaky breath, I reach up to the mouse and

place the cursor over the x to close the Personal folder, when I notice a sidebar in the pop-up box indicating that there is more beneath the whitespace. Curiosity piqued, I scroll down. Sitting at the bottom is one more file labelled 'Brisé'.

Brisé?

White noise fills my ears as my heart starts pounding again. Why is there another ballet reference? One is a coincidence, surely two is significant? Is Ms Hadley playing with me? I double click on the folder and it opens to reveal an unlabelled word document. Something tells me that if I open it I'm not going to like what I see inside. Another thread of doubt pulls inside my chest.

My finger hovers over the mouse. Part of me really wants to open the document, the other part is afraid. There's something about this place. Not just Ms Hadley and her strangeness, but the locked doors and the lack of *people*. It's a big house, surely Mr Sachov has more than just one member of staff? Two now that I'm working here. Yet, this place is empty apart from us both.

A light knock at the door makes me jump, and my hand falls away from the mouse. I straighten myself up. *Just get through today. This is probably a classic case of anxiety,* I think to myself.

"Come in?" I question, wondering why Ms Hadley has returned so quickly, and why she's not just walking in. I look at the time on the computer screen, it's been less than an hour since she left. Another knock sounds, a little more urgent this time.

"It's open Ms Hadley. Please, just come in," I say.

When the door remains stubbornly closed and the knocking becomes more insistent, I get up and stride over, pulling it open.

The corridor's empty.

The hairs on my arm stand as I peer out of the room. I half expect someone to jump out from a hidden alcove and shout 'surprise' whilst waving their hands in the air. Frankly, I'd prefer that to an empty corridor and the muffled sound of a Violin being played in another locked room somewhere in the manor. I freeze, fear chasing up my spine. The music wasn't playing when I arrived this morning, but it most definitely is now. Or at least I think it is. I *thought* I'd heard someone knocking on the office door but there's no one here.

No one but me.

Withdrawing back into the room, I shut the door and lean against it, trying to calm my racing heart. This place is full of ghosts. Ghosts that play violins. Ghosts that want to torture me with references to my past.

CHAPTER THREE

Rose

FOR TEN LONG minutes I stand with my back pressed against the door, my heart pounding erratically. I don't feel safe and I'm not sure whether it's my anxiety kicking in, or whether I really have a right to feel scared. How would the average person react in this situation?

When I think about it logically, I realise that I *do* have a right to feel afraid and that I *should* bring it up with Ms Hadley. If there's someone in this house who thinks it's okay to play tricks on me and scare me like that then I think she should know about it.

Then it occurs to me that it could well *be* Ms Hadley, or worse my own imagination. My anxiety kicks up a notch at the thought. Perhaps bringing it up with her isn't such a good idea after all? Indecision keeps me glued to where I stand. My hands become clammy, my body begins to shake, and I find it hard to breath suddenly.

"Rose, snap out of it," I tell myself angrily. If I let myself spiral now I'll not only be out of a job, but out of my mind too, and I won't allow that to happen again.

Gathering courage, I push myself off from the door, stride over to my desk and pick up the keys knowing I'd feel safer if the door was locked, just like all the others are in this place. I try each key, the final one locking the door. As soon as it's done I feel calmer. The racing of my heart subsides and my breathing returns to a steadier pace.

Now what?

Placing the keys back on the table, I wander over to Mr Sachov's desk. It's as bare as mine. A computer monitor sits on top of it, alongside a keyboard and mouse. A phone accompanies it. There are no photos, no personal items. Not even a pen. I scoot around the desk, running my hands over the thick leather inlaid within the wood. This desk probably cost more than all the furniture put together in my house. I sit in Mr Sachov's chair. It's the same as my own and is comfortable despite the hard wood of the arms and back. The padded leather seat supports my aching joints well enough.

Under his desk, Mr Sachov has three drawers too, and even though I know I shouldn't, I decide to see what's in them. Perhaps there's something, anything, that will allow me a glimpse at the man I'm going to meet in a couple of days. The top draw opens to reveal a pad and pen. I pick up the pad and flip the pages. It's completely blank. Shutting the drawer, I pull on the middle one. Inside, I'm surprised to find a length of red silk. It's not a tie, it's too long for that. Picking it up, I hold it in my hands, allowing the material to run over my palms. For reasons unknown to me, I raise the material to my nose and breathe in.

It smells of florally perfume and a hint of musk. No, not musk...

Sex. It smells of sex.

"Jesus Christ," I exclaim, dropping the red silk into the drawer and slamming it shut. I find my hands trembling a little, anxiety and a thread of something more unnerving running through my veins. Who the hell is this man? And more to the point, why is there a length of silk in his drawer that smells of sex?

I've not had sex in a *very long time.*

Five years to be precise.

Pushing that errant thought away, I give myself a moment to recover, then reach for the bottom drawer.

It doesn't open. It's locked.

"It's locked for a reason, Rose. You need to stop this."

There I go, talking to myself again. Realising that I'm now talking to myself in the third person, I decide that getting back to my own desk on the other side of the room is a far better, far safer option.

Back at my own desk and chewing on my lip, I wonder what I should do next. Ms Hadley hasn't left me any instructions other than to familiarise myself with the files stored on the computer. I think about looking up Mr Sachov on Google but find that there's no internet access on my computer, which is a little odd in and of itself. Surely, I'll need it for my job? Then I remember the three files on the computer and all the information listed in them. Ms Hadley said that Mr Sachov is very particular. Clearly, he likes what he likes, maybe that's why he doesn't have access to the internet? He doesn't need to know about anything other than what he's already interested in.

Or maybe this is some kind of test? Perhaps I'm meant to study the files a little more closely and when Ms Hadley returns at midday, she will have questions about the contents of those three files? I wouldn't be a very good personal assistant if I didn't know all I needed to about my boss in order to assist in the smooth running of his life, now would I? And there really is nothing else I can do.

"That must be it," I murmur, moving the mouse and logging back into the desktop, clicking on the Personal folder once more.

I avoid the file marked *Brisé*.

Yes, my curiosity is begging me to open it up, but common sense and something else, intuition, I suppose, is telling me to steer well clear. I've already uncovered something about Mr Sachov that has unnerved me, and even though I'm trying to forget what I saw, what I smelt, it's proving harder than expected.

I'm not an idiot, clearly that piece of silk has been used in some kind of sexual conquest. I'm not naïve either, just a little surprised as to why it's in his desk drawer and not hidden away in the privacy of his bedroom...

I wonder what that looks like?

A thread of excitement startles me as I imagine swathes of red silk, a darkly decorated bedroom with a four-poster bed and a naked, blindfolded woman tied to the bedposts...

I feel heat rise up my neck and spread across my cheeks. Jesus, what's wrong with me? My imagination is going into overdrive.

I need to get laid.

I swallow an almost hysterical laugh at the thought. Who's going to want me now? I'm damaged goods. Broken a long time before my condition took the one passion I had left.

Turning my attention back to the computer screen, I familiarise myself with the contents of the files, paying more attention this time.

I learn a lot about Mr Sachov from those three files. Of course, he has expensive tastes, I figured that out earlier, but he also appears to prefer Mediterranean food over any other, given the kinds of restaurants listed in the Personal file. He is clearly a very astute businessman given his job and the revenue he earns on all his developments. As far as I can tell he has never made a loss on any of his projects.

The information about his measurements tell me he's well-built, tall, with a toned figure. I'm guessing over six foot, tall enough to tower over my five foot seven inches. Again, money is no object for him. Bespoke suits made by Saville Row tailors seem to be his preference. Last year alone he spent triple my yearly wage on suits. For a personal assistant, I get paid very well. The thought I will be taking home almost two and half thousand pounds a month after tax is overwhelming in itself, but even more so that he spends three times that on suits. This man has way too much money to burn. But, I guess that's his prerogative. Who am I to judge? If I earnt as much as he did, wouldn't I be buying the finest clothes and drinking the finest wines and dining at the finest restaurants around the globe? Being a ballerina in a huge company such as the Royal Ballet afforded me a piece of the highlife, I suppose. Not necessarily in monetary value, but the places I was able to visit and the people I met given my profession.

Now look at me.

Back to my quiet village in Cornwall, surrounded with memories of a past no one will let me forget and working as an assistant to one of the wealthiest men in the area, probably the country. I know I should be grateful, that it could be a lot worse, but I can't help but feel a little disappointed as to how my life has turned out.

I hope I live up to Mr Sachov and Ms Hadley's expectations.

Closing down the folders, I look for a calendar and find one attached to the email. According to the calendar, my new boss spends a lot of time away from Browlace Manor on business trips. This year alone he's been away more weeks than he's been home. He tends to go away, presumably on business, for at least three weeks at a time, returning to the Manor in between, but never staying longer than a month. Ms Hadley hasn't mentioned a wife. I've seen no evidence of one either, at least not in the few areas of the Manor I've been allowed into. But then there's the red silk in his drawer, indicating there is much more to Mr Sachov's personal life that I can establish from the files on the computer. Girlfriend perhaps? That in itself throws up a load of questions. Does she live locally? I somehow doubt that. Perhaps she travels with him and I'll meet her Wednesday too? Or maybe he doesn't have girlfriends, just fuck buddies. The questions I have are endless and will only be answered when I meet Mr Sachov himself. I know Ms Hadley won't be telling me anything, not that I'd ask her, or him frankly. But in time, I'm sure I'll figure it out.

Gazing at the calendar on the computer screen, I can see that he's been away for almost a month this time. Assuming I've interpreted the pattern of his movements correctly, he'll be staying for the same amount of time when he returns on Wednesday. I guess I'll have a month to figure out what really makes Mr Sachov tick.

Strange that I feel the need to do this without having met him, but the small snippets of information have me intrigued enough to want to.

A sharp knock on the door, has me leaping out of my skin again.

"Who is it?" I ask, my voice shaking a little.

"It's me, of course. Why have you locked the door?" Ms Hadley responds, annoyance clear in her voice.

"I'm sorry. Give me a moment," I say, picking up the key and rushing to open the door.

"It's quite unnecessary to lock this room whilst you are in it. Only when you leave," she says, tutting.

I pull open the door and step aside as she bustles in with a tray laden with sandwiches and tea. There's even chocolate cake. My stomach rumbles. I'm suddenly starving. Since being chucked out of the company my appetite has returned and I've put on weight. My body curves in all the right places, I even have breasts now after years of being underweight.

I watch her as she places the tray on my desk before turning around to face me.

"Why did you lock the door?" she asks, her eyes narrowing at me before she casts her gaze about the room. I'm not sure what she's looking for, evidence of theft? Because there's nothing to steal unless you count that piece of red silk. My cheeks flush making me look guilty.

"I thought it was a requirement." I'm not sure why I lie, it just seems the right thing to do.

"Just because the other doors are kept locked, doesn't mean you have the authority to lock this one. I gave you the key so you can get *in*, not so you can lock us *out*," she says, smarting.

"Us?" I ask.

A little nerve in her faces twitches at that, but her gaze remains steady.

"Mr Sachov and I, of course," she responds.

"I see. Apologies, I misunderstood."

"No harm done. Please, come and eat. Tell me what you've been doing this morning," she says, kindly.

Too kindly.

Her question isn't as innocent as it sounds. Something tells me I'll need to be wary of this woman. Very wary indeed.

CHAPTER FOUR

Rose

"SO, do you live in the village?" Ms Hadley asks, as she watches me eat.

I nod my head, swallowing the mouthful quickly. "Yes, I've lived here all my life," I respond. It's not a complete lie. It's always been the house I've come back to, I just haven't lived there for the past twelve years, visiting as infrequently as I could get away with.

"You've been a personal assistant before?"

Picking up my cup of tea, I take a sip, stalling for time. I get the distinct impression she's trying to trip me up somehow. The fact of the matter is, the last time I was anyone's assistant was the summer I turned sixteen and worked for a man who broke my heart. It's not a time I wish to remember, even though everyone else seems intent on doing just that.

"Yes," I say, not willing to elaborate further. If she wanted to interrogate me about my work history she should've done so in the interview.

She nods her head, not pressing further.

"You like living here, in the village?" she asks, as though knowing my answer would be no. The answer *is* no, but no would lead to more questions, questions I'm not willing to answer.

"Yes."

"Family?" Ms Hadley drops that one worded question with a sharp look. A question that could be answered in a multitude of ways. Do I have a family? *Not anymore.* Do I like my family? *Nope.* Do I want a family? *No.* Am I married? *Well, there's no wedding band, so...* Do I have a partner? *Ha, no!* Kids? *Absolutely not.*

"Dead," I respond. She can figure out what that means herself.

She nods again, seemingly satisfied. This woman really *is* crazy.

We both continue eating in silence. Every now and then I catch Ms Hadley looking at me, as though she's trying to figure me out. Well, she can go ahead and try. I'm a closed book, and there's no way in hell I'm letting anyone crack the spine and flip through my dusty pages.

My past is mine, my memories my own. No one is going to shine a light on the darkness I harbour in my heart. I've cultivated it for a very long time and am not about to give up my secrets to some weird old woman.

Ms Hadley coughs, snapping me out of my thoughts. She

looks at her wrist watch. "I must show you the files before I go. They should keep you busy for the rest of the day."

"The ones on the computer? I've familiarised myself with them already," I respond.

She cocks her eyebrow at me. "Not those," she says, annoyance creeping in her voice.

"What files?"

Ms Hadley gets up and walks towards one of the wooden wall panels. I'm about to ask her if she's okay given she's standing in front of the wall, when she presses her hand against a tiny square button I hadn't noticed until now and a section of the wall swings inwards opening into a gaping black mouth. Well, clearly not a mouth, a room or corridor or a secret passageway. I'm reminded of the frantic knocking on the door earlier and feel more than a little unnerved.

"What's this..." I start, standing abruptly.

Ms Hadley reaches forward, her hand and forearm swallowed into the dark momentarily before I hear a clicking sound and a light turns on.

"These are the files I'm talking about," Ms Hadley says, stepping aside so that I can see into what is, very obviously, another room. A room filled to the brim with cardboard boxes full of papers and files, and rows and rows of filing cabinets.

Shit. There's me thinking I'll just be tapping away at the computer, sipping coffee all day. This is more work than I'd bargained for.

Ms Hadley smiles sweetly. "Mr Sachov is a very clever man, but he's not particularly good at this kind of thing."

"What, filing?" I say, probably a little too sarcastically. Thankfully Ms Hadley ignores my remark.

"Most of what he knows is stored up here," she says, tapping her head. "But, he needs someone to keep all his paperwork organised. You're that person."

"What about you?" I ask. She seems to be more than capable of being organised, why didn't she take the job as his PA?

"Me? Don't be silly, I've far more important things to do with my time than filing. Why do you think we hired you? Besides, I run the household."

I almost ask 'what household' given there's only me and her in it, but refrain. I'm already aware that Ms Hadley always has a reasonable answer for everything. I'm sure she'd come up with a plethora of reasons why she needs to run an empty household and why filing is beneath her.

"Now, I've things to be getting on with, and so do you," she says, gathering up the plates and stacking them on the tray. "Your day finishes at four o'clock. I expect you to leave on the dot. Not a moment later, is that clear?"

"Sure, okay," I agree, more than happy to be out of this place in just over three hours. She nods her head, picks up the tray and heads towards the door.

"Oh, one last thing," she says turning back to face me.

"Yes?" I ask, expecting another backhanded insult.

"Please ensure you lock this door when you leave."

"No problem..." my voice trails off as Ms Hadley pulls the door shut on my reply.

Left with a mountain of filing with no real clue where to start, I step into the room and grab the nearest box. Four o'clock can't come around quick enough.

THREE HOURS LATER, tired and with an aching back, I survey my afternoon's work. I've already managed to fill three separate filing cabinets with paperwork all filed in alphabetical order in appropriate sections under business, household and personal, just like the files on the computer. There are still at least half a dozen boxes to go, but I'm proud of what I've achieved, even though my body is cursing me for abusing it.

Rubbing at my back, I push open the door and head out into the main office. Opposite me is a man sitting at Mr Sachov's desk with his head clasped in his hands.

Hands that appear to be covered in blood... I let out a screech, back peddling into the wall behind me.

The man snaps his head up, his eyes widening when he sees me. His loose hair falls about his shoulders, as he stands.

"Who are you?" I ask, trying and failing to keep my voice steady. It occurs to me then that this could be Mr Sachov returned home early, and that I've been incredibly rude. Except something tells me that this man is not my boss, but one of the 'household' Ms Hadley keeps referring too. What I'd initially thought was blood is, in fact, paint, given the paintbrush he seems to be grasping tightly in his hand.

"Who am I? Who are *you*?" he retorts. "And what are you doing in Ivan's office?"

"I'm Mr Sachov's personal assistant. I started today."

"You shouldn't be here," he murmurs, stepping around the table and into the fading afternoon light where I can get a better look at him. He's looks about my age, maybe a few years older, and he's wearing a paint splattered t-shirt with long black trousers that are slung low on his hips. His t-shirt is a little short in length and doesn't quite meet the tops of his trousers, showing a portion of smooth skin, firm muscle and the hint of hair leading lower down... I snatch my eyes up, concentrating on his face.

"I work here," I retort, folding my arms against my chest. There's something about the way he looks at me that makes me feel as though I'm being studied under a microscope. What is it with people in this house and all the staring? First Ms Hadley, now this man.

"What are *you* doing here?" I ask, feeling a little indignant, and a lot unnerved.

I'm pretty sure he shouldn't be here either given Ms Hadley's insistence on locking every damn room in the place. It makes me wonder where he's been hiding.

"You shouldn't be here now," he repeats once more.

"This is my office," I respond, more slowly this time.

Perhaps he's unwell, maybe that's why Ms Hadley is keeping his existence secret. I know families like to keep secrets, mine is proof enough of that. Big, fat, ugly secrets seem to hover over me like a damp mist on Bodmin Moor.

"Ivan won't be happy..." he starts, then clamps his mouth shut.

"Why not?" I ask, taking in the depth of his brown eyes and the dark rings that circle them. I watch as he swipes his paint splattered hand over the beard covering his chin, leaving a smear of red paint across his face

"It's past four o'clock. You shouldn't be here," he repeats, ignoring my question.

"I didn't realise the time. I'm going to go now," I say, taking a step towards the door as he moves closer. He continues to stare at me as though he's purposefully absorbing every detail of my face and storing it away in his memory.

"Yes, you should go," he says, tracking a hand through his hair.

"I will. I'll go," I murmur, backing up into my desk. I feel the hard edge of the wood dig into my backside as this man steps ever closer.

"It's past four..." he repeats, reaching up a hand and trailing a finger across my cheek. I feel wetness against my skin, the same red paint marking me now.

He's so close that I can see tiny shards of blue in the muddy brown of his eyes. He's handsome, yes, with wide shoulders and muscular arms, but he's also a little odd. Odd in a troubled way, like his past is as fucked up as my own.

"You have strange eyes. What colour are they?" he asks, a frown pulling his tawny eyebrows together. They are the same colour as his long chin length hair and stubbled cheeks.

"Green?" I respond, completely unnerved now.

"Green? That's a colour I've not seen in a while."

"What do you mean?" I ask.

He steps back abruptly, shaking his head. "You should leave before Ms Hadley finds you here still. She won't be happy."

"I thought it was Ivan, I mean Mr Sachov, who won't be happy..."

"You'll get hurt, you know," he whispers. "They all do in the end, just like her."

My heart stutters. "What do you mean?" I ask, my voice barely above a whisper.

He steps back quickly. "Ms Hadley isn't someone you should disobey. You need to go," he responds.

I feel like saying that I don't care if Ms Hadley finds me here, that I want to know who the hell he is and what the fuck he's talking about. Instead, I ask a completely different question. "Was that you earlier, knocking on the door?"

"No," he responds immediately.

I don't know this man at all, but I'm pretty sure he's telling the truth even if he does scare me. "Then if not you, who?" I press, expecting more riddles than answers.

"Erik."

"Who is Erik?"

"He lives here too," the man responds. His gaze sweep over me once more before he turns and heads out of the room. For a moment I just remain fixed to the spot, stunned. Then, coming back to my senses, I run after him hoping he doesn't disappear like Erik appeared to have done earlier.

"Wait, I don't know your name," I say, peering out of the door.

He stops, turning on bare feet. I hadn't noticed he wasn't wearing any shoes before. "It's better you don't know. I've said too much already. You should leave. It's after four," he repeats.

"*Please*," I plead, my need to know making me beg a little. It's been a long time since I heard my voice sound so... so desperate?

Submissive, you mean, a long-buried voice says inside my head.

I push the sound of his voice, and memories of that man out of my thoughts. He stopped existing a long time ago, and I refuse to let the memories of him creep back in and haunt me now.

"Anton," the paint splattered man says, before slipping through the door at the end of the corridor and disappearing from view.

CHAPTER FIVE

Rose

THE FOLLOWING morning at Browlace Manor passes uneventfully. More filing and another awkward lunch with Ms Hadley pass the time quickly enough. After clearing another three boxes of files I glance at my watch, it's three o'clock. I've not had a break for the last couple of hours, so decide to take a quick five minutes to stretch out my back and have a drink.

I grab the glass on my desk and take a sip of water, eying up the plate of biscuits Ms Hadley left behind. After yesterday's encounter with Anton I've been even more wary of Ms Hadley today given his veiled warning. I almost didn't come to work, but the very real need to pay my stack of growing bills had me pushing my concerns aside and walking to work in the biting wind. The whole journey I'd been thinking about Anton and the strange way he'd looked at me, about the mysterious Erik, and my very particular boss whom I'm yet to meet.

I've not seen Anton at all today, or Erik. Not that I met Erik yesterday, but there hasn't been any strange knocking on the door at least. Most of me is grateful for that fact, but a small part of me is a little disappointed. There was something about Anton that was alluring beneath the odd behaviour. Then again, I've always been partial to a man who has secrets, and Anton seems to have plenty of those.

I'm guessing he's an artist given the paint and brush, but other than that I know nothing about him. Even Mr Sachov's personal files don't allude to any family and it's not as if I can straight out ask Ms Hadley given her clear need to hide the fact Anton lives here, or Erik for that matter. It's all so odd.

So far today, on the surface at least, Ms Hadley has been nothing but kind. She even asked me how well I was feeling at lunchtime after noticing me rubbing at my lower back. A morning of sorting through Mr Sachov's files has certainly stiffened me up a lot, add that to yesterday's efforts and I'm feeling sore. But despite her concern, I still don't trust her. There's something very unnerving about that woman. I feel like I'm undergoing a test, one where she knows all the rules and I'm oblivious. One mistake and I'm out.

Right now, I'm looking forward to meeting Mr Sachov. His arrival tomorrow can't come quickly enough. At least when he's here I won't have to suffer Ms Hadley's constant scrutiny. She acts as though she runs this house, but when I look at all the information about Mr Sachov in his paper files and the ones on the computer, I get the distinct impression he's not a man who'll let *any* woman run his life, even a woman like Ms Hadley. He seems very certain of himself, I guess you must be to run a successful multimillion pound property business.

Placing the glass back on the table, I walk around the desk to the centre of the room and begin some simple stretches. First, I raise my right arm and lean over to my left, stretching all the muscles in the right side of my torso, then repeat the same movement on the opposite side. It helps a little to relieve the tension in the muscles that run along the sides of my chest but doesn't do much for the pain beginning to radiate from my lower spine and out across my hips.

"Fuck," I mumble, pressing my fingertips into the small of my back, moving them in a circular motion.

I don't know why I bother really, it doesn't help. The pain I feel isn't caused by tight muscles, it's caused by inflammation around the joints in my bones, but still I stretch. Keeping my muscles loose might not help with the pain, but it keeps me supple enough to survive it, supple enough to dance even just a little.

Dreaming of a long hot bath and a glass of wine, this time I raise both my arms above my head then lean forward slowly reaching for my toes. I can feel the muscles strain, and the joints beneath them groan, but still I continue.

Before I was diagnosed with my condition, I could get my forehead against my knees and my palms flat on the ground, now I'm lucky to reach my calves with my fingers.

"Who the fuck are you?" a deep voice says from behind me.

I straighten quickly, groaning with the sharp pain of moving so fast. Twisting on my feet I face the most beautiful man I've ever seen. Beautiful in a dangerous, raw, wild animal kind of way. His blue-grey eyes regard me with a mixture of disdain and mild interest, the kind of interest which precludes a main meal.

"I'm Rose Gyvern," I say, my voice is surprisingly level given my heart has decided to pound like a bass drum. There's something about this man I recognise, he's familiar somehow. He steps into the room, his presence making me feel small. I back up a little. "Nice to meet you...?"

He doesn't respond, he simply waits, crossing his arms over his chest. The shirt he's wearing is white and slim fitting and is tucked into a well-made pair of navy trousers. I see his arm muscles bunch beneath the material as he tenses.

"Don't make me repeat myself," he growls, the dark shadow of his stubble, and dishevelled hair juxtaposing the rest of him that appears so well turned out.

"I'm Mr Sachov's personal assistant. I started yesterday," I reply, wondering if this is Erik.

"Is that so?" he says, regarding me. His gaze trails slowly over my body, starting at my turned out feet. For some reason his eyes narrow at that. I notice how his fingers curl into his palms and his Adam's apple bobs in his throat. Instinctively, I turn my feet inwards, and the tenseness disappears from his face. His gaze rises slowly, and my breath catches at the way he takes in every detail. I feel instantly naked.

Vulnerable.

"I've just finished some filing. Ms Hadley tells me Mr Sachov will be home tomorrow and I wanted to get most of it done before he returns," I ramble, my cheeks flushing as his gaze stops at my chest. The turbulent blue-grey of his eyes darken like an oncoming squall at sea as he watches my nipples pebble beneath my thin silk shirt and lace bra.

What the hell is wrong with me?

My physical reaction to his presence is wholly inappropriate and completely unnerving. He takes another step forward, and I take another step back, crossing my arms over my chest. I feel a red heat flush my cheeks. A strange kind of rumbling noise rises up his throat at that. My arms cross tighter.

Finally, his gaze rests back on my face. His expression is blank, careful.

Controlled, that's the word I'm looking for.

"What were you doing when I walked in?" he asks.

His voice has taken on a dangerous edge. I mean I know it probably wasn't very professional of me to be bent over, stretching in the middle of the office, but to be fair I wasn't expecting anyone to walk in on me doing it.

"I was stretching…" I respond, feeling bloody ridiculous.

"Stretching?"

"My back has been hurting a little from all the filing and lugging all those heavy boxes." I point to pile stacked by my desk. He doesn't bother to look at them, keeping his gaze firmly fixed on me.

"Do you stretch often?" he persists, taking a step closer to me.

"Every day," I respond, feeling more and more intimidated by the glowering look he's giving me.

"Why?"

"Why what?"

"Why do you stretch every day?"

"It's just something I do."

"Why?" he repeats, narrowing his eyes at me.

Is he for real? I frown, feeling increasingly uncomfortable

under his scrutiny. "It really doesn't matter why, it just helps to ease the pain."

"It matters to me. *Tell me*," he insists, glowering at me. There's something inherently dangerous about this man. He reminds me of someone I used to know, someone I've tried very hard to forget. A man who took my virginity, showed me a world I've never been able to forget and broke my heart in the process. Maybe *that's* why he seems so familiar.

Smarting a little at his probing questions and the reminder of my past, I straighten my back, haul in my stomach muscles and pull myself upright. My feet automatically turn out into first position. Somehow standing this way makes me feel a little stronger. Ballet has always been my shield to ward off dangerous memories, and the man who caused them.

"I know, why don't you tell *me* who *you* are and then, perhaps, I'll answer your question," I retort sharply. I know my words come out harsher than I intended but I'll be damned if I answer any more questions if he can't even be bothered to introduce himself.

Something flashes in the man's eyes, then he strides towards me, stopping a foot away. He's so close that I can feel his hot breath slide over my skin. My skin prickles at his nearness.

"Answer me!" he roars. The rage that pours out of his body is terrifying.

Terrifying *and* thrilling.

"Who are *you*?" I repeat, my voice holding steady. I refuse to look away. The last time I submitted to such a man it almost broke me. I refuse to do that again. In this fucking life or the next.

"Answer the damn question!"

"Not until you tell me *your* name," I retort, not caring that my own voice is a few decibels higher than it should be. This back and forth has become more than me giving him a complicated answer to a simple question. This is about power. His over mine.

"You don't get to question me. This is *my* fucking office, *my* fucking house. Now, answer the damn question!" he snarls. The dark curtain of his hair falling into his rage-filled eyes.

"*Your* house?"

Oh, my god. *This* is Ivan Sachov.

This man is my *boss*.

"That's right, Rose. So, if you want to keep your job, you'd better answer me." His voice lowers but is no less angry for it. If anything, it's taken on a sinister edge.

I should be more afraid than I am. I should be running far, far away from him and the other strange occupants of Browlace Manor, but I don't. Instead, I look him square in the eye and answer his question.

"I stretch to keep supple, to keep the pain at bay. I do it because I need to fight the demons that rule my body. I do it because I need to remember who I once was..."

Once was. It's then that I realise I've seen this man before. He may have aged some, he may have bulked up, and his hair might be a few shades darker than it was when I saw him last, but there's no doubting who he is. It would appear I'm not the only one trying to hide from my past. My chest squeezes on the realisation. All the ballet references make sense now.

Ivan blanches at my response, his olive skin turning a shade lighter. He raises his finger and grazes it across my jaw as his head dips lower. The irony of being this close to him is not lost to me given how much I longed to be noticed by him all those years ago. Back then I was just another face amongst many, back then he only had eyes for one woman; Svetlana Ivanov. She was one of the most talented ballet dancers this past decade, until her death, that is.

"Who *were* you?" he asks softly, in a voice so very different to the one that roared at me in anger just now.

"A ballerina. We danced in the same show *La Bayadere*. I was in the corps de ballet, you were the principal dancer, Luka Petrin," I whisper, certain I'm not wrong.

For a split second he remains fixed in place, his body stiff. I watch as a dozen emotions flash behind his eyes, then he jerks back, stumbling.

"Get the fuck out of my office!" he shouts, backing away from me now as though *I'm* the predator and he's the prey.

"I'm sorry... I shouldn't have mentioned," I begin, but he cuts me off.

"GET. THE. FUCK. OUT!"

The sound of clicking heels against a hard floor comes from the corridor, a second later Ms Hadley comes rushing in. She looks between us, her beady eyes taking in the scene before her. I'm trembling violently, as much as Luka is. I mean Ivan, or whoever he wishes to be called now.

"Ivan, be calm. What's going on?" she asks, her eyes narrowing at me as though this is all my fault. I guess it is. I guess he didn't want to be reminded of his past any more than I do.

He points his finger at me, a cruel sneer curling his lips.

"*What's going on?* Rose here is about to leave. She's fucking *fired,*" he snarls, his accent more marked now that he doesn't need to cover it up with pretence.

"But I didn't mean..." I begin, my voice trembling.

Ms Hadley walks up to me, blocking my view from Ivan. Her lips pull back over her teeth reminding me of a feral cat.

"You heard Mr Sachov. Leave at once, and don't come back."

Tears fill my eyes, but I blink them back refusing to let either of them know how upset I am.

"If that's what you want," I respond, picking up my handbag.

I grab my coat, wincing again at the pain in my back as I pull it on. I feel Ms Hadley's stare, but I ignore her and walk right up to Ivan.

"I'm sorry to have upset you," I say.

Then leaning in closer, pressing my fingers against his fore-arm, I lower my voice, so Ms Hadley can't hear. "I know what it's like to run from your past, your secret is safe with me." And with that I walk out of the room.

CHAPTER SIX

Ivan

STANDING at the window of my office, I look out at the woman who just slapped me in the face with a memory of my past I have no desire to revisit.

La Bayadere.

It was the ballet where I met Svetlana. It was the start of our relationship, and the beginning of her destruction. I had been captivated from the first moment I spotted her across the rehearsal room. In an instant I had known that I'd wanted to claim her as mine, and I did. She had no choice in the matter.

I made her love me, and then I fucking destroyed her bit by bit.

Svetlana had played the part of Nikiya and I had played the warrior Solor. It had taken me the length of that tour to seduce her *and* fuck most of the cast. Svetlana had given me her heart easily enough, and I took it, feasting on her love from that moment on. But it was never enough.

I'd wanted so much more, and I took that as well. Except, perhaps, not all of it. Rose had somehow slipped by me.

"Ivan, can I get you anything?" Ms Hadley asks carefully, her voice cutting through the memories.

"No, just leave. I shall speak with you later."

"As you wish," she says, knowing me well enough not to press.

I hear the door click shut, and my attention refocuses on the woman I just fired as she strides down the gravel drive. She seems to be limping a little, her left knee giving way as she walks towards the iron gate and the roadway beyond. Still, she keeps moving with the same determination that she used confronting me. Looking at her now, I wouldn't have guessed a background in dance. Her shoulders are rounded, her step awkward and she holds her body taut as though in pain...

Pain, she had mentioned that, the physical pain. There was something else too, something hidden. I'd seen secrets in her eyes and I'd recognised a piece of me in her that I didn't like. Not one fucking bit.

Demons. She had demons, just like me.

I'd understood immediately that she wasn't just talking about the ones that plagued her physically. No, she'd been talking about the ones that she danced to *forget*. That's why, even with pain, she stretches to remain supple... supple enough to keep hold of her escape mechanism. I'd seen it written all over her face, that for her, to lose the freedom of dance would be catastrophic. Just like taking away my release would be for me.

I need to fuck, like I need oxygen to live. No, that's not exactly right, I need to fuck *and* dominate in order to *survive*.

There is no other way for me. That need has grown into a monster I can't satiate since Svetlana's death, but it's always been there. It'll never be satisfied.

Rose can't work for me, not just because she knows who I really am, but because she will be a constant reminder of what I had to give up. I had known the moment I'd walked in the room and found her bent over double with her hands on her calves that she was a dancer. That was certainly confirmed when she'd stood with her feet in first position with a straight back, her jaw jutting. The pose of every ballet dancer worth their salt.

"Think of a thread pulling up the length of your spine..."

Holding the correct posture at all times is ingrained in dancers from the moment they take up ballet. Christ knows I've tried to rid myself of it. I've bulked up my body to look different. I've allowed my muscles to lose their flexibility. I don't want to dance ever again. I don't want to be reminded of that time in my life.

Yet, you still fuck women in the dance studio where your wife killed herself...

I shake my head of the ugly thought and slam my fist into the wall. I don't even register the pain. How in the hell had Ms Hadley managed to hire an ex ballet dancer? My housekeeper is astute, nothing gets past her, and yet this woman had. It's the worst possible disaster.

"FUCK!" I shout, slamming my fist against the wall again. "FUCK. FUCK. FUCK!"

Rose was in *La Bayadere*. She knows my real name, she

knows about my past and yet, despite touring with the company, I have no recollection of her.

That's unlike me. I remember everyone. How had someone with a fucking ripe arse, full breasts and plump lips like her got past me? I'd fucked most of the damn cast at the same time as I'd chased Svetlana. How had she slipped through my grasp?

Then again, it was over ten years ago, people can change in that time. They can evolve into something more than what they once were, like Rose. Or they can become a darker shadow of their former selves, like me.

I lose sight of Rose as she exits the main gate, and I finally let out a long breath. It's just as well she's gone. I will find another personal assistant. This is the last time I entrust Ms Hadley with my affairs. She can run this damn household, keep Erik and Anton in check, but from now on she can stay the fuck away from hiring staff.

Striding over to my desk I pull open the middle draw and grab the length of red silk I keep in there. Lifting it to my nose I breath in deeply, remembering the nameless woman I'd used this piece of silk on last. My cock stirs.

Grabbing the phone on my desk, I pick up the receiver and dial Ms Hadley's extension.

"Ivan?" she answers.

"I shall be dining in my room tonight."

"I apologise..."

"It's done," I snap. "You have my book?"

There's a moment's pause at the end of the line.

"Ms Hadley, you have my book?"

"Yes. What's your preference this evening?"

"I don't care. You choose, and this time, don't fuck it up," I retort.

There's silence again, before I hear Ms Hadley sigh. "She can't dance anymore. It's the only reason I hired her."

"What makes you say that?"

"She's sick. Rheumatoid arthritis."

"I shall be ready at nine," I reply, slamming the phone back onto its cradle.

Pulling back the sleeve of my shirt, I run my fingertip over the faint white scars that mark my skin. Each one represents the women I've fucked since falling in love with my wife and the hundreds I've used since she stopped living.

Rose may not bear the same kind of scars, but in that brief meeting I got the distinct impression that she and I are more alike than I'd care to admit. We're both running from something in our past, and fuck if I don't want to delve beneath her creamy skin and devour her soul, just like all the rest.

I WALK into the dance studio where my distraction is waiting. The nameless woman is sitting on the wooden chair in the corner of the room. She's one of my regulars and one of the most subservient. I'm not sure how Ms Hadley knew she would be the one I needed tonight, but she chose wisely this time.

The woman is blindfolded, her hands folded in her lap. She sits demurely, her knees and ankles pressed together, her polyester skirt tight around her thighs. Her head is bowed, blonde hair loose, lips parted on a breath. I watch as her chest falls and rises gently, her ample breasts straining against the tight t-shirt she wears. I can tell that she's already wet for me. The way her thighs press together so tightly, the slight pink tinge to her cheeks, the pebbled nipples. She's very receptive, and tonight that's exactly what I need.

This woman is more curved than those who've visited on the last few occasions. She has a rounded tummy and silver stretch marks across her hips and stomach. But I'm not bothered by them. I don't search for perfection in the women I fuck, at least not anymore.

I did once. I spent years chasing the most beautiful, the most perfect of women. I wanted to own the women who were every man's ideal, the women who would make other men hard and insanely jealous because I had them. I'd sought them out, married or not. I'd fucked them. I *owned* them all. Then I left them shattered and broken, a trail of misery in my wake...

Svetlana had been perfect.

Everything about her was just so damn perfect. She had been stunning, kind, warm, talented.

But perfection no longer interests me, I don't even want imperfect. What I want is selfish release.

My attention is drawn back to the woman sitting in the chair waiting patiently. She shifts slightly, aware of another person in the room. I guess she could be described as *homely*. *Motherly*, I suppose, and perhaps she is a mother. I know she's married, I've seen the indent of her wedding ring on her finger. I'm not certain why she bothers removing it. I guess it's easier for her to pretend she's not cheating that way.

None of that really matters to me.

Husband or not, kids or not. I don't ask, and they don't tell me, and that's the way I like it.

Approaching her, I remove my t-shirt and fling it across the room. The cool air scatters over my skin, and my arms cover in goose bumps. Stopping just a metre away, I pull a flip knife from my trouser pocket and open it up. The blade glints in the dimmed overhead lights as I slide my finger over the back edge. A strange feeling unravels in my chest; a mixture of inevitability and relief. I slide the tip of the blade over my bicep and watch as the skin parts, drawing blood. There's no pain, there isn't even release, not in this, that comes later. I watch as my blood slides down my arm and drips onto the floor, seeping between the gaps.

My offering to the wife I had killed.

"You need to say the word," I murmur, folding the blade back into its casing. My voice comes out broken, needy, and I fucking hate myself for showing this woman a glimpse into the hidden depths of me. Fuck that. My fists curl and I grit my teeth.

She raises her head, turning her face to me, then reaches for her blindfold.

"Don't." I warn, and her hand drops immediately. "I didn't tell you to take it off. Do you need reminding of the rules?"

She shakes her head, a rush of colour spreading up her neck. I see her thighs squeeze tighter, and briefly wonder what lie she told her family, so she could be here tonight.

"Are you...?" she starts, breaking another rule.

"There are no conversations in this room, no questions, no talk. You understand that you'll pay the consequences for such flagrant regard of the rules?" I ask, squatting in front of her.

With the knife still grasped in one hand, I slide the other up her calf and between her knees, resting it there. Her breath catches as she waits.

"You need to say the word," I say, more firmly this time. Her knees part at the change in my voice, at the power she wants to give in to.

My fingers edge up the inside of her thigh. The softness of female skin usually has my cock twitching. Not this time.

"Say it!" I growl.

She groans, widening her legs further, giving me access to her wetness. Like all the women who come here, she isn't wearing any underwear. It's one of my requirements. Depending on how I feel, I want immediate access. Underwear just gets in the way.

My fingers hover just beyond the spot I know she's desperate for me to touch. I wait for the word that will open up a world of intense pleasure for us both over the next few hours. Still she remains quiet.

My fingers twirl in gentle circles over her soft skin, and her chest heaves as she fights her own internal battle. Perhaps tonight her delay is the thought of the husband she's betraying or perhaps it's just her way to build the anticipation. Either way, I'm feeling more generous this evening than usual. Though in all honestly, I need time to get my head fucking straight.

By now my cock would normally be rigid, and yet it's barely even stirring.

I'm not ready to fuck her yet. I'm not even sure I will be. My fingers still and I pull my hand back, but her legs slam together, trapping my hand between her thighs.

"Brisé," she says, breathlessly.

But it's already too late. I yank my hand out from between

her legs and stand abruptly. Her mouth opens on a question, but I silence her with my finger.

"No questions, no conversations, no fucking talking. If you ever want to come back here again, I suggest you stick to those three simple rules, got it?" I seethe, angry at this woman. No, not angry at *this* woman, angry at the woman who's turned my head today.

Rose.

The minute I think of her bent over, her round arse high in the air, my cock stiffens.

"Fuck!" I growl, grasping my hand around my cock.

The knife falls from my hand as I yank my trousers down.

"Suck my dick," I bite out, holding the base of my cock and bringing the tip to the woman's lips. She lets out a moan as she reaches blindly for me. Her warm hands find my hips just as her mouth closes around the head of my cock.

"Hmmm," she hums around me, and my balls tighten automatically in response.

With my free hand I grab the back of her head and guide my length as far into her mouth as she can take. She sucks me off, her tongue lapping at me whilst I grind into her welcoming warmth. Her moaning increases as she widens her legs, her way of telling me without talking that she's ready to be fucked.

But she doesn't get to choose when I fuck her, *if* I fuck her.

I watch as her blonde head moves back and forward, and rather than being turned on by the sight, my cock starts to fucking soften. I stop rocking into her mouth, ready to pull backwards but her fingers grip my hips tighter, and she holds me steady as she sucks my cock with utter determination to get me off.

After all, I haven't told her to stop.

I'm torn between chasing that moment of heady release and running the fuck out of the room. In the end, my demons make the decision for me and I allow her to coax my cock back to life. Tonight, I'm taking whatever I can get.

Closing my eyes, I imagine another pretty mouth sucking my dick. I imagine her haunted eyes looking up at me as she fucks me with her mouth. The woman I see has dark hair, green eyes and a body that's as broken as my own messed up soul.

My balls tighten as the rush of my orgasm rips through my body, and for a few brief seconds I find sweet, sweet relief. The woman's groans have me opening my eyes and looking down at her parted mouth. She runs her tongue over the tip of my cock, lapping at the last drops of my cum. I ease out of her hold whilst she drops her head and waits, just like I taught her.

My chest heaves as I battle with the thoughts swirling through my head. I *never* fantasise about another woman when I'm with someone. My head is always in the game. Nothing exists in that moment than the woman I'm with and my need to get off. And yet, somehow, in the brief time I've known her, Rose has managed to creep into my fucking head.

Your soul, a tiny voice says.

"Screw that," I growl, making the woman jump.

This is just a blip. A new piece of arse turning my head. That's all.

There's only one way to get her out, and I intend on making that happen right now.

Reaching down, I grab my flick-knife and pull up my trousers.

"We're done. Ms Hadley will call you a cab."

The woman smarts, her mouth popping open in shock, but I give her no other explanation. I don't have to. Instead, I turn on my heel and stride from the room with only one thought in my head.

I'm going to fuck Rose Gyvern.

CHAPTER SEVEN

Rose

THROWING my coat on the couch I stride into the kitchen, ignoring the stabbing pain I feel in my knee and lower back. Grabbing the bottle of Merlot I started last night, I unscrew the lid and pour myself a large glass.

"Fuck you, Mr Sachov!" I say, before drinking the whole lot in one go.

Smacking my lips, I place the glass back on the counter and fill it up again, knocking the second glass back as quickly as the first. Who gives a crap about a hangover, it's not as though I have a job to go to tomorrow anyway.

I've. Got. No. Job.

I've just been fired by *Luka Petrin*.

Fired by one of the most talented ballet dancers of all time and a man I lusted after in my youth. In fact, the whole company had wanted to sleep with him, even some of the men. But he only had eyes for Svetlana, and I don't blame him.

Yes, I'd heard the rumours like everyone else, but I've no doubt he was faithful to her. I mean, they were *made* for each other. They belonged to one another. Why would anyone want to ruin that?

She was just so *perfect*.

A beautiful dancer, a beautiful woman, and *nice* too. Believe me, nice isn't a trait most ballet dancers have. Competition is fierce, and friendships difficult to maintain. Or perhaps that had just been me. I kept away from most of the social aspects of the troupe. I never joined in on any of the partying or gatherings. I rehearsed, I worked hard, and I slept. Occasionally I would eat, and I never drank.

Rinse. Wash. Repeat.

For ten years, that had been my life, interspersed with a few brief relationships. I'd been happy enough, but I never made it to the dizzying heights Svetlana had. I just wasn't talented enough. She'd had this light that just seemed to follow her everywhere she went, and when the pair danced together... Christ, it was magical.

I remember the first time I'd watched them perform, I'd been a fresh faced dancer and they'd been in their prime. Like the rest of the company we were brought to their rehearsal room and introduced to them collectively, then they'd performed a scene from the ballet. I'd watched in awe, totally taken away by the beauty of them dancing together. They were like gods flying in the stratosphere and the rest of us mere mortals. Mortals who could get hurt, who could feel pain.

My back spasms just at that moment, reminding me of just how ungodlike I am.

Sliding onto my kitchen stool, I pick up the bottle and pour another glass, sipping it slowly this time. My hands are trembling, the adrenaline that had got me home ten minutes quicker than usual, now wearing off. My back and knee throb and I feel feverish.

"Shit," I say, regretting my stupidity. I've overdone it, *again*. I know tomorrow I'm going to feel ten times worse. Groaning, I settle the glass back down and lean my head against the cold marble work surface, gritting my teeth against the pain.

Pain... it's become a part of my life that I can no longer run from.

Ballet had been my escape from this house, from this village, from the memories haunting me. It had been an escape from the emotional pain I felt, and for ten years it had kept my past at bay. I danced to be free of that pain, and now when I dance I'm punished with more. It's a vicious cycle and one in which I can't escape.

Is there really any point in carrying on, Rosie?

That dark voice I know so well whispers in my ear, taunting me.

"Don't fucking call me by that name. She's dead. Rosie is gone."

Ha! Rosie's still within you... that girl who watched her...

"Leave me alone!" I scream.

You'll never dance again.

"Please, leave me alone." My voice catches, and I hate myself for allowing the darkness in.

You'll spend the rest of your life in pain. Aged and broken. Worthless and unloved.

"Stop it."

He didn't love you. Your parents were ashamed of you.

"No more, please."

No one will ever love you, Rosie.. You're too broken to even dance.

"SHUT UP!" Standing abruptly, I pick up the glass and throw it against the wall. It shatters, splattering red wine over the white tiles. But it's not enough to appease the anger and despair I feel, not nearly enough. So, I pick up the wine bottle too and smash it against the counter. It explodes before me, shards of glass and red wine covering the work surface, floor and my clothes.

You couldn't even keep your job filing away someone else's success.

"Fuck you," I whisper, dropping the remains of the bottle on the counter.

Turning on my heel, I walk from the kitchen and upstairs to my bedroom, sleep my only reprieve now.

I AWAKE a few hours later to the sound of thunder and a cold blast of air across my neck. Shifting in bed, I pull the covers up higher, covering most of my head so only a portion of my face is poking out. I should get up and shut the window, but I really don't want to move. My head is groggy from the combination of painkillers, sleeping pills, and wine.

Another loud rumble of thunder sounds as heavy rain pelts

against the window, and as much as I enjoy a good storm, tonight all I want is sleep, though it appears I'm failing at that too.

Rolling onto my back, I shut my eyes and try to coax sleep back, but all I see is Luka, or should I say Ivan, given the man who won't leave my head is not the principal dancer of eleven years ago, but the man I'd stood toe to toe with not a few hours before.

Ivan is completely different to the person I remember. He's brash, rude, angry, and nothing like Luka. Okay, maybe not nothing like, he still has the same allure. Except this time, it's the dangerous kind. I guess the loss of his wife has changed him. Loss does that, it changes a person. Ivan is living his own kind of hell, just like me.

No wonder he's so angry. He's clearly spent a lot of time and effort trying to forget his past and put his wife's death behind him. He's built a life without her, a successful one by all accounts. Then he's confronted with me, a reminder of a time when they were happy, when she was alive. I can almost understand his reaction.

She'd 'died in tragic circumstances', that's what we'd all been told at the company. I know none of the details, I don't think many people do. Her death had made the news for a few days, but after the funeral Luka and Svetlana were forgotten and he'd disappeared from the ballet scene, confessing that he would never be able to dance again, not without her.

My heart squeezes at that. I've often wondered what it would feel like to be loved so completely... to give up his passion because he'd lost his one true love.

There's been only one time in my life I believed that I had

been loved just as much. My foolish sixteen year old heart had been so trusting, *gullible*. I'd been wrong, so very wrong. That wasn't love.

Sighing heavily, I sit up in bed. The digital clock on my bedside table tells me it's ten pm and deciding that sleep isn't going to return anytime soon, I get out of bed. Hobbling towards my bedroom door, I pull on my dressing gown and head back downstairs into the kitchen, my head pounding in time with the ache in my knee and hips. Flipping on the kitchen light, I am faced with the carnage of my earlier anger. I step gingerly into the kitchen, trying to avoid the shards of glass scattered over my floor, and grab some paper towels and the dustpan and brush.

Crouching down I pick up the larger pieces of glass and place them in a pile. Reaching for a rather sharp looking shard, I gingerly grasp it when a loud knock on my door makes me jump. I drop the glass, managing to slice open the pad of my middle finger in the process.

"Shit!" I exclaim, as blood slides from the cut. It's deep. Fortunately for me, the pain doesn't register given the drugs, alcohol, and painkillers still in my system.

The door knocker bangs sharply again.

"Hold on a minute!" I shout, grabbing a tea towel and wrapping it around my finger. Blood seeps through the material.

Another couple of sharp raps on the door has me hobbling down the corridor, ready to give Mrs Samson a piece of my mind. She has a habit of knocking at my door at all manner of hours asking for sugar or milk or something similar. One time she even asked if I had some cigarettes knowing full well I don't smoke. The woman is a royal pain in my arse, and now finger. Clutching my hand to my chest, I yank open the front door to find Ivan

Sachov standing in front of me soaking wet and with a thunderous look on his face. Without giving me a moment to ask what the hell he's doing on my doorstep looking like he wants to murder someone, Ivan pushes open the door and strides into my hallway.

"Who do you think you are, barging in here like that? How dare you!" I shout, turning on him.

I'm so pissed off that I forget to hold the tea towel against my finger, and it drops to the floor. Blood seeps from the wound and drips down my hand.

"Shit!" I say, moving to pick it up, but Ivan gets there before me and snatches it up in his hand.

"What happened?" he barks, grabbing my wrist and wrapping the towel back around my bleeding finger. Ivan stares me down, his eyes dark and smouldering.

For a moment I can't speak, I'm so caught up in the look he's giving me and the weird affect it seems to be having on my body. I don't recognise this man; Ivan is a different beast to Luka, principal dancer and ballet god.

"Well?" he demands, still holding onto my wrist.

His hands are cold and wet, but it's his touch that makes me shiver. His clothes are completely wet through and his hair is plastered to his head. I watch as a raindrop rolls down his cheek and falls from his jawline.

"I cut it on a piece of broken glass. Now, can you just leave?" I say, yanking my hand back.

His grip tightens. "What were you doing with broken glass?"

He peers down at me, his eyes narrowing. Then he does something strange, he pushes back the sleeve of my dressing gown and pulls my arm out towards him, running a finger over my skin.

"What are *you* doing?" I retort, trying and failing to get out of his grasp, trying and failing to ignore the pleasant sensation of his touch.

"You need to sort out that cut. Where's your medical supplies?" he snaps.

What the hell is his problem? He fired *me*, he has no right to come into my home acting in such a way. Come to think of it, how does he know where I live?

"If you let go of my arm, I might be *able* to sort it out!"

He makes a noise that's a mixture between a snarl and a snort, then proceeds to drag me along my *own* hallway and into the kitchen.

"Watch the glass!" I yell as he steps straight onto the pile I'd just cleared. I yelp as my bare foot steps on a shard I'd missed. He looks at me holding my foot up, then down at the pile of broken glass before finally resting his eyes on the red wine covering most of the kitchen surfaces.

"What happened?"

"Shit, that hurts," I say, completely ignoring his question. His presence has certainly sobered me up sharpish because now I feel *all* the pain. My finger and foot are throbbing and my knee and back are aching. Not to mention the little voice in the back of my head intent on bringing me further down. The black clouds aren't just gathering outside.

Ivan lets go of my wrist and I hobble backwards trying to get away from him as much as the broken glass all over the floor. I don't get very far before he grips me around the waist and lifts me up onto the section of worktop that isn't covered in spilt wine and broken glass.

I let out a tiny sound of indignation and push at his chest for having the audacity to manhandle me. He ignores my attempts to shove him away, and simply grips my hips tighter. I fight the urge slap him.

"Get your hands off me," I grind out, caught between being completely pissed off for his audacity and uncomfortably turned on. Who the hell does he think he is?

"Do you have a medical box or not?" he asks, still grasping hold of my hips. Somehow, he's managed to work his way between my open thighs. I glance down, aware that my dressing gown has fallen open and I'm only wearing a pair of boxer shorts and a camisole, without a sodding bra. His gaze follows mine, and his mouth presses into a hard line as he takes a good look at my breasts.

"The medical box?" he snaps, stepping back quickly.

"Over there in the cupboard above the sink," I reply, slamming my knees together and yanking my robe back around me. I know I'm bright red, I can feel the familiar heat rise up my chest and neck. Ivan strides over to the other side of the kitchen and a couple seconds later he has pulled the box from the cupboard, the same stony expression plastered on his face as he returns with it.

"Give me your foot," he barks, placing the box of medical supplies next to me on the counter. He rummages through and pulls out some antiseptic wipes and a plaster.

"I'm perfectly capable of sorting myself out," I say, pulling my foot up onto my knee so that I can see if there's any glass stuck in it. I suck a breath through my teeth at the sudden sharp pain in my finger and foot, as well as my knee which is already beginning to swell up. *Shit.*

"Where does it hurt?"

There's something in the way he asks that question that makes me think he isn't just talking about the physical pain. I glance up at him, but although I'm certain he knows I'm staring at him, he refuses to meet my gaze. Instead, he opens an antiseptic wipe and slides it over the cut on my foot. I grit my teeth as he cleans away the blood.

"There's a bit of glass embedded in your foot. I can feel it," he says, his eyebrows drawing together as he attempts to pull it out.

"Ow!" I flinch, trying to yank my foot out of his grasp. He just grips it tighter.

"Do you have any tweezers?"

"Why?"

"So I can pull the glass out, I can't get it with my fingers."

I don't respond right away, I'm too distracted by the way his thumb is massaging my foot just by the ankle bone. I don't think he even realises he's doing it. *Why* is he doing it? I zero in on that simple touch, at the heat building beneath his thumb as it moves over my skin. Jesus, what is happening here?

"Rose, do you have any tweezers?" he repeats, snapping me out of my troubling thoughts.

I nod, swallowing hard, trying not to show how affected I am by his touch.

"Upstairs in the bathroom cabinet... Look, you can go, I can manage on my own," I say, attempting once more to get rid of him.

He makes that odd noise again, then releases me from his

grasp. "I'll get them," he says, before striding down my hallway and disappearing up the stairs.

I watch him leave, my mouth gaping like a goldfish and my heart galloping. What the hell is going on? Why is he here? And more to the point, why isn't he bloody leaving? I think I've made it clear that I don't want him here.

Haven't I?

Then I remember the sudden flush of heat from his touch, and the awkward moment when our eyes met earlier. Leaning my head back against the kitchen cabinet, I close my eyes and try to calm my breathing. Upstairs my bathroom door slams shut.

CHAPTER EIGHT

Ivan

I STEP into Rose's bathroom and slam the door behind me. Staggering over to the washbowl, I turn the cold tap on and splash my face with water. I've *never* felt so out of control around a woman before. Not even with Svetlana.

What the fuck is she doing to me?

Collectively, I've been in her presence no more than half an hour, and in that time, she's managed to well and truly fuck with my head. The feel of her skin, the way her lip curls up when she's angry, the flush of red heat at my touch, the shape of her legs and her glorious breasts... the way her gaze cuts right through me. Those eyes. *Fuck.*

Gripping hold of the washbowl I lean over, fighting the urge to throw up. "What the fuck is wrong with you, Luka?" I ask myself.

Luka? I haven't referred to myself as Luka for more than two years now. Things really must be bad.

"Get a hold of yourself."

Taking in several deep breaths, I make myself stand upright. Above the sink is the mirrored cabinet Rose mentioned. I stare at the man reflected back at me.

"What the fuck are you doing here?"

I mean, I know *why* I came, that desire hasn't changed. I want to fuck Rose more than I've ever wanted to fuck any woman. But something is stopping me from trying to make that happen. Okay, that's not true, I'm trying to make it happen, I'm just not trying hard enough.

Why is that?

It doesn't help that she seems to be battling herself. Her body tells me she wants me just like all the other women I've had, but her actions and her words are telling me to back the fuck off. Whilst that would normally present as a challenge to me, and who doesn't love a good fucking challenge? This time I feel differently about it. I'm unsure, and it isn't a position I like being in. Uncertainty isn't in my vocabulary. I'm a very certain man. Certain about what I want, what I need, what I like and what I don't. Then why here, with Rose, am I so fucking uncertain?

"What are you doing here, Luka?" I ask again, more calmly this time.

I half expect my reflection to respond. Except the person I see isn't Luka, it's Ivan and he doesn't answer to anyone, even himself.

. . .

WALKING into the kitchen with the tweezers grasped in my hand, I find that Rose has cleaned up the spilt wine and cleared away the remaining pieces of broken glass. She's nothing if not stubborn. I get the distinct impression she's looked after herself for a long time, and accepting help isn't something that comes naturally to her. I swallow a laugh, *giving* help isn't something that comes naturally to me either, yet here I am doing exactly that.

"I've made *myself* some tea," she says, hobbling over to the kitchen island with a mug in her hand. She settles down on the stool and looks at me. Her expression is deadpan, the earlier anger, and flush of red heat, gone. She's managed to school her emotions, hiding herself behind a mask, and damn if it doesn't want to make me dig deeper for them. I'm used to women giving themselves up to me without even having to ask. I'm used to women entrusting me with their bodies and their hearts. I'm used to taking everything I need then leaving them, I've never had to work for it.

"Did you find them?" she asks, her gaze moving from my face to my hands as she takes a sip of tea. I notice there isn't a cup for me.

"Yes."

"Took you long enough," she responds a little sharply. I can see that her hand is no longer covered in a tea towel and that her finger is dressed in a plaster. The cut must be deep because blood still seeps through.

"Sorry," I mutter.

Sorry?

Where the fuck had that come from? I don't do apologies, ever. My mouth clamps shut, and I grit my jaw. The last time I apologised was when I held Svetlana's limp body in my arms. That apology had been like acid on my tongue, it had changed everything for me. That night, I'd discarded Luka Petrin and had become Ivan Sachov.

Now I'm apologising for taking too long to find the damn tweezers.

"Whatever." Rose shrugs her shoulders, unaware of the rarity of such an apology. I cross my arms over my chest, pissed off with her, with myself. In fact, I'm fucking furious.

"I tried to get the glass out, but it was a little difficult with my knee..." her voice trails off as she watches me glance at her bare legs. She attempts to cover herself with the dressing gown, but it isn't quite long enough, and I can see a good portion of creamy thigh. A beauty spot sits just above her swollen knee on her inner thigh and my cock stirs again at the thought of pressing my tongue against it. Forcing myself to look away, my gaze slides lower to her knee which is swollen and red. She must be in a lot of pain with it. I've suffered a few injuries in my time as a dancer and that knee is going to hurt like a bitch once all the alcohol has worn off.

"What's wrong with you?" I ask.

"*She's sick. Rheumatoid Arthritis.*" That's what Ms Hadley had said, but I ask the question anyway.

"Not that it's any of your damn business, but I have an autoimmune disease. That's why I had to give up ballet. I've not danced for over a year." She reaches down and gingerly rubs her slim fingers over the inflamed and swollen joint.

"You don't dance at all?"

"No." She sighs, looking away. Something tells me she's

lying about that. Ballet is ingrained in her very soul, she can no more stop dancing than I can stop fucking.

I look her over, apart from two slightly swollen knuckles on her right hand and knee I can't see any other obvious signs of the disease. That doesn't mean to say that she isn't in a great deal of pain, it just means the outward signs aren't as obvious yet.

She holds her hand out. "Now that you've had a good bloody look, would you give me the tweezers, so I can get this damn glass out." she growls.

"No, let me."

Ignoring her suspicious gaze, I crouch down before her and grasp her ankle. The second my fingers touch her skin, something fucking crackles inside my chest. Call it chemistry, call it overwhelming attraction, call it lust. Whatever the fuck it is, I'm not sure I like it. Yes, I've had similar reactions to other women, but nowhere near as intense. The moment I've fucked them the feelings subside, absorbed by the demon inside. Rose appears to be poking the beast.

"What are you doing now?" she bites out.

"Helping you."

She laughs bitterly. "I don't need *your* kind of help."

"Well, you've got it, whether you like it or not." I inspect the cut, gently feeling for the piece of glass beneath the skin.

"You don't strike me as the kind of man who helps others. In fact, you don't strike me as the kind of man who ever gets on his knees for anyone, let alone a woman. So why are you doing it now?"

I snarl. The sound literally releases from my mouth before I can stop it. She's not wrong, in fact she's absolutely right. I don't help anyone unless it benefits me. I don't get on my knees for a woman unless I have an ulterior motive. Frankly, it's normally the women kneeling before me, not the other way around.

"Did you just snarl at me like a fucking animal?"

She attempts to pull her foot back, but I grab hold of it tightly, running my thumb over the arch. "Stop talking," I grind out.

"Ha! This is my house, remember. If you don't like what I have to say, you know where the door is."

"Right now, I'm just taking a piece of glass out of your foot, that's it."

Rose snorts. "What do you take me for, Ivan? Do you honestly think you can demand my attention, my *respect*, from a few hot glares and well placed touches? I *see* you. I've known men like you and I won't fall for it again."

And there it is... *again*. So, there *is* more to Rose than she lets on. I knew it. I sensed that.

"Well, do you?" she persists.

"No, actually, I don't," I respond honestly.

Yes, I might want her attention but I sure as hell don't need her respect. What I want is to fuck her. I ignore the snort she makes, choosing to run my hand over her instep and up her ankle. Rose draws in a breath at the touch but this time she doesn't try to pull free from my grasp, a feeling of self-satisfaction turns my lip up into a smile.

"Don't flatter yourself," I hear her mutter with disdain. "I want the glass out. So if you're insistent on doing that, I suggest you get on with it."

The smile I have slips, and I squeeze her foot tighter than I should. She's beginning to piss me off. How dare she fucking reject me? Pressing my thumb onto the sole of her foot beside the wound, I feel for the shard of glass. The hard edge isn't too far beneath the surface.

"Shit," she says, jerking her foot.

"You need to keep *still*, or I won't be able to get it out."

"That hurt!" she snaps back, glaring at me, and fuck if I don't want to pull her off the stool and into my arms. My fucking cock stirs, and all I can do is squeeze her foot tighter, harder. One more snide remark from her and I'm not going to be able to control my actions. She needs a good fucking spanking.

"It's going to hurt more if you don't hold steady," I snap back, a veiled threat even if she doesn't recognise it.

"Just get it out, then you can leave."

I almost respond with a smart remark of my own but decide against it. Her absolute determination to send me on my way has my blood pumping and my anger boiling. No one fucking rejects me.

"Fine!" I grip her foot tightly and ignoring her yelp, dig the tweezers into the cut. I find the piece of glass and pull it out quickly.

"Fuuuuuuckkk!" she cries, as the shard slides out, blood following its release.

I look up at her wide eyes and bite back down on another apology. What's wrong with me? I hurt people, that's what I do best. This is no fucking different.

"Pass me the antiseptic wipes," I say, dropping the pair of tweezers on the floor. I press the pad of my thumb over the cut as I try to stem the flow of blood.

"Here," she says, passing one to me.

I take it from her and clean the wound. "I need some wadding and a bandage too."

She passes me both and stays quiet whilst I wrap up her foot. Once I'm certain it's going to stay in place, I release her foot and stand. We look at each other, neither of us saying a word. For the first time in my life I'm not sure what I'm going to do next.

I came here with every intention of fucking her then leaving her wanting, *needing* me. I came to mess with her head and her heart... I still want to fuck her. I want to tear that dressing gown from her shoulders, rip her shorts down and fuck her up against the kitchen island.

This is the first time I've come close to wanting to take without getting consent. The demon inside me fucking roars to life at the thought. I take a step back from her. That's one step too far, even for me. I'm not a fucking rapist.

"Why are you *here*, Ivan?"

She asks me the same question I asked myself not five minutes ago. The fact that she doesn't use my real name surprises me. Then I remember her promise to keep my past a secret. I don't doubt that she will. I can already tell she's someone who keeps her promises, just like I'm the kind of person that breaks theirs.

"I thought that was obvious. I came here to fuck you," I say.

CHAPTER NINE

Rose

"I CAME HERE TO FUCK YOU."

Did he actually just say that? He stands before me, his arms folded across his chest, refusing to look away. The cocky, arrogant bastard.

Most of me is indignant, pissed off, some of me is flattered, turned on. Another part is *scared*. Okay, that's a lie. A very large part of me is scared. I don't trust him. I don't trust myself around him.

"I don't even know you," I say, surprising myself with my response. What I should have said was 'get out of my house, you self-serving dick', but my brain doesn't appear to be computing right now.

"I'm your boss. We know each other," he replies.

"*For all of five minutes*. You fired me, remember?!"

A muscle flicks in his jaw as he regards me. He doesn't mention the other way we know each other. Discussing *La Bayadere,* and the fact that he was one of the most gifted ballet dancers of our time appears to be off the table.

"Then work for me." He unfolds his arms and steps towards me once more.

I automatically want to shrink back because his presence is so overwhelming. Instead, I sit up straighter and hold my hand up, barking out a laugh.

"So you can *fuck* me, then fuck me over? No thanks. Been there, done that." I slam my mouth shut on my response, realising too late I've let out another snippet of my past without meaning to.

His eyes snap to mine and I look away. Why do I persist in hurting myself? I don't want to think of him, I don't want to remember how my foolish sixteen year old self had been used by a man just like this one. Ivan steps closer, he grips my jaw in his hand and forces me to face him. I'm about to push him away when the fire in his gaze stops me. Is that jealousy? How can he possibly be jealous? It doesn't make any sense, he doesn't know me enough to warrant such a reaction.

"Who? A director, one of the troupes? *Who?*" he demands, the low growl of his voice rumbling up his chest.

I jerk my chin out of his hold and push upwards, ignoring the throbbing pain every-fucking-where. Pulling myself up to my full height, I stab my finger into his chest. "It's none of your damn business. Now. Get. Out. Of. My. House."

To my surprise, he steps back.

"You can have the rest of the week off to recover, but I

expect you back at work Monday morning eight am sharp," he says, taking another step backwards.

"No," I say, stalking *him* now. For every step I take towards him, he steps back down the hall.

"*No?*"

"You heard me. I'm not in the business of fucking my boss just because he orders me to!" I snap.

Ivan doesn't even flinch. Seemingly oblivious to my very obvious distaste. He backs away from me, as I limp towards him. My dressing gown has managed to undo itself and even though I know I'm on show, I'm past caring.

He needs to leave. Now.

"In fact, I'm not in the business of fucking any man just because he orders me to. I'll find another way to survive, thank you very much."

His fingers might have felt like fire and ice on my skin. His gaze might make my insides quiver, his presence might make me want to submit myself utterly to him and he might just be the most alluring man I've ever met, but that doesn't mean to say I *will* give in to him. I'm thirty fucking years old, not some doe-eyed teenager who believes that love conquers all. Love fucking tears you up and spits you out. It fucking shreds your heart and devours your soul.

Love fucking hurts.

"Then don't," he says, stopping so abruptly that I almost collide into his chest. I would have if he hadn't held his hands out to stop me. I feel the warmth of his palms seep through the robe covering my arms.

"Don't what?" I tense under his touch. Don't think about

where I want those hands to move next? Because that's *exactly* what I'm doing right now. He's dangerous. Poisonous.

This man is not for you, Rose. This time that little voice in my head has a point.

"Don't fuck your boss..." He sighs, lifting his hands off me. "Come and work for me, and I promise I won't touch you."

"What?!"

"Be my assistant, come work for me, and I swear on Svetlana's soul I won't touch you," he repeats. It's the first time he's mentioned his late wife, and a flash of pain slices across his face.

"I don't understand," I say, pulling my robe tightly around me. "A few hours ago, you fired me because I know who you really are, because I remind you of your past." He blanches at that, but I continue regardless. "Then you come here because you want to fuck *me*, and now you're offering my job back on the promise that you'll never touch me? What the hell is wrong with you?"

"If I knew that, then I'd know how to fix it," he admits, surprising himself at the admission given the look of shock that follows it.

"You're messed up."

"I know."

"Why would I *want* to work for you now?"

"I'm a man of my word."

I laugh at that. "Tell me something, Ivan. When we danced together in *La Bayadere,* there were rumours that you fucked the entire cast of dancers." *Except you,* the same dark voice says inside my head. I ignore it and continue. "I never believed it, until now..."

"You didn't?" he asks, swiping a hand through his damp

hair. Strands stick up in different directions making him look like a dishevelled school boy, but it's just another ruse to hide the danger within.

"Why would I? I saw the way you were together. I don't think I've ever seen two people more in love. Why would you want to jeopardise that?"

He looks over my shoulder, avoiding my gaze, and I know instantly that he'd done exactly that, jeopardise their love. Perhaps Luka wasn't so different from the man standing before me now. With that knowledge, the memories of the man I once admired, shatter. I'm guessing at nineteen I was still as naïve as I was three years before. Well, I've grown up a lot since then.

"It's complicated..." he admits.

"You fucked all those women despite the love you shared, because I know that *can't* be faked. You *did* love her, I saw that, but you fucked her over anyway. You're a piece of work."

Ivan stares back at me. I wait for the lie to come. I have a feeling he's been lying to himself for a very long time. What he says next surprises me most of all.

"I'm fully aware that I'm a bastard, but in my own way I loved Svetlana very much. Did I betray her? Yes, yes, I did. I fucked every woman in the troupe, except one it would seem," he says.

My arms tighten around me, but I don't allow myself to react any more than that. Ivan doesn't need to know how much he affects me. In fact, I'm going to make it my sole aim to ensure he never knows how attracted I am to him.

"I cheated on my wife before we were married, I cheated on her after. I stole her heart and made her love me. I ruined her. That's what I do. I take things and I ruin them."

"And this makes me want to work for you because?" I ask.

"Because I swear to you now, I won't touch you. I won't ruin *you*."

"Why? If this is who you are, what makes you think you won't even try?"

"Because you see the demon within me and you aren't afraid of it. I can't promise I won't try, but I know you're strong enough not to let me succeed. Tonight, you've proven that to me. I always get what I want. This is the first time ever I've been denied."

"Jesus, bighead much?" I mutter. That draws a smile, or perhaps it's a grimace, I'm not really sure. I don't think his face knows either.

"Will you work for me, Rose?" he asks, and I swear if I didn't know any better, that there's a vulnerability to his request. This man is an enigma.

No, not an enigma, he's *dangerous*, but I know that already.

The hallway fills with silence as he waits for me to answer. But I don't answer immediately, I take my measure of him, devouring him with *my* gaze this time. He stands still, barely even breathing it would seem, whilst I figure out whether I can do what he's asked.

Am I attracted to him? The simple answer is yes. Yes, of course I am. Who wouldn't be?

I remember the length of red silk in his desk drawer and the way it had made me feel. The excitement, as well as the anxiety. It was another reminder of the girl I've buried deep inside the pit of my past. Can I be around that kind of person again? Can I work for a man who's admitted to cheating on his wife, admitted that he came here tonight with the sole purpose of fucking me, just like all the other women he's conquered? I think back to the vulnerable, naïve sixteen year old girl who believed love was the *only* thing that could conquer all. I remember that same love I'd felt for a man twice my age, a man who'd taken away my innocence and left me broken. I remember the night he was taken from me too, and the dark cloud that always lingers nearby, looms over me now.

"What's it to be, Rose?" Ivan presses, his voice barely above a whisper.

It's uncanny how alike Ivan is to the man I once loved; handsome, controlling, charismatic, domineering, sexy, passionate, dangerous, twisted, *fucked-up*.

But, I'm no longer that innocent girl. I'm a grown woman with a lifetime of experience behind me. I made the mistake of trusting a beast hidden beneath sexy smiles and intense stares, I won't do that again.

Staring straight into Ivan's eyes, I give him my terms.

"Working for you requires danger money it would seem, so I want double. I also want to be formally introduced to the other men hidden away in Browlace Manor. I want to know who's in the building with me and why all the doors are locked."

His eyes widen, that muscle ticks in his jaw once again. "How did you know about them?"

"It doesn't matter how I know, I just do."

"Anything else?" he bites out.

"Yes. I want to know about the red silk in your drawer. I want to know how often you use it, on who and why."

"That's personal," he snaps.

"You wanted my terms, so here they are. Take it or leave it."

He presses his lips into a hard line, thinking it through.

"Oh, and one more thing..."

"There's more?"

"You keep Ms Hadley away from me. I don't trust her."

Ivan narrows his eyes at me, anger flaring behind them. Half a minute later, he nods his head sharply. "I shall send a cab to collect you Saturday night, seven pm sharp. I shall ensure Ms Hadley has the night off so that I can introduce you to Anton and Erik formally. Then I shall answer all your questions."

"And the money?" I ask.

"Isn't an issue."

"Then we're in agreement?"

"We're in agreement, Rose," he says, turning away from me. In four strides he's at the front door and is yanking it open. Outside the rain still pours. He glances over his shoulder at me. "But I have something I'd like to add to our new agreement."

"What's that?" I ask.

"No ballet."

"What?" My heart lurches.

"If you fail. If you *succumb* to your need to dance. I get to make you mine." And with that, he walks out of the door leaving me gaping after him.

CHAPTER TEN

Ivan

I WATCH Rose step out of the taxi that's just pulled up outside. She's wearing a dark, floor length coat, and her hair is loose around her shoulders. She opens her purse and pulls out a twenty pound note, but the taxi driver waves off her money.

Did she think I'd expect her to pay? Something about that infuriates me. I may be a bastard when it comes to women's hearts, but I look after my staff.

Stuffing the note back into the purse she smiles at the driver, then turns and walks up to the front door. She doesn't notice me staring at her, though that's no surprise given I'm standing in my darkened office. I laugh at myself, hiding in darkness so she won't see me staring. What am I, a fucking teenage boy stalking their crush? I need to get a hold of myself. This is getting ridiculous.

It's been four days since our stand-off in her kitchen.

Four days of torture.

Every night I've requested the company of a woman. I've fucked them for hours and reached release, but Christ knows my head was elsewhere every time. All because of this woman who refuses to fall for my charms. My cock stirs just watching her as she takes the few steps up to the front door and I recall how determined she was to get what she wanted. Double the pay, meeting Anton and Erik, knowing all my fucking secrets. That part isn't going to be easy, not because I'm going to find it hard not to tell her the truth, but because I've got to make sure what I tell her convinces her enough not to see through the bullshit. There are some things that are meant to stay locked behind walls of lies. My soul is one of them.

Turning my attention back to Rose, I notice that she still has a slight limp and I wonder briefly what medication she takes to ease the symptoms of her condition. If she's going to work for me then I need to make sure she's as healthy as she can possibly be, so I make a mental note to look into finding her the finest doctor money can buy. I'll be damned if I pay her double to stay at home all day in bed, unless of course I'm with her, and then maybe she'd be worth the money. I'm pretty fucking certain she'd be worth it. My cock certainly thinks so.

Rose stops at the door and raises her hand to press the bell. She hesitates, her finger hovering in the air. She stands there for a good twenty seconds before the door swings open and Ms Hadley steps out.

Fuck. I'd told her to leave an hour ago. Why is she still here?

Rose takes a step back as Ms Hadley steps towards her. The wind is whipping up Rose's dark hair and I'm finding it difficult to catch her expression, though I can see my housekeeper's well enough. She's scowling. It's a look I recognise, and normally proceeds a good dressing down. I don't know what Ms Hadley is saying, but I can tell by the sneer she's not exchanging pleasantries. Rose's hand lifts, and she swipes her hair behind her ear. I notice that her cheeks are bright red, though not with embarrassment given her equally angry expression. She folds her arm across her chest and I watch as her eyes narrow.

There's the Rose I'm beginning to recognise. The one that doesn't take any shit. Something tells me she's had to fight her corner more than once in her life. It's just as well she has a backbone, demure and prissy just won't cut it here. Ms Hadley is like an overbearing, overprotective mama bear, and she doesn't take kindly to interlopers. It took Svetlana a year to soften Ms Hadley towards her and even then, she was still guarded.

Two pink spots darken the old woman's cheeks as Rose steps toe to toe with her. Now it's Ms Hadley's turn to blanche at the onslaught. There's no doubt Rose is giving as good as she gets. I admire her gumption.

My spying is disturbed when I hear a knock on the door, there's a strip of light beneath it and the shadow of feet moving.

"Give me a minute, Anton," I call, knowing it's him by the way he knocks. He knows not to open the door unless I give him permission to do so. We're used to living with each other. Anton understands my need for privacy, like I understand his need for space.

"She's here," he responds.

"I know that. Just bring Erik to the dining room as planned. I'll be there in a minute."

"Fine," he agrees. I hear his steps as he walks away.

Turning my attention back to Ms Hadley and Rose, I frown when I realise Rose has already entered the house. I'm about to go and greet her when something in Ms Hadley's gaze stops me. Stepping further into the shadows, I take one last look at my housekeeper. It's the first time I've really observed her unawares and a little voice of caution sounds in my head as I watch her expression turn from angry to downright murderous. Something tells me I'm going to have to watch my housekeeper a little closer from now on.

***

"ROSE, MAY I TAKE YOUR COAT?" I ask, striding into the entrance hall.

She jumps at my sudden appearance. "Do you sneak up on everyone like that?" she asks me, immediately indignant.

"Apologies. It wasn't intentional." There I go again, apologising to this woman.

"I just bumped into Ms Hadley," she says, undoing the buttons on her coat. She struggles a little with each one. "I thought we agreed that you'd keep her away from me? It's not a very good start, is it?"

"She wasn't supposed to be here. I asked her to leave over an hour ago. What did she say to you?"

"Nothing of any consequence," Rose responds, undoing the last button of her coat.

She lets it part, her hands falling away. Beneath I spot a red silk shirt, paired with a short black skirt that sits mid-thigh. Her shapely legs are covered in black tights and knee high boots. Even though she's dressed for a day of work rather than dinner,

I still have to swallow the sudden lump in my throat. Whether it was a conscious decision to wear that red shirt or not, it still has the same effect on me. My cock stirs as I imagine a similar length of silk wrapped around her wrists.

"I'll make sure you don't cross paths from now on," I say, ignoring the urge to grab her by the hair, and drag her to my studio to fuck.

"Thank you," she says, handing me her coat.

I take it, feeling the warmth of her body heat still lingering in the material. It takes all my self-control not to lift it to my face and breath in her smell.

"Follow me," I say, turning on my heel and striding towards the dining room. Rose follows, the sound of her heels clicking in time with the ever present pulse in my cock.

The dining room sits at the end of one of the corridors that lead off the entrance hall. Earlier, I made sure that Ms Hadley unlocked all the doors leading to the room, not wanting to remind Rose of the fact that the rest of the doors in the Manor remain locked. Maybe she's forgotten her need to know why they're locked, and I won't have to lie to her. I'm not averse to lying usually, I'm not really averse to lying now, but if I can avoid it, I will.

"Am I the only one who works here that doesn't get a set of keys to all the doors?" Rose asks.

"Yes," I respond, holding open the door to the dining room.

She stops on the threshold of the room, both of us standing in the doorway. The nearness of her is making my skin itch. She smells delicious, of coconuts and warm summer nights. It reminds me of Mauritius, a place I haven't been to in years, and probably one of the only places in the world where I don't feel suffocated by my past. I never even took Svetlana to my hotel there. I stopped going the moment she stopped living. I didn't deserve the freedom of my soul whilst hers was damned to hell.

"So you expect me to work here with you in this house whilst all these secrets lurk behind closed doors?"

"I expect you to work as my assistant. You only wanted to know *why* the doors were locked, your terms didn't include access to the rooms beyond them," I remind her.

"That's just semantics," she retorts, her forehead creasing in anger. That feisty women begins to surface, and I find myself wanting to provoke her more, just so I can see her get angrier still. It fucking turns me on.

"No, it's not. I'm not willing to give you access to the rooms beyond those required for your job. I do it for good reason."

"Fine, then you'd better start explaining."

Rose strides past me, her arm brushing against my chest in her haste. I see her flinch from the contact and my cock stirs once more. She might be able to deny me, but I know the attraction is there, she's just better at fighting it than I am.

"Any particular place you'd like me to sit?" she asks pointing to the table that is dressed to seat four.

"Next to *me*, here," I say, pulling out a chair.

She raises her eyebrows at the veiled ownership, but sits down anyway, eyeing the two empty chairs opposite us.

"Anton is bringing Erik. They'll be here momentarily," I say in answer to her silent question.

"Bringing? You make it sound like he needs babysitting."

"He does. That's why we lock the doors, to keep him safe," I say.

"You keep the doors locked because of your brother Erik?"

"Brother? He's not my brother. What gave you that idea?" I ask, leaning over to grab the bottle of Merlot. I pour us both a glass and add wine to one of the glasses opposite. Erik doesn't drink. Actually, up until recently Erik did drink, quite a lot in fact, but he's lost himself to another addiction that is far better for his physical health, if not his mental health.

"Ms Hadley said that she's worked for the Sachov family most of her adult life. When I met Anton and he told me about Erik, I just assumed they were your brothers..."

I nod my head, understanding now. "Ms Hadley was telling the truth when she said that she's worked for the Sachov family her whole life, but Anton is the only real Sachov in this house. He and I have been friends since we were kids and subsequently I've known Ms Hadley for as long as I can remember too. When I became a successful dancer and was earning more money than I knew what to do with, I bought this house and hired Ms Hadley. She was about to retire but decided to take me up on my offer when I asked her to work for me."

"So why is Anton living with you now?"

I watch her pink lips part then slide over the rim of the glass as she takes a sip. Even that has my balls tightening. Ignoring my physical reaction to such a simple act, I answer her question.

"After Svetlana..." my voice trails off as I note the look of compassion in Rose's gaze. That one look guts me, she may as well have picked up the knife from the table and stabbed it in my heart. I don't deserve her compassion.

Taking a mouthful of wine to calm my torrid emotions, I continue. "Anton came to live here with me, to give emotional support I suppose. He had his own reasons too, but that story isn't mine to tell. He allowed me to adopt his family name, so I could start a new life."

"That was good of him."

"He might not be my brother by blood, but we are family. That's the way it's always been."

"And what about Erik? You said he was the reason for all the locked doors. Why are you keeping him prisoner?"

"They're not keeping me prisoner. They're keeping us safe."

Rose's head snatches around as she watches Erik enter the room. Behind him Anton follows, gently clicking the door shut. A warm blush rises up her neck, spreading out across her cheeks at the sudden entrance of my friends. In that moment she looks just like a summer rose blooming in the winter sun; a rare and unusual beauty.

She stands, her chair scraping across the hardwood floor as she does so.

"Hello again," she says to Anton, almost shyly.

He nods briefly in her direction. Something flickers across his face in the split second it takes for him to imprint her in his memory, something that has me scowling.

Interest.

I'm hoping the interest he shows is due to his artistic eye and nothing more. I know he appreciates beautiful things, and Rose is most certainly beautiful, but that's where I draw the line. He may be a gifted artist who can paint an extraordinary image from memory alone, but I'll be damned if she becomes his latest muse.

No fucking way.

Luckily for him, Rose is distracted by Erik who's gripping

his violin in one hand, the bow in the other. He too is staring at her. Perhaps this wasn't a good idea after all.

"Hello Erik," she says, walking around the table towards him.

What is she doing? I should've warned her about his state of mind before they came in, but I'm captured by the way she approaches him. She moves slowly, her entire body language completely changed. Her eyes are downcast, her steps slow, cautious. She moves as though understanding instinctively that he is to be dealt with care. It's mesmerising to watch.

Erik watches her warily from behind the curtain of his chin length hair. He may be clean shaven and dressed smartly, but it's obvious he's unwell. The tenseness of his body, the wild look in his eyes. Erik is like a dog who's been beaten daily and then introduced to a new, kinder owner. No one knows whether it will bite the hand of friendship or accept it.

I watch as Erik clutches his violin and bow against his chest, stepping away from her. She stops within reaching distance and I stiffen with tension. Anton does too. Yet neither of us make any move to stop her.

"So you're the violinist? You play beautifully," she says, her voice is low, gentle.

There's something about the way she holds herself, and the soothing tone of her voice that makes me wonder who in her past she had to speak to in the same way. There's experience in her actions and this only serves to interest me more.

I hold my breath as she stands before Erik, her gaze lowered, not looking up into his eyes. She waits, absolutely still, silent.

That silence may be a balm to Erik but to me it's deafening. I'm waiting for the bomb to explode, I know Anton is too.

But it doesn't.

Instead, with a calmness reserved only for the brave, Rose reaches over and brushes her fingers over Erik's arm. Her hand lingers there, her touch light, her head still bowed. Erik steps forward, his huge frame towering over her smaller one. He looks at her fingers as though he has no idea how they got there. All the while, Rose remains perfectly still. I should probably stop this, say something at least, but for the life of me all I can do is watch to see how it unfolds.

"I'd love to hear you play a full piece one day, if that's not too much to ask?" she requests softly.

Erik looks from her hand touching his arm back up to her bowed head. It's *exactly* too much to ask, but Rose has no way of knowing that. The words I have to tell her as much are currently stuck in my throat, as are Anton's, given he's not uttered a word either.

The air bleeds with tension as we all wait for Erik's response. This is such a bad fucking idea.

"One day, perhaps," he replies.

Anton looks at me in shock, raising his eyebrows. I grip the chair in front of me to steady myself. Rose nods her head, then without looking at Erik removes her hand, turns slowly on her feet and returns to her seat by my side, completely oblivious to the miracle that's just taken place. Without saying another word, Erik sits at the table and places the violin and bow on the floor by his feet.

"Were you all childhood friends?" Rose asks me, as she settles at the table.

"Yes, we were... Erik is Ms Hadley's son."

CHAPTER ELEVEN

Rose

HER SON?

"You're Ms Hadley's son?" I ask Erik. He simply nods his head, watching me.

I can't see how this beautiful man is made from the same gene pool as Ms Hadley. Where she's dark, he's blonde. Where she has a sharp stare and black eyes, his are the burnt colour of autumn leaves with hidden depths of gold, not unlike the wood of his violin. But there is something else about him that draws me in. It's something I recognise.

Despair.

I see it in the shake of his fingers, the tightness of his shoulders and the jitter of his leg beneath the table. A bead of sweat rolls from his hairline down the side of his face. This man is fighting something with every breath of his being and I can't believe they brought him here in this state. I'm about to suggest they take Erik back to his safe space, but Anton begins to talk.

"Erik was adopted by Ms Hadley when he was five, and consequently by my family too. He lives here with us so that we can take care of him," he explains.

I rip my gaze away from Erik and turn my attention to Anton. The last time we met, his hands were covered in red paint and he was anxious that I hadn't left the Manor. Well, it's long past four pm now, and nothing untoward has happened. This time the length of his hair is pulled back from his face in a high bun and his beard is groomed and tidy. Everything about him is more presentable. He seems like a different man altogether except for the fact that his hands are still spotted with paint. Green this time, not unlike the colour of my eyes.

"I see," I respond, not certain that I do.

Why would Ms Hadley agree to her son being locked up in this house? In fact, given what she said to me when I arrived, I'm pretty certain she wouldn't be happy about me having dinner with him either. She's already warned me off Ivan, which is ridiculous considering I have no intention of getting involved with him romantically. Ivan isn't capable of a loving relationship and there's no way I want to revisit the darkness of my past with him, or anyone else for that matter.

"Erik, are you okay with this?" I ask him.

He doesn't answer me. Whatever lucidity he had a minute ago has disappeared. I can see the darkness closing over him, and my heart aches. This is cruel.

"Ivan, please..." I say, looking between him and Erik.

"Erik has post-traumatic stress disorder from his time serving in the army," Anton explains.

"He shouldn't be here," I respond, keeping my voice calm even though I want to scream at Anton and Ivan for bringing him to this meal when he's clearly not ready to be around people he isn't familiar with.

"You wanted to meet him," Ivan accuses, defensive now.

"Not like this, not at his expense."

Erik stands abruptly. "I need to go." He bends down, picks up his violin and bow and clutches them to his chest once more. His grip is so tight on the bow that it bends under his grasp.

"It was nice to meet you..." my voice trails off at the look of agony in his eyes. He knows as well as I do that nothing about this meeting was nice, for him particularly.

"I should go." He turns on his heel and strides from the room. His tall, strong frame in such contrast to the vulnerability leaching from him.

"Anton, see him back to his rooms safely, please," Ivan asks.

"Rose, forgive me. I won't be but a moment," Anton says, before rushing off after Erik.

The moment they leave I turn on Ivan. "What the hell was that?"

"That was Erik."

"You know what I mean, Ivan!"

"Rose, these are *your* terms. You wanted to meet Erik and Anton. Well, now you have."

I watch him take a sip of wine without any sense of regret at putting his friend through such an ordeal.

"You really are an arsehole, aren't you?" I ask incredulously.

"I've been made aware that I am on more than one occasion, yes," he responds, a flash of amusement in his eyes.

I want to scream at him for being such a pig. If this is how he treats his friends, fuck knows how I'll be treated as a member of his *staff.* I get up and stride over to the corner of the room, grabbing my coat from the chaise longue.

"Erik doesn't need to be locked up in this house. He needs professional help, he needs fresh air and kindness, he needs *care.* Given everything you've admitted to me about your torrid little fucks, kindness and care aren't part of your vocabulary. I'm leaving."

Ivan stands, blocking my path to the door. He grabs hold of my arm and squeezes.

"I look after my own, Rose. Erik gets the best possible care money can buy, I assure you he is very well looked after."

"You lock him in! You brought him to this dinner with no thought to how it would affect him!" I shout, not able to keep my voice down.

I know what it's like to be kept prisoner at the whim of someone else. Those weeks were the darkest of my life. *But you never felt more alive before or since. Isn't that what frightens you more?* that little voice inside my head reminds me.

I ignore it.

Ivan crosses his arms defensively. "You wanted to meet him..."

"You could've just *explained* the situation. Are you that insensitive to other people's needs?"

"Yes," he admits. "I don't know how to be any other way."

His honesty knocks the wind out of my sails a little. We look at each other, another unspoken conversation going on between us, one that I have no idea how to handle. He's not a nice man, he freely admits that. He messes with people, with women. He hurts the people he claims to love, and he has no regard for his friends. So why the hell am I still standing here? Why am I drawn to him so completely?

Because the darkness has always attracted you, Rose, that little voice taunts.

"I don't think I can do this," I say, mainly to myself.

Don't lie to yourself. You want him. You crave the darkness.

"We had an agreement," Ivan responds sharply.

"I might have bled on you accidentally, Ivan, but you don't *own me*. There's no contract written in blood anywhere that says I have to do a damn thing."

"Perhaps there should be," he mutters.

I pretend not to hear and move towards the door ignoring the voice in my head and Ivan's angry stare. I reach for the handle, but it swings open and in walks a middle-aged woman with greying hair. She's carrying a tray of food. I let out a surprised sound.

"Should I come back in a few minutes, Mr Sachov?" she asks, glancing between us both.

"No, Fran, please serve the starter. Erik will take his in his room, he's no longer dining with us tonight."

"No problem," she replies.

We both wait whilst she places three plates on the table. She glances at me quickly and smiles. Her eyes are kind, there's no hidden agenda in them. Not like the man before me, or Ms Hadley.

"I thought you didn't have other staff?" I ask, distracted by Fran's appearance.

"We have two cooks, a handful of maids and three grounds-men. That's the household Ms Hadley runs. I will introduce them to you all when you start back on Monday."

"*If* I decide to start on Monday," I say.

"*When* you start," Ivan insists.

Fran shuffles past us both, leaving the room with a gentle click of the door as it shuts behind her. The moment she's gone, Ivan steps closer to me. He frowns, no doubt trying to figure out a way to manipulate me into staying.

"Get out of my way, Ivan." My body flushes with heat at his nearness, and I despise myself for it.

"We had a fucking deal, Rose," he says, looming over me.

"Like I said. There was no contract. I'm under no obligation to stay," I respond coolly. *If* I choose to work for him, it will be because *I* decide it's worth the risk, not because he wants to bully me into it.

"You can no more walk away than I can. I know you want me, Rose," he retorts, arrogant enough to believe he's right. I laugh, covering up the fact that he may well be. Am I really considering this after everything he's said, everything I've seen?

But he is right, isn't he? You couldn't walk away from Roman and you won't with these men either. Stop lying to yourself, Rose.

Roman... My heart aches just acknowledging his name after all these years.

"You know nothing about how I feel," I respond, trying to keep my voice steady.

Ivan clamps his jaw shut as he looks at me, the tension between us is overbearing. I step backwards needing a little space, Ivan breathes out heavily as though glad of it. At least one of us has the capacity to think with their head and not another part of their anatomy. But that's just the thing, isn't it? I might be level headed enough to take myself out of this situation, out of the desire already growing between us, but for how long? Ivan admitted he might not be able to stop himself from trying to seduce me, but he's relying solely on me to fight it. That's not fair, and neither is the fact part of the "deal" is that I never dance again. That if I do, he thinks he can just "have" me. It's just bullshit. I need to dance, just like he clearly needs to fuck.

And yet you still came tonight despite that. You know what you want, Rose. Stop lying to yourself.

"This was a bad idea. You just don't get it," I say, shaking my head. Stepping around him I head for the door and escape.

I don't get very far.

"Rose, stop," Ivan says, grabbing hold of my shoulder.

I stiffen under his touch, but for whatever stupid reason I don't move. My feet remain glued to the floor. He steps up behind me and I have to press my eyes shut at his nearness. His closeness sets my skin on fire and I hate him for it.

"Rose, you're right, bringing Erik here to meet you probably wasn't the best idea I've ever had. But those were your terms and I need you to stay..." he says quietly.

The difference in the tone of his voice is marked. Something about it makes me turn around to face him.

"Why? So you can hurt me too?" I ask, looking up into his beautiful face. His kind of beauty is the deadly kind, like a venus flytrap, or a mythical siren. Both lure their prey before devouring them.

"Yes," he blurts out. "It's what I do..."

I laugh at his response, shaking my head. "Goodbye, Ivan."

"Wait!"

From the other side of the room Anton enters. He flashes a look at Ivan that I can't interpret before striding over to me. He stands between us both, blocking Ivan from my line of sight. Behind him, I hear Ivan snarl. Anton ignores him.

Looking up into Anton's dark eyes, I wait. What now? What can Anton possible say to make me change my mind? More to the point, why would he care enough to do so?

"Erik's okay now, Rose. I understand why this has upset you, but please know he wanted to be here. He wanted to meet you, Ivan didn't make him. Erik *chose* to come. He's trying to get better."

I open my mouth to protest, but Anton continues.

"Look, I can see that you're the type of person who truly does give a shit, believe me I've met many who pretend they do, but most definitely don't. I'm asking you not to leave because you think you understand who Ivan truly is, because you never will... He's complicated. We all are, Rose."

"Anton, for fuck's sake," Ivan begins, but Anton holds up his hand, cutting him off.

"I know exactly the kind of man he is. There's nothing complicated about him. In fact, I'm pretty sure he's just an arsehole," I retort.

"You're absolutely right, he *is* an arsehole, there's no denying that."

"Fuck you, Ant," Ivan snaps.

"But you wouldn't have come here tonight if you didn't think you could handle him. Honestly, if I hadn't seen how Erik reacted to you earlier I would've taken you home myself. I know enough about Ivan to know he's no good for you."

"That's right, you warned me about Ivan the first time we met. You said he would hurt me, just like *her*..." I know now that Anton was talking about Svetlana. All those affairs, her heart shattered because Ivan didn't love her enough to be faithful.

"What the fuck, Anton?!" Ivan says, stepping to the side so I can see the expression on his face. He looks like he's about to commit murder.

Anton ignores the rage emanating from Ivan. "I should probably still take you home, warn you off, but selfishly I want you stay for Erik."

"For Erik? What do you mean?" I ask, frowning.

Ivan cuts off Anton, answering my question before he can.

"Erik never lets women touch him, let alone get close to him like you just did. You're the first person aside from Anton and me that has been able to do that," Ivan explains, scraping a hand through his hair. He glances at Anton who's staring at me in that unnerving way of his.

"Is this true?" I ask Anton, not trusting a word that comes out of Ivan's mouth.

"Yes. Erik suffers with flashbacks. Occasionally those flashbacks can become more real than the world around him. It's at those times when he's a danger to himself, and others. He was in the special forces, he saw things that can't be unseen, experienced things that can't be forgotten. During the day when we're not around we keep the doors locked for his safety," Anton explains.

"And after four you let him out? Well, isn't that generous of you all?"

Ivan crosses his arms, narrowing his eyes at me.

"He isn't a prisoner, Rose. We include Erik in every decision. He agreed to this. He needs routine, he needs clear boundaries whilst he recovers. So yes, during the day he remains in his rooms and has more freedom when the staff go home."

"And at that point you let Erik *roam free* like some animal allowed out of its cage?"

Ivan flinches.

"It's not like that, we make sure that one of us is always here to keep him company. We take it in turns. We want him to get better," Anton insists.

"And the violin?"

"Part of his recovery. Erik played before he went into the army. He was good, really good, but despite what he promised you, Erik hasn't managed to play a full piece since before he was conscripted to Afghanistan. The trauma he suffered and the memories that plague him are bound up so tightly within his love of classical music that he can't play the violin without dredging up the horrors of war. His ability to play a full piece is both the key to his healing and the lock that binds him to his past and the memories that make him so unwell."

"That's so sad," I say, my heart aching for him.

"And yet, today, for the first time in two years he's allowed a woman to touch him," Anton says.

"Woman?" I frown.

"I meant person."

He's lying. He meant woman. Why would Erik have an issue with a woman touching him? Why would Anton lie about it? More mystery, more secrets. So many secrets. I have too many of my own, am I really willing to be surrounded by more?

Anton cocks his head and stares at me with the same unnerving look he gave me when I first met him. There's something about the way he looks at me that makes my hair stand on end and my skin prickle with heat. It unnerves me. It's as though he's absorbing every detail.

Not for the first time I wonder who this man is. If I'm honest, all three have me intrigued in different ways.

Ivan and his sexual prowess, the overwhelming chemistry I feel around him. There's an undeniable darkness within him. It's intoxicating. It calls to a long suppressed part of me, a part that wants to tame it.

Anton and the mystery that surrounds him, the intense way he looks at me. The two seemingly different ways he presents himself; the self-assured man in front of me now, and the man I met on the first day.

Erik and his heartbreaking vulnerability. A man who's more dangerous than Ivan and Anton put together.

These men each represent a piece of a man I once loved. A man who gave me the memories I've been running from for the last fourteen years. Memories of dark rooms filled with pain and release, fear and joy, lust and love. It all comes flooding back and I don't know how I feel about it.

Actually, that's a lie. I know exactly how I feel. I feel afraid, but worse than that, I'm excited. The darkest parts of me begin to come alive and I already know that if I pursue them, I may not survive this time.

If I give in. If I *truly* let go, perhaps none of us will.

"Rose, did you hear me?" Anton says, pulling my attention back to him.

My eyes focus once more as Ivan grips Anton's shoulder.

"Let's sit, we'll talk more," Ivan demands, nodding his head to the empty seats.

I look between the two men and think of the third who's missing now, and despite all common sense I decide to stay.

That maniacal little voice inside my head starts to laugh.

CHAPTER TWELVE

Ivan

I *SHOULD* HAVE LET her leave.

A good man would've let her go. I'm not that man, and neither is Anton.

Both of us have our reasons for wanting Rose to stay. I know what mine are, but Anton's aren't quite clear yet. That's a conversation for later. I look across the table at him. He's talking to her about Erik and the support he gets from us all, and whilst it's all true, Anton's motives for telling her are shady as fuck. At least I'm honest about why I want her.

I may be a fucking arsehole, but I don't hide that fact.

Yes, I want to bury my cock inside her warmth. I want to fuck her until nothing else exists apart from our release. I want to redden every inch of her skin with my mark. I want to bruise her heart and her soul. I want to take everything she can give and then when she's satiated, I want to take even more.

I want to own her.

I want it all.

I don't hide that fact. I never have with any of the women I've fucked.

Anton is telling her what she wants to hear. I tell her what she doesn't, or maybe she does, but she's not willing to admit that to herself.

Yet.

Rose glances at me, her green eyes tearing at my fucking skin. Her presence is like two hands wrapping around my throat squeezing the life from me. I've never wanted anyone as much as her.

She's fucking bewitched me.

Rose has turned my head unlike any other, even Svetlana. This woman is a fucking mystery and I want to delve into her depths and never come up for air. I want her so bad I can barely breathe. I want to devour her and make her mine. I want everything she can give, and more.

"Rose, you okay?" Anton questions.

Rose smiles at Anton, and my fucking stomach curdles. *He can't fucking have her.*

My fist crashes against the table making Rose jump.

"What?" she accuses.

I find myself growling from between my teeth. "He can't fucking have you," I seethe, unable to stop myself.

Anton's head snaps around as he glares at me.

"Ivan, what the fuck has gotten into you?" he asks innocently.

It's been a good few years since I've wanted to punch Anton. I love him as much as a man without a heart can, and yet in this moment I want to fucking kill him.

"Don't fuck with me, Anton," I snarl.

"Stop this. Now!" Rose says, standing.

"Where are you fucking going?" I demand, standing too.

Rose narrows her eyes at me and pushes her fingers into my chest. "If you can't behave, I'm going home, and I won't return."

My nails dig into the flesh of my palms. She isn't pretending, she means every word.

"I'm sorry," I say eventually. This time the apology comes out as a hiss.

I can't even look at Anton because I know he'll be shocked to hear my apology. What is it with this woman and her ability to make me want to say sorry for every shitty thing I've ever done? Why the fuck do I feel like she owns me and not the other way around?

"Please sit back down..." I ask.

She glares at me and though her cheeks are flushed, it's not with anger, but with *lust*.

I fucking feel it.

The chemistry between us is so intense I can barely concentrate. Anton observes us both and for the first time in my life I find that I can't read him. What's he up to?

"Please, Rose," I repeat.

"Fine." Rose sits back down and returns her gaze to Anton.

"Tell me what you meant when you said Erik hasn't allowed a woman to touch him in two years."

Anton shifts uncomfortably in his seat. I can see he's trying to figure out a way to tell her what she needs to hear without giving her the complete truth. At this point in time it's better he tells her this truth than reveal the one that we're all intent on hiding.

"Erik dislikes physical contact," Anton says, looking over at me.

"I gathered that, but you implied that a woman's touch, specifically, is what he dislikes. Yet, he allowed me to touch him. Why?"

Anton glances at me once more, and I shrug. "You may as well tell Rose. If she's going to work here, she needs all the facts."

Rose waits.

Anton lets out a long sigh. "Erik was captured and tortured on a routine reconnaissance mission in a remote village in Afghanistan. The rest of his squad were either killed when they were ambushed or murdered during their own interrogations. He was the only one to survive."

"What happened to him?"

"We don't know all the specifics, because it's been too traumatic for Erik to recount the details. What we do know for certain is that Erik was tortured by a woman. The scars he bears physically are bad enough, but the ones he holds inside are far, far worse."

"He was tortured by a woman?!"

"Yes. From what we've gathered she was particularly cruel, in every way imaginable.

"I'm sorry." Rose lifts the glass of wine to her lips and drinks it in one long gulp.

"You don't need to apologise, this isn't your doing. But you understand now why it's important to me that you stay. Erik is my friend and for just a second back there I saw the person he was before that bitch broke him."

"I can't fix him. I can't fix anyone," Rose mumbles. She glances up at me, those secrets I'm desperate to unravel flashing behind her eyes, taunting me.

"I'm not asking you to. I'm asking you to take the job, spend some time with Erik whilst you're here, with one of us accompanying you, just in case..."

"You want me to spend time with Erik?" She looks across at me, her brows pulling together.

"Ivan?" Anton asks me. I know what he's asking and I fucking hate him for it.

Rose is mine.

I don't answer right away, mostly because the word 'no' sits heavily on my tongue. Yet, I'd seen how Erik was with her. I've seen how he's suffered over the years and despite my selfish need to keep her to myself, I find myself nodding my head.

"Rose," I say, turning to look at her. "We'd appreciate it if you would at least try. I can give up an hour of your time every day. Of course, that all still depends on whether you want to take the job or not."

Rose looks between us both, her hands are still clutched around the glass as she considers our request.

"Thank you for explaining everything to me, Anton. I appreciate your honesty," Rose says, eventually.

"You're welcome," Anton responds with a genuine smile. "Part of the reason I'm glad you've stayed is because of Erik's positive reaction to you. It's a huge thing. The other part is because, for the first time in two years, I've witnessed a change in Ivan. His apologies are rarer than a red diamond."

"Red diamonds exist?" Rose asks, bemused by the reference.

"Yes, they're the rarest diamond in the world and like you, incredibly alluring," he replies with a low voice.

The heat in the room has just risen a notch, and this time it's Anton who's causing it. I squeeze my hand into a tight fist.

What. The. Fuck.

He really needs to stop looking at her like that. She really needs to stop looking back at him in the same way. I've never felt more on edge.

Ready to fight. Ready to bolt. Ready to fuck.

What is she doing to me? What is Anton doing?

I watch as a flush moves up her chest and neck and not for the first time this evening I fantasise about swiping my arm across the table and fucking her against it. I imagine her cheek pressed into the white linen whilst I press a hand between her shoulders forcing her flat against the hardwood, my cock filling her.

"Fuck," I say out loud, shifting uncomfortably in my seat.

"You alright, Ivan?" Anton asks, cocking an eyebrow.

He knows full well I'm not fucking alright. He knows I've had blue balls for the last four days despite the women I've taken to try and relieve the tension.

"I would be if you stopped fucking with Rose," I say.

Anton laughs. His smile tells me he's not at all bothered by my accusation, but the tightness of his shoulders and the side look he gives me as Rose turns her gaze away from him tells me otherwise. She looks at me, her eyes narrowing before turning back to Anton.

"Are you fucking with me, Anton?" Rose asks outright.

"No," he lies.

"Anton!" I warn.

"Rose is our guest here tonight. She's asked me questions about Erik, which I've answered honestly," he says to me before turning his attention back to Rose.

"I'm not talking about that. I believed what you said about Erik," she responds.

I watch as she places the palms of her hands flat on the table. She leans forward towards Anton. Her hands sliding across the table, so that they're within reach of his. I'm unable to take my eyes off the glimpse of breast I see as her shirt falls forward slightly. Beneath she wears a matching red lace bra.

"Anton, are you fucking with me?" she repeats.

"I'm not fucking with you, Rose."

On the table his forefinger and thumb are pinched together and moving as though he's holding a pencil and is outlining a new painting. Rose doesn't appear to notice his hand movements, but I know him well enough to know that Rose has sparked the muse within him. I've seen his paintings and through them I've seen into the deepest pits of his soul.

Clenching my jaw, I try to control the possessiveness I already feel for Rose. If he thinks he can fucking have her, then he's got another thing coming.

I don't give a shit.

Erik I can cope with, just. Not Anton, not *him*.

She's *mine*.

The look Rose gives Anton slices into my skin as jealousy rises within me. I watch as she takes in his features as much as he memorises hers, then nods her head.

"I guess only time will tell," she says, neither confirming nor denying outright that she believes him.

"It's only fair you know everything about Erik, about us. Working here won't be easy," he says looking at me, daring me to deny it.

"I still haven't decided whether I'm going to take the job," Rose says.

She looks between Anton and I, taking her measure of us both. She's not foolish and I respect that. The thought that she could still walk away has me biting on the inside of my cheek. The metallic taste of blood fills my mouth and I reach for my glass of wine, swallowing back a mouthful.

"What can we do to reassure you?" Anton asks.

I laugh at that, so does Rose. I catch her eye, and a look of understanding passes between us. Smiling inside, I realise she's not fooled by Anton. She sees the danger he presents, just as she sees it in me. I wouldn't be surprised if she sensed it in Erik too. Something about her innate ability to see into us, *me*, has my cock stirring and my balls tightening.

Rose is looking into the eye of the demon, she can see the darkness, and still she remains.

As she gazes between us both I realise one fact. To be able to sense the darkness, the danger, you have to hold it inside as well. Just like a tightly budding rose, the very core of her, the truth in her heart, is protected by layers of petals.

And by god, I want to peel them back one by one, because I'm certain that right at her core is a person not so dissimilar to my own dark soul.

Rose leans back in her chair before twisting her body to face me, her fingertips gently pulling at the cuff of her silk blouse. She hesitates a moment, before she looks up, locking eyes with mine. I read a thousand emotions in the depths of them. Some of them scare me, some thrill me, others make me want to pull her into my arms and fuck her here with Anton watching.

"Tell me about the red silk..." she says, her voice no more than a whisper now.

Beneath the surface, I hear the unmistakable sound of desire lacing her words, but more than that, I sense the power she holds, and it takes everything in me not to pull her into my arms and kiss that beautiful mouth of hers.

I don't kiss, *ever*. It's too personal. Yet, I'm willing to cast that rule aside so I can kiss her until my lips are bruised and my heart has bled out.

Out of the corner of my eye I see Anton's mouth drop open, his eyes darkening with unmistakable lust.

There it is.

That's what Anton has been trying to hide from Rose. He wants to fuck her as much as I do and we both know what happens when he becomes obsessed with a woman. His past is littered with a trail of shattered hearts just as much as mine. The only difference is that I paint their hearts with pain whilst he captures it on a canvas.

The room descends into a silence so thick with electricity that neither of us are able to utter a word. We both watch as Rose lifts her finger to the corner of her mouth pulling at her lip in a gesture so erotic I must grip hold of the seat to prevent me from launching at her. Anton shifts forward, his fingers stilling as his eyes take in the provocative gesture, committing it to memory. At first, it appears to be an innocent gesture, that she's unaware of how sensual, how fucking *sexy* she is, then Rose smiles languidly and there's no doubt in my mind that she's very aware of the power she has over us both. Her knowing green eyes survey Anton then me, and I begin to question just who the predator and who the prey really is.

"Tell me everything," she repeats softly.

And if Erik hadn't run into the room covered in blood, I would've done just that.

CHAPTER THIRTEEN

Rose

THE RAGGED THUMP of my pulse beats in my neck as I gaze at the men before me. Something in the room has changed, or maybe something in me has. I'm not sure at what point it happened.

Either way, the Rose of old, the one I've buried deep inside begins to bloom. I can feel myself unfurling, unravelling under their scrutiny. I've spent so long hiding her away, burying her within that I almost forgot what it was like to be her.

I've been ashamed of her. Ashamed of the need I hold inside.

Over the years I've trained myself to ignore the impulses I felt, so I danced to express myself instead, to have an outlet. This past year that outlet has diminished with every ache and pain. The memories have been creeping back in and with it the darkness. Maybe that person I've tried to bury inside has been unravelling ever since I stopped dancing professionally and that tonight, for some reason, she's finally found a way to appear.

Surrounded by these men, I feel those protective layers strip away. I feel *free*.

Lifting my fingertip to the corner of my mouth, I pull at my lower lip. I'm not sure what in that moment makes me do it, but the effect is immediate.

Intoxicating.

Both Ivan and Anton react to that simple touch, and a swell of heat pools low in my belly. Anton's pupils enlarge, his fingers stilling on the table. Ivan grips the seat of his chair, his body shaking with repressed lust.

I haven't felt this powerful for a very long time.

The flash of red at my wrist reminds me of that piece of silk I'd held in my hands and the smell of sex drifting into the air. It reminds me of similar binds that had tied me to a man I've spent so long trying to forget.

Here, right now in this moment, I'm not disgusted by it, I'm turned on. So turned on that if Ivan were to pull me against him, I wouldn't be able to resist. I would welcome his touch, I would endure the pain I hold inside just so I could have him.

Maybe, just maybe, I'd let it out.

But it isn't just Ivan that is making me release the mental binds that have held me together all these years, it's Anton too. His gaze rakes over me and I squirm under the intensity of it. To be studied like this, like I'm the only living soul in the universe... It's a heady aphrodisiac. The more I sit here in their company the more I'm aware of the layers protecting the person I've been running from, disintegrate.

How can these men have such a potent effect on me? But it isn't just Anton and Ivan, it's Erik too... his tortured soul is like a beacon, one that I find very hard to resist.

"Tell me everything," I repeat.

Ivan's mouth pops open, the story I need to hear just a whisper away.

Then the door slams open and Erik rushes in covered in blood.

In his hand is a knife.

The second it takes for Anton and Ivan to rush to their feet, the cage snaps back into place, locking down the blooming flower within me. Everything seems to slow down as Erik looks wildly about the room. He may be physically here with us, but mentally he's somewhere far, far away.

I should be afraid.

I should be afraid for my life like any normal human being would be in this instance. But how can I be frightened of such cruel beauty? I wasn't with Roman, and I'm not with these men.

You revel in the darkness, that's why.

"Fuck!" Ivan snaps, yanking me to my feet as time seems to speed up once more.

I'm not able to get a word out as he hauls me against his chest and forces me back away from Erik. He practically lifts me from the floor, my toes barely touching the ground. The moment my back hits the wall, he grasps my face in his hands.

"Don't say a word," he warns me, his voice low, soft. "Let Anton and I deal with this."

I nod my head as Ivan's fingers slide into my hair, curling around the strands. The heat of his palms warms my skin and despite the very real danger from Erik, I'm more turned on than I've ever been in my life.

Ivan leans over me, pressing his body against mine. I can feel his arousal thick and hard against my stomach.

Despite the danger, he's turned on too.

His eyes darken, the pupils enlarging as his mouth hovers over my lips. For a moment I think he's going to kiss me. Instead, he steps back slightly as his fingers tug on my hair, pulling my head back so that my face is tilted upwards towards him.

"He won't hurt you as long as you remain quiet. Stay here and don't move."

Letting me go, Ivan turns on his heel and walks slowly towards his friends. Anton has his palms held up in a submissive gesture as he stands before Erik.

Erik is shaking violently, the blunt knife clutched in his hand. There's a wild look about him but instead of being afraid, I feel nothing but the very real need to go to him. To soothe his pain, his fear, to absorb it as my own.

Inside me, the flower begins to bloom once more.

Erik's head snaps around the moment he notices Ivan approach. Automatically, his hand jabs forward, the knife glinting in the light as red droplets of blood splatter against the white linen of the table cloth. There's so much blood.

Too much blood.

"Erik, it's me, Luka," Ivan says gently.

It's the first time I've heard him refer to himself as the person he once was. Why not say Ivan? Why Luka now? His manner is entirely different. He moves and talks as though trying to calm a child in pain. I see a glimpse of a man so contrasting to the one presented to me in the past few days.

Erik twists around, a flash of recognition in his eyes before it's lost again beneath the nightmare he's living.

"Erik, you're safe," Anton says gently.

Erik's chest heaves as he pants heavily. I see him rock on his feet, the weight of his fear forcing his body to move, whilst his memory holds him firmly in place.

"It's worse this time," Anton murmurs as Ivan approaches.

"You think it's..." Ivan's voice trails off.

Me? I think.

I touched him. I caused this and I need to fix it. Pushing off the wall, I take a step forward.

Anton catches my movement from the corner of his eye. He shakes his head.

"No!" he says a little too sharply, a little too loudly. That sudden noise breaks through Erik's haze and his head snaps in my direction. Our eyes meet. My breath catches.

The pain I see within him is swimming in fear. Fear so overwhelming, so expansive, so deep that he's drowning in it. But beyond that, in the deepest darkest depths, is rage, and that rage is directed at me now, or at least the person he sees in his memories.

"You!" Erik snarls at me, baring his teeth.

"Erik, don't," Ivan warns, as he reaches out his hand towards him. "This is Rose, you just met her."

But he doesn't hear Ivan, he doesn't hear Anton either. In fact, neither can I. All I hear is the pounding beat of my heart and the whooshing sound of air as I push off the wall and step forward. I don't think about anything other than the fact that in this moment Erik needs to see me as someone other than the woman who tortured him. Someone so completely different to the woman who broke him. I need to shatter the darkness and pull him up from the depths, and the only way I know how to do that is through ballet.

It's saved me too many times to count.

I hope it will save him too.

Without thinking about the consequences, I place my arms and feet into fifth position, then lower into a demi-plié before brushing my right foot across the floor. The bottom of my shoe slides across the wood as I leap forward into a brisé, my shirt rippling with air as I spin on my toes finishing with a pirouette. I land lightly despite the heavy ache I carry with me always. My arms are still held wide as the three men freeze. It takes just a couple of seconds to complete the move, but that's all it takes for everything to change.

Pandora's box has been opened.

Erik drops the knife from his hand and falls to his knees, a cry of pain ripping up his throat as his hands press against his right flank.

Anton rushes forward, kicking the knife out of the way as he crouches beside him.

"We need a doctor now!" Anton shouts at Ivan who's staring at me with a mixture of shock, lust, awe and despair.

"Ivan, now!" Anton repeats.

Ivan's head snaps around to Erik cradled in Anton's arms. He pulls out his mobile phone and punches in a number. In a few sharp commands he's called for an ambulance.

"Is he badly hurt?" I ask, as my hands begin to shake uncontrollably now.

"There's enough blood to suggest he is," Ivan says, kneeling before Erik. He shrugs off his suit jacket and hands it to Anton who grabs it and presses it against the wound.

"Press it tight against him. I'm going to check she's okay," Ivan says quickly.

"Make sure who's okay?" I ask, taking Ivan's spot on the floor by Erik. His face is pale, his eyes pressed shut as he mumbles nonsense. Anton eases Erik backwards so he's lying on the floor.

We lock eyes. "You think he's hurt someone?"

"Fran took Erik his supper," Ivan says quickly, giving Anton a look I can't interpret. "I'm going to go and check on her. Stay with him," he orders before rushing out of the room.

"That damn ambulance better hurry," Anton bites out, fear and agony rippling across his features.

"How did this happen?" I murmur, looking between Erik's pale face to Anton's concerned one.

"He must've had an episode. A flashback..."

"This is my fault. I touched him."

"No! No, this isn't you. He *let* you touch him. That doesn't happen, *ever*, Rose."

"But you said he was tortured by a woman. I must have set something off in him. God, this is my fault," I say, my hand flying to my mouth.

"No, not you..." Erik grinds out.

I snap my head around to look at Erik, who's staring up at me with wide eyes. The amber orbs have lost some of the wildness now, and all I see is that deep ocean of sadness. My heart constricts, and the breath tightens in my chest. I know I shouldn't be thinking it, but I want to dive into his pain, submit to it. I want to wrap myself in the undercurrent of it and make it my own. The deepest parts of me, the shores of my soul, drawn to it inexplicably.

"Erik, what happened?" I ask. I want to touch him, my hand reaches forward, my fingers hovering over the bare skin of his arm.

"She came to my room... Why did she come?"

"Oh, fuck!" Anton exclaims.

"Is Fran okay? Is she hurt too?" I ask, not taking my gaze off him. I remember the older woman's kind, genuine smile and worry for her.

"Fran? I don't..." Erik's eyebrows pull together as though trying to make sense of my words.

"It's okay, Erik. Don't think about that right now..." Anton says, his voice trailing off as he looks at me.

Could Erik have hurt Fran? Is he really capable of that? Then I remember the wildness in his eyes, the sheer fucking terror, and I know that it's possible. Probable even.

"I'm sorry," Erik mutters, his eyes losing some of their focus as he reaches for his friend.

"It isn't your fault, Erik. None of this is," Anton replies.

Erik doesn't seem to hear him. Instead he turns to me, a grimace marking his handsome face. "Thank you," he murmurs.

"For what?"

"For dancing..." then his eyes flutter shut but not before his fingers graze gently against my

own.

. . .

IT TAKES A FURTHER ten minutes for the ambulance to arrive and for Ivan to return, his face sombre, pale. As pale as Erik's is now.

"Fran?" Anton asks the moment Ivan steps into the room. He stands, giving the paramedics space to deal with Erik. Medical paraphernalia litters the floor as they attempt to stem the flow of blood and ease Erik's pain. Not that he's lucid at all now, he passed out not long after Ivan left the room.

Ivan's gaze flicks between us. "She's absolutely fine. He didn't hurt anyone apart from himself."

"Thank fuck," Anton murmurs, letting out a long steady breath.

"How is he?" Ivan asks.

I notice a smudge of blood on his cheek. I don't remember seeing it when he left the room, but there's so much blood everywhere it's no surprise he's got some on him too.

"They've managed to stem the bleeding, at least enough to get him into surgery."

"We're going to take him now, Mr Sachov. Will one of you be accompanying him?" the paramedic asks.

Ivan glances at Anton. "Go with him. I will call Ms Hadley, let her know what's happened. I need to ensure Fran gets home safely, she's a little shaken up."

"I thought you said she was fine?" I ask.

"Physically, yes, but she witnessed his episode. By all accounts it was more than a little disturbing. In the end, she had to lock herself in his room."

"Jesus Christ," Anton says, swiping the back of his hand against his forehead leaving a smear of blood in its wake. "This could have been so much worse."

"Yes, it could've. I'm guessing somewhere deep inside, Erik's instinct was to protect Fran. That's why he sought us out."

"But I thought..." I begin, not understanding how he could stand to be alone with her given his issues with women.

"Fran has been one of the few people Erik can tolerate in small doses. She's not been able to touch him since he returned home, but she's never triggered an episode before now... *Fuck!*" Ivan says, swiping a hand through his hair.

"You weren't to know he'd react like this," Anton says, trying to ease his conscience.

"Don't make excuses for me, Anton. Rose was right, I pushed him too hard. I fucking caused this."

Anton doesn't try to dissuade him. I'm guessing he agrees with Ivan deep down, and despite what he'd said to me earlier, I feel just as responsible. I'd seen how broken he was when he'd been introduced to me. I'd recognised his damaged soul and despite that, despite my outward concern, for selfish reasons I'd wanted to reach out to him. I'd wanted to touch his darkness so mine wouldn't feel so bottomless.

The paramedics slide Erik onto a carrier and lift him off the floor.

"We need to get him to hospital. We've radioed ahead to the surgical team who will be prepped and waiting for him," the female paramedic says.

Ivan nods sharply. He steps forward and rests a hand against Erik's bare arm, squeezes gently before letting go. They carry Erik out, Anton following behind, leaving me alone with Ivan once more.

CHAPTER FOURTEEN

Ivan

"ARE YOU OKAY, IVAN?" Rose asks, approaching me.

I'm standing by the window, looking out as the ambulance drives away with Erik, my friend, a man who is family, a man who is so scarred by a woman's cruelty that he hurt himself to try and block out the pain.

A sickness rises in my throat as I remember Svetlana's limp body, the wounds she inflicted on herself, and the pain in her eyes before she passed out with blood loss. I remember the heartache caused by *my* emotional torture and realise that I'm no different from that bitch who tortured Erik...

"Ivan, are you okay?" Rose repeats, as she settles in the chair beside me.

I think about what she's asking me, and that question seems

too big to answer. I've no idea if I'm okay or not. I've no fucking clue.

What does that even mean; '*Are you okay?*'

Am I okay that my friend has stabbed himself? Am I okay that this woman has shaken me to my very core? Am I okay that Anton appears to want her too? Am I okay that Erik allowed her to touch him? Am I okay that she broke through the one barrier no other woman has since he returned from Afghanistan? Am I okay that Rose has crept into my psyche in such a short space of time? Am I okay with the fact she just danced to stop Erik from doing something stupid, to save him from attacking us? Am I okay that she's opened a festering wound that fucking *hurts*? Am I okay with the fact that she's mine now, whether she likes it or not?

I don't know the answers.

For the first time in my life, I don't know myself, and it fucking terrifies me. Holding the glass of wine in my hand, I take a long drink, doing everything in my power to stop my hands from shaking.

"Perhaps I should call a cab?" Rose says, reaching for her bag.

She opens the zip and pulls out her phone. I snatch it from her, shoving it into my suit pocket.

"No!" is all I manage to say.

I don't want her to go anywhere. She can't leave, not until I figure out what's wrong with me. I almost laugh at that.

Everything is wrong with me.

I'm a twisted fuck, if I weren't I wouldn't be thinking about the thousand ways I'd like to fuck Rose right now. I wouldn't be thinking about the creaminess of her skin coloured pink by the hard slap of my hand, or her ankles and wrists tied together with ribbons of silk. I wouldn't be thinking about her legs stretched wide and my face buried in the lushness of her thighs, my mouth tasting her essence. I wouldn't be thinking about all the ways I can make her mine, and all the ways I could take what doesn't belong to me... her heart, her love, her passion, her fucking soul.

"It's been a long night... I think it's best if I go. Will you let me know how Erik is doing once you hear?" She moves to stand, but my hand flies out gripping her thigh instinctively.

"You're not going anywhere," I mutter, my fingers squeezing a little too hard.

This time Rose doesn't try to escape my hold. Instead she remains still, tense.

"Ivan... you're in shock," she whispers.

She's right, but not for the reason she thinks. This isn't the first time Erik has hurt himself and it won't be the last. There's more to how I feel and all of it is wrapped up in her.

"I still haven't told you," I say, lifting my gaze to meet hers.

"Told me what, Ivan?"

She tips her head to the side. There's a softness in her gaze and I'm not sure I like it. Where has that woman gone? The one who looked as though she could devour me and not the other way around. The look she gives me now reminds me too much of Svetlana. Sweet, sweet, Svetlana.

I remove my hand from her thigh and take her hand in mine.

"Come with me," I say, pulling Rose to her feet and leading her from the room. She doesn't protest, she simply follows me as I lead her through locked doors and dark hallways.

Each time I stop at another door, unlocking it, I expect her to bolt, to run. But the deeper we move through the house, the closer she seems to move towards me, entwining her fingers with mine, her body pressing against my side.

Stopping at the door to the studio, I let go of her hand and lean my forehead against the wood, my palms pressing against the frame. I breathe in deeply, knowing that the moment I step over the threshold the demon I've been keeping at bay all night will be set free. It will escape free from its cage and it will fucking devour her.

"Ivan, what's behind this door?" she asks softly.

There's a noticeable tremor in her voice. It holds a mixture of fear and excitement, making for an intoxicating combination. The demon within me begins to stir.

"A place I'm not sure you're ready to see," I respond, pushing back off the door and turning to face her.

She looks up at me, curiosity flashing in the meadow-green of her eyes. Those eyes that make me want to be someone else. Someone who can give rather than take, who can give love rather than steal it. I rip my gaze away, choosing to look at her cherry red lips instead.

"Is this to do with the red ribbon?"

"It's to do with *everything*," I respond.

She nods her head, folding her arms over her chest. A move I've come to recognise, to protect herself.

"Am I making a mistake?" she asks.

Her question isn't directed at me, it's a question she asks herself. The fact is, it doesn't really matter if she is or she isn't. She could turn around right now, walk out of this house and I would respect that. After the events of tonight I owe her at least one night's reprieve.

But that's it. That's all she gets.

Four days ago, we made a deal. She had her terms, and I had mine.

Tonight, Rose may have danced to distract Erik, to save him from himself, but she opened the door to the demon within me and I know myself enough to know that once released it won't stop until it gets what it wants, and it wants Rose.

I want Rose.

Stepping around her, I back Rose up against the door, my hands resting on either side of her head. I already feel the darkness within me begin to unravel. My need to take from her a sickness that will devour me if I don't set the demon free. It's her or me, and self-preservation is kicking in.

"Agreeing to come here tonight was a mistake, but you know that already, Rose."

Her lips part on a breath as I push my hips against hers. The pink flush she always gets, that turns me the fuck on, blossoms on her cheeks.

"Ivan..." her voice trails off as I circle my hips, rubbing my cock against the mound of her pussy. She must feel how hard I am for her. Fuck, I want to rip off her clothes. I want to bury myself into her. I want to dive beneath her skin. I want to lure out the darkness that glitters like an obsidian stone within her chest.

"There was a moment just before Erik appeared that I saw something in you, something that called to me," I say, tracing my finger along the length of her jaw.

"And what was that?" she whispers.

"Hunger..."

Her breath catches as I dip my head, sliding my lips against the curve of her neck. She twists her face away from mine, baring her most tender spot. Whether she understands it or not, it's a sign of submission, that expanse of skin where her pulse thrums telling me all I need to know. Everything about the way she's reacting now is submissive and whilst it turns me on, the other side of her, the hungry side, the sharp mouth and will of steel calls to me even more. She has the power to rule me.

That's a first.

As I run my lips lower, swirling my tongue into the dip of her neck and sliding my lips and fingers out across her collar-bone, I understand something about Rose.

She's a contradiction.

Like a garden rose she has the delicate fragility of velvety petals, soft to touch, layered, but easily plucked. Yet, I need to be careful because one wrong move and the sharp thorns that protect the truth of her have the ability to make a person bleed, to fucking shred the skin.

Like she's shredding mine now.

CHAPTER FIFTEEN

Rose

HUNGER... that word hangs in the air between us as Ivan bends his head and presses his mouth against the sensitive skin of my neck. The soft caress twisting my stomach in knots. I could let him take me. I could let him devour me.

A part of me *wants* him to, and yet...

Yet, there's another part, a part that's growing bigger with every passing moment that wants something different. To own such a man, someone so strong, powerful. To make him mine. To tame the demon within. I want that more.

But I know if I walk into that room, if I truly immerse myself in his world, I could lose myself permanently this time and I'm not sure I'm strong enough to survive it. Ivan hasn't lied about who he is. He's a man who sees what he wants and takes it and be damned to the consequences. If I let him in, he will break the last shards of the person who can survive in this world leaving behind a person who shouldn't. Mustn't.

Ivan's fingertips slide across my collarbone, his mouth tracing the same path. The knots within my stomach tighten, whilst a warm heat pools between my legs. Half of me wants him, the other half is desperate to get away.

Inside an internal battle rages, and he knows it. He's using my indecision against me.

I need to be stronger than this. I may have let Ivan and Anton see a glimpse of the old me in the dining room. I'd been so close, so close to letting her out once and for all.

I'd *wanted* to set her free.

For the briefest of moments, I almost had. Then Erik had entered, vulnerable, broken, desperate, and all I could think of doing was dance.

Snapping him out of his nightmare had been the only thought on my mind.

Liar! You knew what would happen if you danced. You want to be set free.

"No!" I push against Ivan's chest, and he stumbles backwards. My response is to the voice in my head more than the feel of his body pressed against mine.

"No?" he questions, swallowing hard. His eyes narrow, the demon within him riled, rising to the challenge. Inside me, my own demon stretches, ready and willing to meet its match.

"No more," I say, swallowing the lump in my throat, desperately trying to quell the darkness in me.

"You don't get to say that to me, Rose. You knew the consequence of your actions." Ivan scowls, his eyes almost black in the dimly lit hallway.

"I did it for Erik. He would have hurt someone."

"It doesn't matter why you did it, it makes no difference to me now."

"It matters to *me*," I retort, pushing off the wall, trying to ignore the throbbing between my legs and the scrape of claws behind my ribcage.

"It's too late. You've poked the demon, there's no going back, Rose."

"There is. I still don't know about the red silk, I still don't know what happens behind this door. We'll call it even. I won't ask, and you don't get to take a damn thing."

Even I'm impressed by the calmness of my voice because it really doesn't represent the turmoil inside.

"No. No fucking way!" Ivan snarls, and in one step he's gripping my wrists and forcing my arms above my head. "It's too damn late, Rose."

"Fuck you," I snap back, twisting my body beneath him, but he forces his knee between my legs, pressing his whole length against me. The brute strength of him keeping me trapped.

He's aroused... and god help me, so am I.

This, this dangerous passion igniting between us, this is what I'm trying to avoid. Like a wildfire, this kind of passion is all consuming. It devours everything in its path leaving nothing but charred remains behind.

It took me the best part of fourteen years to recover from the last time I'd been consumed so thoroughly. Roman's beautiful but twisted smile enters my thoughts at that exact same moment.

"Let me go, Ivan!" I shout.

"No. I won't," he growls, squeezing my wrists painfully hard. "I *can't*."

"Ivan, I don't want this. I won't survive it this time, *please*." My words break on a sob, but I swallow the pain and press my eyes shut against the darkness of his stare and the memory of Roman's hand closed around my throat.

His body shudders against mine as a single tear slides down my face.

I'm so close to giving in, so close to letting myself mould against him. I'm staring into the mouth of a fucking lion and I'm about to let it devour me.

"Don't do that. Don't fucking break," he growls, breathing hard.

His chest expands against my own, and though his words seem comforting, he still doesn't let me go.

I'm still trapped, inside the darkness cracks.

Give in. Let the demon devour you.

"Please," I whimper again, but this time I'm not sure whether I'm asking for him to let me go or asking him to fuck me.

"What are you afraid of? Is it me?" Ivan asks, brushing his lips against my forehead. It's a tender gesture and so contrasting to the heavy, oppressive weight of his body against mine.

I shake my head. "It's not you I'm afraid of, it's *me*..."

Ivan stills, his breath fluttering over my skin. My pulse is ragged, a heady mix of lust, desire and fear bleeds into the air around us.

"I'm afraid of the demon in *me*," I whimper.

Ivan makes a strangled noise as his hands fall away from my wrists. For a moment I think he's going to let me go, but what he does next has my legs buckling beneath me. Ivan slides his hands into my hair, yanks my head back and crashes his lips against mine.

He kisses like a man possessed by the devil himself. He kisses as though I am the oxygen he breathes, as though he will drown if he doesn't. His tongue probes my mouth, his teeth scrape against my own. There's no tenderness in this kiss. I don't think he's capable of it.

Right in this moment, I'm not even sure I care.

If this was a horror movie, if this was a story of two twisted creatures, then Ivan and I would be nothing more than dark entities shredding the skin of their outer shell and devouring each other. The darkness within me cracks and splinters as the Rose of old begins to unfurl once more. Ivan's demon calls to mine and I know if one of us doesn't back away there'll be no saving either of us.

I kiss him back with the same animalistic need. My own desire breaking free. Our tongues battle for dominance, my hands reach up and grasp his head, pulling him closer. He groans into my mouth as I spread my legs wide, rocking my hips against his thigh. A rumble releases from his mouth as his hands fall lower. Ivan grasps my breast and squeezes hard, pinching my nipple. In response, I bite his lower lip, enough to draw blood.

Something in me releases, something powerful.

Something *dominant*.

Using my body weight and the element of surprise I force Ivan around so that I have him pinned against the wall instead. The sound that escapes his throat is a cross between a growl and a whimper. It's a sound that seems to surprise him too, given the way he pulls back sharply, his eyes widening with shock.

I pull his head back towards mine, not giving him a moment to even contemplate what's happening. Then I practically climb up his body, my legs wrapping around his waist as I consume him with my mouth. Ivan's strong arms hold me in place, pinning me against him, but even though he easily could, Ivan doesn't flip us back around.

I can feel him surrender to me.

This kiss between us started out one way, with Ivan very much leading, and now, now I can feel his muscles relax as a long sigh parts his lips. He's allowing me to take charge and he's fucking enjoying it.

"IVAN!" A shrill voice shouts.

Ivan forces me off as though burnt. He's panting heavily, just like I am. Neither of us can remove our gaze from the other. Everything about him calls to me.

Dangerous, passionate, powerful, *deadly*.

He's all of that, yes. But there's more, he's broken, vulnerable too, and I want nothing more than to cut myself on his jagged edges.

"Ivan, what are you doing?!"

At the other end of the hallway is Ms Hadley. I don't need to look at her to know that she's calculating how quickly she can be rid of me. Earlier, when I'd arrived, she hadn't just warned me away from Ivan, she'd threatened me with my past, told me that if I didn't obey *her* then my dirty little secrets will be revealed not only to Ivan, but to the whole ballet world.

I don't know how she found out, but she did, and if she has

her way, the gossip mongers in the village will finally get to hear the truth after all these years.

She briefly looks at me. Her eyes narrowing as she approaches us both. I can read her thoughts clearly. She's ready to ruin me. She *will* ruin me if I give in to Ivan, to myself.

"Fran called, where's Erik? What happened?" she snaps, striding along the hallway towards us.

Ivan pulls himself up straight, shoving his hands into his trouser pockets, restraining himself. I know how close he is to reaching over and pulling me against him, because I feel the same way too. I never thought I would say that I'm glad to see Ms Hadley, but right now I am.

"What happened?" she repeats, a thread of warning lacing her words.

"Erik's been taken to hospital. He suffered an episode. He stabbed himself..." Ivan says, flinching at the look of disgust Ms Hadley gives him.

"And neither you nor Anton thought to call me?"

Ivan grits his teeth, a muscle in his jaw jumping.

"He's *my boy*, Ivan. You should've called me immediately."

The way she says 'my boy' has my skin crawling. Ivan doesn't appear to notice, too wrapped up in his own guilt to recognise the ownership in her voice. A feeling of disgust washes over me as a loud warning bell sounds inside my head.

"I'll take you to him now," Ivan says, striding past Ms Hadley and down the hallway.

He doesn't even glance my way. I move to follow him, but Ms Hadley holds out her arm in front of me, preventing me from moving.

"This is your fault. I warned you."

"I had nothing to do with this," I respond tightly.

"I'm not talking about Erik. I'm talking about Ivan. He doesn't need another manipulative bitch in his life. I will ruin you if you fuck with him."

My head snaps around as I look at the twisted snarl of her lips and in that moment, I understand her, I *get* it. As her beady eyes regard me, I see very clearly into *her* fucked up core. The demon inside me bares its teeth.

"You're right, he doesn't. None of them do. So let this be a warning to you, Ms Hadley. I'm not a pushover. I'm not someone who is scared by empty threats. You and I both know there are too many secrets buried in these walls for you to reveal mine without consequences," I say, giving her a warning of my own.

"You wouldn't dare..."

"Try me," I retort, pushing past her and striding after Ivan.

The truth is, I would never reveal the secrets Ivan holds within that locked room. I'm nothing if not loyal, perhaps to a fault. Being with Roman proved that much at least.

"You have one more chance to do the right thing," Ms Hadley murmurs as she hurries to catch up with me.

Ivan pushes through the door at the end of the corridor and we lose sight of him for a second. I stop walking, Ms Hadley pulls up sharp.

"I'm taking the job, and there's nothing you can do to stop me," I respond, only realising in that second what my decision is.

"You can't. You mustn't," she hisses, her gaze flicking to the door then back again.

"I've already made my mind up, so back off!"

"You'll regret that decision, Rose. Mark my words."

I laugh. "Oh, don't worry, Ms Hadley, I have you marked. The only bitch manipulating these men appears to be you."

Her eyebrows rise at that remark, doubt crawling across her features. Like everyone else in my past, she's misjudged me. I'm not a wallflower or a fucking pushover and she can think again if she believes she can blackmail me into backing off.

"You know nothing about me or these men," she retorts.

"I know enough," I respond, stepping around her and pushing open the door. As I step out into the entrance hall, I'm more than certain this house holds secrets far darker than anyone would care to admit.

CHAPTER SIXTEEN

Rose

I'VE BEEN SITTING in the darkness of my front room, mulling over the evening's events for the past couple of hours. It's well past midnight and despite the time, and the exhaustion I feel, I can't sleep. I keep thinking back to Ms Hadley's warning and my response to it. She's dangerous, I sensed that when I first met her, and know that for certain now. Yet, she's such a big part of their lives, the men of Browlace Manor, and I'm not sure they sense the wickedness in her like I do.

But it isn't just Ms Hadley that's keeping me awake, it's Ivan too.

Tonight, I had allowed the darkness to show itself and I'd *enjoyed* it. Ivan believed that I was strong enough to fight his advances, I thought I was as well.

Now I know I'm not.

The way he'd kissed me. I've never been kissed like that. Not even Roman had kissed me so thoroughly, without restraint. He'd always been so particular. A kiss from him had been honed, deadly. The kiss of death, I used to think, and in some way, it had been.

Ever since Roman, the only thing that has ever been able to keep my past at bay is ballet. I may not have been the most talented, never advancing past the corps de ballet, but I'd loved it nonetheless. It kept me sane when my past tormented me. It kept me centred when thoughts of Roman rocked me. It kept the demon from escaping.

Now, now my only saviour has opened the door to another demon... and this one is determined to make me his.

I lean my head back against the armchair and close my eyes for the hundredth time this evening, willing sleep, knowing it won't come.

With a sigh I give up, instead I watch the rain as it patters against my window. The street lamp outside is reflected in every drop that slides down the glass pane, like hundreds of little golden jewels cascading from the sky. My eyes catch something beyond the glittering raindrops, a shadow. A man-shaped shadow.

I sit forward in my seat, my heart all too loud in my ears. Has Ivan returned to finish what he started? A sharp rap at the door has me standing abruptly, pain in my lower back making me draw in a breath. I'm already paying for dancing earlier. Those few steps will cause me days of pain, especially since I hadn't stretched beforehand. But none of that really matters now. The pain within, without, none of it.

I'm damned if I do, damned if I don't.

I hear another sharp rap at my door and I hurry to open it. May as well get this encounter over with. Ivan won't leave unless he says his peace, the last time he came here he practically battered the door down. With carefully schooled emotions, I pull open the door.

Except it isn't Ivan, it's Anton.

"Rose. May I come in?" he says, asking for permission instead of barging in like Ivan had a few nights ago. That simple gesture of respect tells me a hell of a lot about the man Anton is.

"I... sure," I say, stepping aside to allow him entrance.

"Is everything okay? How's Erik?" I ask, leading him to my kitchen.

I flip on the light switch and automatically fill the kettle with water, if only to give me something to do with my hands. Anton's silence is unnerving. He's still covered in blood, his shirt stiff where it's dried.

"Anton? How's Erik?" I question again.

He takes a seat on a kitchen stool and places his head in his hands. His shoulders are rounded, his body slumping. My throat constricts. Surely, he isn't... *dead?*

"Stable," he says eventually, his voice muffled. He lifts his head to look at me as I let out a sigh of relief.

"Thank goodness."

"Fortunately for him he hit muscle and not any internal organs. He's out of surgery now. Ivan and Ms Hadley are staying until he wakes up."

My mouth presses in a hard line at that. I know she's his mother, but I don't want her anywhere near Erik, Ivan nor Anton for that matter.

"Ms Hadley is pretty shaken. It's the first time I've seen her so worried. It could've been so much worse."

I almost snort at that. *Worried?* That would mean she cares, that she *loves*, and honestly, I'm not sure she's capable of either.

"Can I ask why you all still call her Ms Hadley? I mean you've known her for years. It just seems an odd thing to do. Why not call her by her first name?" I ask. What I really want to know is why none of them can see the poison in her heart. Maybe one day I'll ask, I guess that day is not today.

"Because she insisted on it when we were kids, and it stuck," he responds, shrugging. "Why does it matter?"

"It doesn't really. I was just curious," I say, placing two mugs on the counter and popping a teabag in both. The kettle is still boiling so I rest against the counter opposite Anton. He looks as exhausted as I feel.

"Thank you for coming here and letting me know how Erik is. I appreciate it."

"You're welcome."

Silence stretches out between us, neither of us trying to fill it. Instead I busy myself with making the tea, pouring the boiling water into the mugs and adding milk to both. I place the bowl of sugar on the counter and help myself to a spoonful. Anton merely picks up the mug and takes a sip, sugar clearly not his preference.

We both sit waiting for the other to speak, but time stretches out, the only sounds filling the space is the clock ticking on the wall. It's already half past midnight.

Normally in situations like these I'd try to fill the silence with useless conversation, but honestly, I'm not even sure what to say. Anton is a little bit of a mystery, and he unnerves me, more than a little actually. Here in close quarters with him, without another person to break up the strange tension, I begin to feel a little uneasy. Which is ridiculous given that I was happy to be in his company at dinner not more than a few hours ago. He had seemed 'normal' then, like a regular guy happy to entertain his friend's guest. Now, normal seems to have been replaced with odd once more.

I haven't forgotten about the weird way he acted when I first met him or the intense way he seems to look at me. Though this time, that intensity seems to have dialled down a notch. Tiredness and worry have dampened that, it would seem.

"You didn't just come here to tell me about Erik, did you?" I ask, finally breaking the silence.

Anton reaches up and runs a hand over his hair. In the bright overhead light of the kitchen I can see that a good portion has dried blood in it. He laughs a little, but it isn't filled with mirth, merely a grim acceptance.

"No, I didn't."

"So, what then? What do you want to tell me?"

"Not tell you, *ask*..." His voice trails off as he looks down at the mug clasped in his hands. If I didn't know any better, I could've sworn I heard a little vulnerability in it, and I wonder why.

"Ask me what?"

Anton looks up at me, his brown eyes searching mine. "I came here to ask you not to abandon us."

"Abandon you? What do you mean?"

"I meant what I said before, working for Ivan, for me and Erik by extension, won't be easy."

"No kidding," I retort with a light laugh, trying and failing to ease the tension.

"I'm serious, Rose. You can still back out."

"Look, I'm not a complete idiot. Believe it or not, I know what I'm getting myself into."

This time.

Anton nods his head sharply. I watch as he pulls at a loose nail on his finger. "Are you certain of that?"

"Pretty certain, yes. Ivan wants to fuck me, Erik wants to kill me and you... well, right now I'm not sure what you want, but I'm guessing you didn't just come here for a cup of tea?"

"Erik didn't want to kill you. In fact, I'm betting my inheritance that when he wakes up you'll be the first person on his mind," Anton responds, choosing to ignore my last statement.

That kind of throws me a bit, the fact he believes that the first person Erik will think about when he comes around is me, but before I get chance to question it, Anton continues.

"You're right about Ivan, he does want to fuck every woman he comes across. It's a sickness, Rose."

I blanche at that, suddenly feeling a little sick myself. There's me thinking I'm special, and I'm no more than another notch to gain on his bedpost.

"No offense meant," he adds quickly.

I laugh it off, trying not to show how that statement has affected me. "None taken... So, what about you? What do *you* want?"

His shoulders tense as the silence stretches out between us once more.

"Just one thing... well, two actually." His voice trails off as he looks up at me. This time that odd stare is back, the one where I feel like he's committing my face to memory, taking in every blemish, every flaw, every goddamn piece of me.

"What's that?"

He takes in a deep breath, before blowing out the air noisily.

"That you agree to become my muse."

Muse?

"Muse?" I say, out loud this time.

"Yes. Exactly that. The first moment I saw you I wanted to paint you. I've been trying to capture you on canvas ever since." He holds up his hand, wiggling his fingers. "I just can't quite do you justice and it's driving me insane."

He gives me a lopsided smile at that and it changes his face completely. He should smile more often. He doesn't seem so odd when he does.

"You want to paint *me*?"

"Yes. I want to paint you. You have such an expressive face. One that holds many truths and even more secrets. I see them bubbling beneath the surface. It's quite fascinating to watch..."

My cheeks flush at that. I certainly feel like he's peering into my soul every time he looks at me, just like the way he is now. I squirm under his gaze, suddenly unable to return his stare. Despite what I'd said to Ms Hadley to throw her off her game, my privacy is important to me and Anton seems to know just how to look past the walls I've built to protect it.

"Your skin is flushing again, isn't it?" he asks.

What an odd thing to say. Surely, he can see that for himself. I frown, not understanding.

"I'm colourblind... I have Monochromatism. I see only black, white, and shades of grey. There's no colour, not even a glimpse of it," he explains

My hand flies to my mouth in shock. "I'm sorry, that's awful."

Anton shrugs. "When you don't know any different, it's not so bad. I was born this way."

"But you're an artist. How is that even possible if you don't know what colours to use?"

"Not the best career choice, is it?" He laughs a little at that, but there's a sadness beneath the laughter. What is it with these men and their sadness? It draws me in like nothing else.

"No, it isn't," I agree, trying to rid myself of such dangerous thoughts. "But then again, being a ballet dancer wasn't a choice for me either. I had to dance in order to live."

"And now?"

"Now I dance to survive, I guess."

He nods his head and takes a sip of his tea, regarding me beyond the rim of the cup. As we look at one another, I begin to feel as though I *understand* him better. He's not staring at me to be creepy, he's staring because he's desperately trying to figure out the colours that bring me to life. Colours he'll never be able to appreciate. Something about that makes me inexplicably sad.

"Why torture yourself?" I ask before I can stop myself, because it seems to me that's exactly what he's doing.

"Because I have to, because it's all I have. Why do any of us do the things we do? Why do you continue to dance when it pains you to do so?" he asks.

"How do you know...?"

"Being colour blind makes you observant out of necessity. I saw what it cost you to dance tonight," he says, looking at me pointedly.

I'm pretty sure he isn't just talking about the ache in my back and knee. He knows Ivan better than anyone, I suspect.

"Yet, we do these things anyway..." My voice trails off as I mull over the truth of his words.

He sighs heavily. "It's like wanting something you'll never be able to have. Just because you can't have it, doesn't stop you from wanting it, from trying to get it."

"You sound very similar to another man we both know," I mutter.

Anton laughs. "Ivan and I are similar in that respect, yes, but that's where it ends."

He looks at me sharply, trying to establish whether I believe him. And whilst I don't think he's lying, I don't think he's telling the whole truth either. Lying by omission is still lying, no matter how you look at it.

"There's no cure?" I ask, moving on. Not willing to get into an internal argument about whether this man is lying for the right reasons or the wrong ones.

"I've tried every treatment possible. None have worked. That's why I need a muse, I need someone who inspires me, but more than that, someone who can help me to *see*..."

"And you want me to be that person?"

"Yes, very much so," he replies, honestly this time.

"But I'm not sure how I can do that. Starting Monday I'll be working for Ivan. He doesn't seem like a man who's able to share."

In fact, I already know he's not a man who's able to share. The way he kissed me told me that even if his words hadn't.

"You're correct in that assumption. Ivan has always been

possessive. When we were young he would never share his toys... that hasn't changed."

"There's a but isn't there?"

Anton chews on his lip. "He's already agreed to you helping Erik. He loves him enough to do that... Despite all his faults, and believe me there are a few, he understands how integral you are to Erik's recovery. We both agree that it's important you spend time with him."

"And you think he'll allow me to help you in a similar way?"

Anton shakes his head. "Christ, no. There's no way he'll agree to that."

"So, if I agree to be your muse, how's this going to work then?"

Anton swipes a hand over his beard as he mulls it over.

"Ivan goes away for weeks at a time on business trips. You'll need to look after his affairs whilst he's gone. I'm hoping you'll agree to helping me then. Just an hour or so a day..."

"I'm not sure about this," I say, remembering the possessive, hungry way Ivan had kissed me. That kiss wasn't from a man who would readily give up his possession, despite that possession's own free will. I'm certain that what I want wouldn't even register as something to be concerned with, let alone considered.

Are you admitting you're his possession? That dark little voice asks me. I shake my head trying to free myself of it.

"*Please*, I'll do anything..." Anton says, taking that shake of my head as a no.

He stands abruptly, moving around the kitchen island so that he's standing next to me. I look up at him, as he stares at me. Slowly he raises his hand to cup my cheek.

"So beautiful," he murmurs, as the rough calluses on the palm of his hand scrape against my skin. *"Please,"* he repeats, running the pad of his thumb over my cheekbone.

To my surprise, I lean into his palm a little, enjoying the tenderness I find there. What is wrong with me? One minute I'm craving the fierce touch of Ivan, the next I'm basking in the gentleness of another.

"And if I say yes, what do I get in return?" I manage to murmur.

"Whatever you want from me..."

I smile at that. I know he's lying, even if he isn't aware that he's doing it. He's easier to read than he thinks. I've become an expert at reading people, I learnt from the best. It's why I am the way I am. As a naïve teenager, I may have believed everything Roman had said in the beginning, but by the time our sordid love affair had ended I'd learnt that behind every lie lived a truth far more harmful.

"I'll do whatever you want," he continues.

Another lie.

It's funny, normally I associate people who lie with pain and heartache. My parents had lied to me most of my life. Roman had lied the whole time he'd known me, and I'd lied to myself for years. I guess that's why Ivan is a breath of fresh air. Even though he's still dangerous, he's not lied to me once since I've met him. Yet, somehow with Anton, who I know is lying to me now, I get the distinct impression that he's doing it for my own good, whatever that may be. It's more than most in my life have.

"Okay," I say.

"Okay?" Anton questions, his hand dropping from my face as though he's only just realised he's been touching me.

"Okay, I agree to be your muse, on one condition."

"What's that?" he asks.

"That in your presence, I'm allowed to dance."

Anton chews on his lip as he considers my terms. I seem to be making a lot of them lately. First Ivan, now him.

"I agree," he replies.

The sense of relief I feel is great, as though a heavy weight has been lifted off my chest and I can breathe again. Thank God, I can breathe again.

"And Ivan?" he questions.

"Tonight I've already failed the one and only condition he set, so what difference does it make? Besides, he isn't going to find out... is he?"

"No," Anton agrees, returning to his stool.

"That's settled then. I will become your muse, I will help you to see in exchange for the freedom to dance," I say, knowing that this is the only way I'll be strong enough to protect myself from Ivan, and from the demon in his heart.

Anton stands. "Thank you, Rose," he says, moving to leave. He gets to the kitchen door, then turns on his feet. "I almost forgot, here's your phone. Ivan had it, he wanted me to give it to you."

"Thank you," I respond, taking it from him.

"I guess I'll see you Monday sometime?"

"Yes, Monday," I confirm.

A minute later I'm alone once more.

Absentmindedly, I push my phone back and forwards between my hands on the countertop. My thoughts flick between the three men of Browlace Manor, so very different from one another and yet with a familiar thread running between them all. I know if I really try and dissect who they are as men, I'll be up all night. What I need is mindless distraction, so I turn my phone on with every intention of finding my e-book app and reading one of the books I downloaded recently. Instead, I'm distracted by a red dot above my telephone icon indicating I have a voice message.

Putting the phone on loudspeaker I press the button.

"Rose, it's Ivan... I thought you'd like to know that Erik is going to be okay, at least physically. Ms Hadley is with him now. She'll make sure he has company when he wakes up and whilst he recovers in hospital. I, I just..."

There's a heavy sigh and a long pause, and for a moment I think Ivan has hung up. I'm about to press the delete button, when he begins talking once more.

"I'm going away for a week or so. There's some business I need to attend to..." Another long pause. *"I understand from Ms Hadley that you still want to take the job. After everything that's happened tonight... I'm, I'm glad, Rose..."*

In the background I hear the sound of a male voice call for Ivan's attention. Ivan covers the mouthpiece, muffling the conversation between him and whoever he's talking to. Half a minute later he's back on the line.

"Sorry about that..." A long sigh. *"What is it about you that makes me want to apologise for every little thing I do?"* he blurts out, then rushes on. *"Look, you don't have to start until I'm back, there won't be a great deal for you to do anyway until I return, but if you want to, you can. I'll pay you either way."* Silence ticks away once more. *"Rose... about the kiss..."*

There's confusion in his voice, uncertainty. But thinking better of it, he coughs and starts again. *"If you want to start work*

Monday, call Fran. I've texted the number to your phone. Ms Hadley will be staying in a bed and breakfast near the hospital, so she can be close to Erik. If he's released before I return, I've asked Ms Hadley to give you space. She's agreed to that at least. I've not mentioned our discussion about you visiting with Erik. Maybe that should wait until I'm back. Anyway, I'd better go. Goodbye for now, Rose," he says finally, before hanging up.

I replay the message another three times before I finally press delete. Why is he going away now? Is it really because he has a business trip, or is he running away? I know if I think too much on it, it will drive me crazy. Instead, I haul my tired arse out of the kitchen and upstairs. It takes me a long time to stop thinking about the men of Browlace Manor and an even longer time to fall asleep.

CHAPTER SEVENTEEN

Rose

MONDAY COMES AROUND QUICKER than I'd expected. The whole weekend I kept my mind off the men of Browlace Manor by reading and scrubbing every inch of my house. Both served as a welcome distraction. This morning I was up, washed and dressed before sunrise. Now as I sit and wait for the clock on my kitchen wall to tell me it's seven o'clock and time to leave for work, I wonder whether returning to the manor is really the best idea I've ever had.

There are so many arguments against it. I'm sure if I had any girlfriends they'd all be telling me to sell up and move as far, far away from the men of Browlace Manor as I possibly can. But the argument is moot. I have no girlfriends, or common sense it would seem, because as soon as the clock strikes the hour I'm out of my seat, pulling on my coat and heading out the door.

Fifty minutes later, filled with adrenaline and a little achy from the long walk, I step up to the front door. Yesterday I called ahead to Fran, like Ivan had suggested, and told her I would be coming this morning, so it isn't a surprise that when I reach the front door, it's open.

Stepping into the warmth, I hear the sound of drum and bass music coming from one of the other doors to the left of the entrance hall. Ignoring the rules, and the voice inside my head that sometimes likes to obey them, I follow the sound. To my surprise, the door to the corridor is unlocked, though it stands to reason given Erik is in hospital and there's no need for locked doors. Pushing it open, I make my way along the hallway towards another door at the end. Through the gap I can see a room filled with natural light and splashes of startling colour.

This must be Anton's art studio.

Feeling like a lurker and that I'm somehow encroaching on his sacred place, I get halfway down the hall and decide better of it. Just as I'm about to turn on my feet and slope off to my office, the music turns off and the door swings open. Anton stands before me bare chested, his hair hanging about his face with a paintbrush clutched between his teeth.

For a second, he stares at me in shock, then he grabs the paintbrush whilst simultaneously running a paint covered hand through his hair.

"Shit, I wasn't expecting to see you today, at all this week, in fact. If I'd known you were coming, I would've made more of an effort," he says, apologising for his state of undress.

"I'm the one who should be apologising. I heard the music... I was intrigued, I suppose."

"Is that so?" Anton smiles lazily, crossing his arms as he

leans against the doorway. "You do know that curiosity killed the cat?"

I laugh a little at his playfulness. "Yes, my mother used to remind me of that fact regularly as a child."

"So, you're here now. Do you want to come in?"

I hesitate. Despite the amusement in his eyes, my mother's voice lingers in the back of my head. Every time my curiosity got the better of me as a kid, I ended up knowing things that were better kept secret.

"No, I really should get to work. That filing in Ivan's office won't get done on its own. Whilst he's away I may as well make myself useful."

Anton pushes off from the door and steps into the hallway. The natural sunlight coming from the studio behind him making a halo of his tawny hair, and just for a moment I am struck dumb by how attractive he is. He has a different kind of beauty compared to Ivan's. He's not as tall, or as muscular, but he's still fit, strong. I can't help but appreciate the light tan of his skin pulled across the taut muscles of his chest and stomach. There's not an ounce of fat on him and no chest hair to speak of, despite the copious amounts growing on his head and chin. He's beautiful in his own way, not unlike an oil painting himself, though without any of the softness that oils often imbue in the canvas. Anton is more like the sharp tones of acrylics; potent, powerful, bright, which is even more heartbreaking given his condition.

"That's why this is the perfect opportunity for you to see my studio, my artwork. You haven't changed your mind, have you?"

"No!" I say, a little too quickly. "No," I repeat, avoiding the look of satisfaction in Anton's gaze. "Like you said, Ivan's away. What harm could it do?"

Walking towards Anton with a confidence I don't feel, I plaster a neutral look on my face. Just before I reach the door, Anton's arm flies out preventing me from entering. The heady smell of his scent filters through my senses as I take in the smooth chocolate of his eyes. On the surface he smells of apples, but beneath that is a more intense smell, of incense and smoke. It's a strange combination, but not unpleasant. It reminds me of Bonfire Night and the delicious warmth of a roaring fire. I lean towards him almost involuntarily.

"You remember what we discussed?" he asks, the soft warmth of his breath fluttering across my cheek.

"Yes, I get the freedom to dance and I help you to see..."

"*And*," he prompts.

"And I become your muse..."

Anton smiles, his arm dropping. "Please, come in."

I STEP INTO HIS STUDIO, immediately accosted by a rainbow of bright colours and half finished canvases. Strewn about the room are bottles of paints, pencils, charcoal, paint-brushes, half finished sketches and more art paraphernalia that I can't name. For a minute I can only take in sections at a time. My gaze moves from the high glass dome above, letting in all the light, to the huge six foot canvas that rests against the wall on the other side of the studio. Half of it is covered with a large piece of material, the beige sheet falling haphazardly to the floor. There are smaller canvases stacked against another wall, the one in front is covered in blocks of colour. I stare at it trying to figure out if there's some kind of meaning behind the design.

"That was my Piet Mondrian phase. It didn't last long," he chuckles.

I watch as he walks into the middle of the room and leans across a huge art desk, reaching for something on the other side. I don't pay attention to what he picks up, instead stepping towards his desk to look at the multitude of half complete sketches that lie across the surface. The outline of a face, a headless figure, the back of someone's body. I see a sketch of Fran smiling whilst holding a tray of food, a light charcoal drawing of a woman bent plucking a flower from a wild hedgerow. So many sketches, all of them beautiful, detailed. One in particular, catches my eye. It's nothing more than a room with a panelled wall of mirrors and a chair situated in the corner, but what intrigues me the most is a long stretch of wood that crosses one side of the mirrors to the other, a barré. This is a sketch of a dance studio, and that has me reaching for it, but Anton quickly picks up another one, distracting me with a portrait of Erik.

"My god, you drew this?" I ask, my mouth popping open as I take it from him.

He's got the likeness spot on. The angular cut of Erik's jaw, the full lips of his mouth and the heavy set eyebrows drawn together over troubled eyes. Erik is holding a violin between his chin and shoulder, the bow pressed against the strings, his fingers forming a note along the neck.

"You sounds surprised?"

"Not surprised... impressed. This is amazing, incredible, Anton."

"Thank you."

I hand him back the sketch. He takes it and lays it on the table, covering the drawing of the dance studio. I want to ask him about it, but then he raises what looks suspiciously like a joint to his lips and lights it, drawing in a lungful. The end lights up a bright orange as the weed crackles and burns.

"Are you smoking a joint" I ask, taken aback.

"Yes, this is a joint. Do you want a toke?" he asks, puffing out a thick stream of smoke.

It has a particular smell, just like weed always does, but there's an undercurrent of apples. That explains the strange scent I'd smelt earlier.

"No, thanks. Never really been into drugs."

Anton shrugs. "Fair enough. So, what's your poison?" He looks at me curiously when I don't answer immediately. "Come on, everyone has one."

"Red wine," I say. Even though that really isn't my poison of choice. Vulnerable, powerful, evocative men are. But I'm not about to spill that little secret right now.

"Well then, I'll make sure I get some in for our next session. No use me getting high if I haven't got someone to join me."

Anton draws on the joint one more time before stubbing it out in a saucer that he's using as an ashtray. Then he picks up a bottle of water and takes a long drink.

"May I look at some of your stuff?" I ask, heading towards the wall where the majority of canvases are stacked against it.

"Sure," Anton says, cutting in front of me. He reaches up for the sheet that's covering half of the large canvas and pulls it up to cover it completely. "But not this one. It's for a client, it isn't finished."

"You sell your work?" I ask, looking at a painting of a young boy running through a meadow of poppies. It's incredibly life-like, but the colours are off, a little too stark to be a real represen-tation of the image he's trying to capture.

"Yes. I've sold a few over the years."

"And your condition? How have you managed with it and getting the colours right?"

"Fortunately for me, art appreciation is subjective. Some people will like my work and the oddity of the colours, others not so much. I've been lucky so far."

"Then why do you need me? If you're able to make a living out of the artwork you already produce, why do you need my help?"

Anton sighs. "Because I want perfection. For once I want to produce something that everyone will appreciate."

"But that's impossible. Like you said, what one person might think is a stunning piece worthy of hanging in their home, another person might dislike intensely. You're setting yourself up to fail."

Anton smiles, though it doesn't reach his eyes. "When I say everyone, what I actually mean is my father..."

"He doesn't support you?" I ask, almost dumbfounded. How could he not? Anton has a medical condition which means he's never been able to see colour, and yet every single piece of artwork in this room is utterly stunning.

Anton barks out a laugh. "No, my father doesn't support my need to create in this way. He never has."

"I'm sorry about that."

"Me too."

For a moment the tension between us returns as Anton stares at me openly. His eyes rake over my face and I can't help but notice the way his pupils dilate, and his lips part on a breath. The light flirting is replaced suddenly with a man that is dedicated in making me feel bare under his scrutiny. I feel naked when he looks at me like this. Naked and raw.

"What are you doing, Anton?"

"Committing you to memory. Having you in my space like this, so relaxed, is quite the inspiration."

"Well, I'm glad I could help," I respond, stepping backwards as he steps towards me.

"Perhaps tomorrow when you come to work, you'll bring your ballet shoes? I'd like to see you dance."

"Perhaps," I murmur, my cheeks blazing with colour. It's been a long time since I've performed for anyone. Honestly, I'm not even sure I'm capable of dancing the way I did before. My body is so very different now. Whilst the passion for dance hasn't lessened and the thought of being able to dance freely excites me, my agility and failing strength have me more nervous than I have any right to be. I shouldn't be dancing at all. My body won't appreciate it even if my soul will.

Glancing at my watch, I can see that I've already lost almost an hour talking with Anton, and with the sudden need to leave his studio, if only to get away from the growing appreciation I have for this man, I make my excuses.

"I should go. I've a lot to do..."

Anton relaxes. The almost obsessive stare gone now.

"Sure, you've already given me enough to work on. Same time tomorrow... I'll bring wine?" he asks, trying to ease the tension flaring between us.

"As tempting as that sounds, the only drink I consume at eight in the morning is tea."

"Then how about when you've finished your shift. A glass of wine at four o'clock isn't so bad?"

I laugh at his tenacity. "For a drunk I'm sure it's positively acceptable."

"You can't deny me now, not after I've shown you the place where I keep *my* soul..." his voice lowers a little at that, a dangerous, powerful darkness leaching into his tone.

"Fine, four o'clock tomorrow." I agree. "But on the agreement, I have space to dance."

Though the room is huge, it's filled to the brim with stuff. Frankly, I'm almost positive he won't be able to manage to tidy it. Part of me is counting on it, the other part hopes he makes room for me somehow.

With that agreement in place, I turn on my heel and stride from the room. Halfway down the hall, the drum and bass switches back on, louder than before, and I'm pretty sure that beneath the din is the sound of a man dragging a table across a hardwood floor.

CHAPTER EIGHTEEN

Ivan

SLEEP HAS EVADED me for two nights now. I left for London the moment I knew Erik would be okay, catching a direct flight from Newquay. Now, I sit with my bare feet propped up against the balcony of my hotel room still unable to rid myself of the intense heat that my body roars with every time I think of Rose and that kiss.

That fucking kiss...

It had been electrifying, all consuming, everything I wished it wasn't because now all I want is more. I'd broken the one cardinal rule I insisted on keeping with the women I fucked.

Absolutely no kissing.

It's just too personal, too intimate, too fucking emotional.

And yet, I'd cast that rule aside and kissed her.

That fucking kiss had cleaved open my chest and ripped out

my heart, pulverising it in one easy motion. Now my chest is still gaping, an open wound I've no idea how to fix.

What is she doing to me?

More to the point, why am I letting her?

"It's not you I'm afraid of, it's me. I'm afraid of the demon in me."

That one statement had been it for me. For reasons I'm unable to fathom right now, those few words had unlocked my resolve and made me weak.

I need to gain back some power, or I'm fucking lost.

She must never know what that kiss meant, and I sure as hell won't be kissing her again. Not in this fucking lifetime.

"Damn it to hell," I mutter, slinging back another double shot of brandy. The alcohol does nothing to dull the ache I feel in my cock at the thought of Rose and her sharp tongue, her will of steel, her fucking... *dominance.*

"Fuck!" I slam the glass tumbler on the table in my anger.

That kiss had started with me ruling her. I could feel her mould against me, welcoming my mouth and then, when I touched her beautiful plump breasts something changed...

She'd fucking bit me!

Then, catching me off guard she'd flipped me around and climbed up my damn body.

And I'd fucking let her.

If Ms Hadley hadn't walked in on us I've no damn clue what would've happened next. Would she have continued to rule me? Would I have continued to let her?

"Rose, what have you done to me?"

Aside from making me talk to myself like a crazy man, Rose has slipped beneath my skin like no one since Svetlana. I don't even think Svetlana made me feel as confused. I know who I was with her. With Rose, I don't know who I am anymore.

Who the fuck am I? Ivan? Luka? *Who?*

"Pull yourself together!"

I'm like a fucking madman, unable to control my thoughts let alone the words that spill out of my mouth. In an hour I'm meeting with the Freed brothers to talk business. Fuck knows how I'm going to get through the night with thoughts of Rose on my mind. Getting up, I stride into the bedroom and pull off my clothes, the sound of the city drowned out by the thumping of my heart. Walking into the bathroom, I turn on the shower and stare at my reflection as the water heats to the right temperature.

"What the fuck is wrong with you?"

Pulling my spine straight, I force myself upright and look at myself. *Really* look.

Years of dancing has kept me trim, muscular. I have a body most men would envy, and most women want to fuck. My muscles have bulked up more since training them in a different way. I'm not as graceful as I once was, but the shadow of the dancer in me still lingers. For the briefest time, I wonder what it would feel like to dance with Rose... It's a dangerous thought, so I bury it.

"Why her? Why Rose?" I ask myself.

I think of her wicked sharp tongue, her soft lips, her shapely legs, curvaceous body. I think of her demanding kiss and the *power* within it. I think of the way she felt towering over me a full head height taller as she clung tightly to me with her legs wrapped around my waist. I think of the way her hands pulled at my hair, just on the side of painful.

My fucking cock comes to life at the memory.

Automatically, I reach for it, squeezing the base with my hand, trying and failing to temper the raging hard-on. Thoughts of Rose scatter across my mind as my hand moves up the hard shaft of my cock; her plump lips, her ripe arse, the way she'd stood up to me in my office when we first met, and later in her kitchen... The way she'd danced so gracefully, despite what it meant, despite how it hurt her.

That damn kiss.

She'd rubbed herself against me with abandon and I'd almost come there and then in the fucking hallway. My hand moves down, squeezing with just the right amount of pressure.

She'd fucking bit me.

My balls twitch, precum beading on the tip of my cock. I let out a moan as I run the pad of my thumb over it, smoothing it over the bulbous head. I'm so ready to fuck, so damn fucking needy. Slamming my palm against the bathroom unit I lean over and start running my hand up and down my cock, fisting myself like a fucking teenager.

Self-pleasure isn't something I've done for years now given I have women at my beck and call. But I need to get Rose out of my damn head, otherwise the meeting tonight will go to shit. It's hardly professional entering a meeting with tented pants.

"I'm going to fuck you out of my head, Rose," I growl, imagining her softness beneath me, imagining taking everything from her, breaking her open and holding her bleeding heart in my hand. I imagine tasting the salt of her tears and absorbing the sighs of pleasure.

"You're *mine*."

The room heats up from the steam of the shower, and I begin to lose myself behind a cloud covering the mirror. It's okay though, I don't want to look at myself getting off, it's only distracting me from thoughts of Rose.

Rose and her luscious arse.

Rose and her shapely legs.

Rose and her soft breasts and creamy skin.

Rose and her meadow-green eyes.

Rose who stands up to me, when everyone else fucking cowers.

My hand moves quicker, my fist twisting as I move my hand up and down to a steady rhythm. I feel my balls tighten as I imagine Rose on her knees before me, her face pressed against the hardwood of the studio floor back home. She's naked and bare, her arse high in the air. I imagine turning the ripeness of her beautiful curves a bright pink as I spank her with the flat of my hand. I imagine the sting across my own palm, the loud slap reverberating around the room, only drowned out by her cries and the whimpers that follow when I stroke the same spot with gentle fingers. While I stroke her pussy until it glistens with her juices.

A low moan releases from my lips as my eyes roll back in my head with the heady intoxication that thoughts of Rose cause me. My legs begin to tremble with the oncoming orgasm, so much so that I fall to my knees onto the soft bath mat.

"Rose," I utter on another moan.

Then the fantasy begins to change, and it's no longer Rose kneeling on the floor, it's *me*. My hands are tied behind my back, and Rose is standing before me, her green eyes boring into my fucking soul. In her hand she holds a paddle. She lays it across her palm, caressing it with the flat of her hand.

My fist pumps harder, as my fantasy unravels, my breathing

comes in short gasping breaths as Rose walks behind me, trailing her fingers over the bare skin of my shoulders. This fantasy is so real, so desired, that when I imagine her kneeling beside me, her berry red lips whispering in my ear, I can almost hear the soft cadence of her voice.

"You're mine, Ivan. Submit to me."

And with the echo of those words in my head I come harder than I've ever done in my life.

CHAPTER NINETEEN

Rose

BY THE END of the second day, my back is killing me, and my stupid knee is swollen once again. Walking to and from work, as well as lifting and hauling boxes of files is taking its toll on me physically.

Today, I hate my body.

I hate that I can't do what I used to. That I can't dance the way I want. I miss the way I always felt so beautiful dancing, so unencumbered, so *free*.

I'd felt that way once with Roman... at least my sixteen year old self had. The version that's me now doesn't feel anything but pain when I think of him.

Sighing I shut the computer down, more than ready to go home. Except I can't. I have an agreement with Anton. One that I promised to fulfil.

Grabbing my bag and coat from the hook on the back of the door, I head out of the office and towards Anton's studio.

I hear music the moment I step into the hallway leading to his studio. This time it's pop. I recognise the song, it's *Wild Love* by James Bay, and one of my favourites.

It's the kind of song that seeps into your consciousness, the kind of song that fills you up from the soles of your feet to the tip of your head. Leaning against the wall, I close my eyes, allowing the sound to wash over me, but the music stops abruptly. Anton pausing it for whatever reason.

Taking that as my cue to enter, I push open the door to Anton's studio gasping at how tidy it is. The huge central table has been pushed up against the wall on the other side of the room. The numerous canvasses that were spread out all over the space yesterday are now stacked neatly next to it. Every single bit of rubbish, empty paint bottles, discarded sketches and art equipment have been tidied away.

Anton has managed to clear a space big enough for me to dance in.

"You like it?" he asks, a grin spreading across his face.

"It's certainly tidy. If I knew you were this good at organising, I would've got you to help me file away Ivan's mess," I laugh.

"That man is about as organised as a piss up in a brewery."

"He runs a multi-million pound empire, how on earth has he managed?"

"It's all up here," Anton replies, tapping his finger against his head. "If anything were to happen to him, all that would be lost."

"That's a little worrying..."

"Not now that he's got you, it isn't."

"I'm just his assistant," I reply, my cheeks colouring slightly at the compliment.

"We both know you're more than that. I've never seen Ivan more enamoured. You've certainly turned his head."

My cheeks blush an even deeper shade of pink at the memory of Ivan's kiss and at the way I acted. I'd climbed up his body like a bear climbs a tree. I'd wanted to claw at him, I'd wanted to devour his mouth like a bear would a hive full of honey. Another part of me had taken over in that kiss. A part of me I'm afraid of.

"Seems like you might be a little enamoured with him too?" Anton muses, tapping the end of the pencil he's grasping against his mouth.

"What do you want me to do?" I ask, ignoring Anton's remark and dropping my bag and coat on a chair by the door. Opposite the open space is an easel with a canvas fixed to it. I suddenly feel nervous that I will be under such close scrutiny, especially by this man. When Ivan looks at me, I know what he wants. When Anton does, I'm not so certain. That makes being with him alone more than a little uncomfortable, not because I think he'll do something to hurt me, but because I'm not sure how to protect myself.

"Did you bring your ballet slippers?" he asks, settling himself on a stool behind the easel.

"Pointes," I correct him, pulling them from my bag.

"And you can dance comfortably in that?" Anton eyes my office attire with doubt. I purposely wore a skirt with tights, but the fitted shirt and jacket aren't particularly conducive to dancing.

"I'll remove my jacket and shirt," I say, stopping when Anton's eyes darken a shade. "I have a camisole on. I can move more freely without them."

"Go ahead," he approves, watching me with interest.

With my gaze focused on Anton I drop my pointe shoes to the floor then shrug off my jacket and place it with my coat and bag. Reaching up, I slowly undo each button of my shirt. By the time I'm finished a flush of heat has spread out over my skin, and my nipples have pebbled with the heat of Anton's gaze.

Anton mutters under his breath, and scrapes a hand over his thick beard, twisting a few strands as he watches me. Right now, I can't seem to get a grasp on what he's thinking, so I decide to just stop worrying about it. I agreed to do this.

Sitting down on the polished floor, I slide my feet into my pointe shoes. The moment my toes hit the platform a calmness scatters over my skin and as I lace up the ribbon, the frayed pink stark against my black tights, excitement settles in my belly. Standing as gracefully as I can with a body that aches in places I wish it wouldn't, I face Anton.

"Did you bring the wine?" I ask, breaking the sudden tension as his gaze lingers on the automatic way my feet turn out into first position.

The last time I'd stood like this Ivan had fired me. Fortunately for me, Anton doesn't appear to want to do the same.

"Merlot okay?" he asks, ripping his gaze away from me, as he leans to the side and reaches for the bottle behind an upturned crate next to him on the floor. He unscrews the cap, offering it to me. I walk over to him, taking it.

"That's perfect," I respond. "Did you bring a glass?"

"I have a mug?"

I crinkle my nose. "Perhaps not."

Anton laughs. "I'm kidding, here," he says stretching to the side again. This time when he sits back up he's holding a large wine glass, and by large, I mean the ones that can hold almost half a bottle.

"Are you trying to get me pissed?" I ask, taking it from him and filling it a quarter of the way.

"Maybe," he shrugs.

"Well, good luck with that, I can drink a bottle of this stuff and not even get tipsy. Better luck next time, eh?"

"You don't look the Alcoholics Anonymous type, Rose."

"I'm not. I know my limits..." I mutter.

"And what are they... your limits?" Anton lifts his foot and rests it on the crate, watching me, waiting for my answer.

"We're not talking about alcohol anymore, are we?"

He shakes his head.

"That's for me to know, and you to find out..." I let that statement hang in the air, before asking him a question of my own. "Where's your poison?"

Anton grins, giving me a cheeky wink that seems oddly out of place, then reaches into the top pocket of his shirt, pulling out a rolled joint and a lighter.

"Bottoms up," he says, lighting it.

"Cheers," I respond, raising my glass and gulping back the wine I poured myself. Anton regards me closely, but if he's surprised about how I've knocked it back, he doesn't say anything.

The wine is full-bodied, smooth. It tastes of wild berries and oak, with a slight bitter taste of tannin, just enough to give it a kick, and exactly how I like it.

"Delicious," I say, placing both the glass and bottle on the table, careful not to put them on top of the sketches piled neatly on the surface.

"Only the best for our Rose," he says.

Our Rose? He says it like I belong to him, to *them.* The last time I belonged to anyone was Roman, and that didn't turn out so well. Back then I was a child, naïve. Things are different now. I'm different.

Anton takes a long toke of his joint, holding the smoke in his lungs, before breathing it out in one slow breath. The smell of apples and bonfires fills the air once more. It seems to go perfectly well with the berries and oak of my wine.

I stand awkwardly as Anton continues to smoke his joint. "I've never been a muse before... What exactly would you like me to do?"

"You came here to dance, so dance," Anton says, all playfulness gone now. Picking up a pencil, he points to the middle of the space he's cleared. "Please," he adds.

"I'll need to warm up first, it's been a while."

"Do what you need to do. I'll be sitting here, watching your every move," he murmurs, his words taking the form of a blue tinged dragon as smoke billows out of his mouth.

Turning my back on him, I walk to the centre of the floor and begin to stretch, just like I had that first day I met Ivan. A sudden shooting pain in my back has me gasping loud enough to catch Anton's attention.

"What is it?" he asks, getting up.

I feel defeated before I've even begun. "I have Rheumatoid Arthritis. It's why I had to give up dancing," I tell him, a heavy weight sits on my shoulders at the admission. Here I am, hoping to be able to dance in order to protect myself from Ivan, from the demons of my past, to *survive*, and my body won't even allow that.

"You're in pain? Where?"

"Mainly my lower back, but also my knee."

"Which knee?" he asks, kneeling on the floor before me. He looks up at me with his liquid brown eyes and for moment we just stare at each other. It's an interesting position to be in, there's something so empowering about having a man on their knees before me. It only ever happened a handful of times with Roman, but each time is clearly etched in my memory.

"The left, but it's no use, there isn't anything you can do to help," I mutter.

"I won't touch you unless you give me permission, Rose," Anton murmurs, lowering his gaze.

My heart constricts, and inside my demon roars. Does he realise what he's doing?

"Do it," I whisper.

Anton slides his hands up from the base of my ankle, over the curve of my calf until they settle around my swollen joint.

"You shouldn't be dancing like this," he admonishes.

"I know that, but we made an agreement and I need to dance. I *need* to."

The warmth of Anton's hands seeps into my skin, but he doesn't try to move them or take advantage of the situation like I know Ivan would. He simply keeps his head bowed and his hands around my knee. Ever so slowly his thumbs gently massage my swollen joint. Both pain and pleasure courses through me as a slow, steady warmth builds in my stomach.

"Then you need to let me look after you, Rose."

"I don't need looking after."

"Everyone needs someone, Rose," he replies, gently.

I should tell him to stop. I should tell him to get up. But I don't do either. I allow him to gently caress my knee and wonder what it would feel like if I allowed him to touch other parts of my body. What it would feel like, if I ordered him to?

"Tell me what you want, Rose," Anton asks.

"I want you to paint."

Anton lets go of my knee and stands, striding back to his stool. He sits down and waits. Despite myself, I feel bereft of his touch.

Eventually, finally, when my pulse rate has decided to calm down I carry on stretching. Out of the corner of my eye I see Anton relight the joint.

"I know you're not into drugs... but weed is known to help relieve the pain of arthritis. Maybe you should try some." He cocks his head and waits for me to answer.

"I've heard that," I respond, looking between Anton and the plume of blue-grey smoke twirling upwards from the joint.

"Do you want to try?" he asks.

I bend my knee tentatively, and the pain expands. "Yes," I say quickly before I can change my mind. Perhaps the joint will relax me enough to do what I must. I approach him and reach for the joint.

"No, let me," he says, picking up the joint. He holds it up to my lips. "Go easy the first time. It might make you cough a little."

Nodding my head, I open my mouth and take the end of the proffered joint, closing my lips around it, the warmth of his fingers pressing against my parted lips.

Taking in a deep breath, I draw on the joint, holding the smoke in my lungs. Anton's hand falls away and I breathe out, a long plume of smoke billowing from my lips.

Anton raises his eyebrows in surprise.

"Just because I said I don't use drugs, doesn't mean I've never tried them, Anton. I was a teenager just like everyone else."

Anton laughs. "You never cease to amaze me, Rose. There's so much more to you, isn't there?"

"Perhaps," I respond, taking the proffered joint and finishing it off.

Anton doesn't try to press me further, he simply waits. It isn't long before the effects of the joint begin to take hold. I begin to feel a little light headed, but in a good way. Floaty, I suppose. Handing the joint back to him, I move to the centre of the room.

When I move, the pain is still apparent, but it's no more than a distant ache rather than a sharp stab. No different to how I usually feel day to day. I start warming up again, this time finding the movements much easier than before.

Once I feel loose enough, I begin to practice the five positions, moving through each one as fluidly as I can manage. I avoid looking at Anton, instead focusing on a spot just behind him.

"Would you like some music?" Anton murmurs.

Something has changed in his voice, there's a soothing calm about him now. Whether it's because of the joint, or the fact that he's genuinely grateful I'm here as his muse, I can't really tell. Either way I feel myself begin to relax more. My limbs feel lighter, and the stiffness in my joints has lessened further.

"Please," I respond, rolling my head on my shoulders and enjoying the heady feeling.

Anton nods his head and picks up a remote control from the crate next to him. He presses a button and *Wild Love* begins to play once more. I watch him as he settles back in his seat. Taking that as my cue to begin, I slide my left foot out in front of me, my toe pointed towards him, then stand on pointe. For a moment I just allow myself a moment to get used to moving this way again. I pull in my core and lift my chin as my arms form and arch above my head. Anton draws in a breath, his eyes widening as they rove over my body. Then as though a spark has been lit within him, he turns his attention to the canvas in front of him and begins to draw.

Closing my eyes, I let the music wash over me and just dance. I don't follow any rules, I just give myself the freedom I desire, the freedom to move without worrying about what it will cost me. At home I don't have the space to dance this way, but here in Anton's studio I let myself go. Nothing enters my head but the peaceful calmness that dancing brings. I don't distinguish one song to the next. I merely let my body move as I twirl and twist over the wooden floor. The pain I felt when I first began to move is nothing but a distant memory now.

With every step, with every stretch of my hand, and point of my toes, with every arabesque, every demi plié, I feel the tension I've been holding release.

I feel as though I can finally breathe.

Really, truly, breathe.

It's as though these last few months I've been holding my breath, never expanding my lungs completely. Now I can move fluidly, all the aches and pains gone, or at least not registering beneath the haze of weed.

I feel as though I'm floating, flying.

I'm not sure how long I dance for, but the natural light leaving the room and the darkness pooling around us both reminds me that I should get home soon. When I finally stop moving I realise that I don't want to leave. That I want to stay here in this room with Anton.

When he rolls another joint and silently offers it to me, I take it, greedily drawing in a lungful of apple flavoured smoke and chasing it down with more red wine.

Between us the bottle is soon finished and the joint smoked. I find myself sitting in the middle of Anton's studio, my legs stretched out in front of me, not really knowing how I got there. Anton is sitting crossed legged next to me and a deep sense of calm envelops me as I relax.

"You okay, Rose?" Anton asks.

I nod my head, trails of light and colour moving in front of my eyes before they become too heavy to keep open. I'm vaguely aware of Anton shifting closer, his arm wrapping around my shoulder as he pulls me against his side.

"Hush now, sleep," he says.

Those are the last words I hear as I float off into the darkness.

CHAPTER TWENTY

Rose

I WAKE up in a dimly lit room, shards of light breaking through a gap in the curtain. Groaning, I sit up, having no recollection of how I got home. The last thing I remember is sitting with Anton on his studio floor smoking a joint and finishing off a bottle of red wine.

My mouth certainly backs up that memory. Urgh, the taste is disgusting.

Sliding my feet off the bed, I reach for the light switch just above the headboard of my bed. Except I can't feel it. Maybe I'm still high, or drunk, or both. Standing, I test out the strength of my knee. Oddly, neither my back, nor my knee hurt as much this morning. What in God's name was in that joint? Realising I probably don't want to know, I pad over to the window and yank open the curtains.

"What the fuck?" I say, taking in the view.

That certainly isn't my small back yard... I'm still at Browlace Manor and it's well past morning. Twisting slowly on my feet, I take in my new surroundings. The room is sparsely furnished with only a bed, a side table and a small wardrobe with a few clothes hanging up in it. There's nothing on the walls apart from a faded photo of three young boys about ten years old. All three are glaring at the camera. They look very much like the younger version of Ivan, Anton and Erik.

Feeling a sudden chill on my arms and legs, I look down to find that I'm only wearing my panties and vest top. Nothing more.

Who the fuck undressed me? Did I manage it myself? Did Anton do it?

My question is answered when the door to the bedroom unlocks... *unlocks*? Anton walks in holding a tray piled with toast, tea, and two plates loaded with eggs and bacon.

"Morning, Rose," he says, cheerfully.

"What's going on?!" I half shout, half screech. "And why's the door locked, Anton?"

Anton kicks the door shut behind him and places the tray on the side table.

"Shit, sorry, Rose. This must be a bit weird for you. Let me explain..."

"Explain? Explain what... did we?" I ask, looking from the dishevelled sheets on the bed to Anton's sexy 'just got out of bed' look and half undressed body.

"No!" he responds quickly. He pulls a face, looking more than a little guilty. "You kind of passed out and I figured it best you sleep in the spare room. I slept in my own room down the hall."

"Oh Jesus, thank fuck!"

He frowns at that. "Is the thought of spending the night with me that bad, Rose?"

"No, that isn't what I meant... I just meant that I'd want to remember if I spent the night with you..." my voice trails off at the admission.

"Perhaps," Anton responds.

"Perhaps?" I ask, wanting to know what he means by that. Why wouldn't I enjoy it? Sex is sex, right? What an odd thing to say. He doesn't try to answer the question hanging in the air. So, I ask an easier one.

"Did you undress me? Or did I manage that myself?"

"I helped, you were a little... inebriated," he finishes.

"Well, thanks." I feel my cheeks warm again as I look down at my bare legs. There's a streak of blue paint just above my ankle bone.

Anton seems to notice it at the same time I do. A strange look moves across his face, one I don't understand. It looks a lot like guilt.

"Sorry about that. The paint must've come off my hands when I was removing your tights."

Perfect, I think a little ungratefully. Looks like I'm going to have to get my clothes dry cleaned, because if there's paint on me, there's bound to be paint on them.

"So, are you hungry? I know I'm ravenous, especially after all that weed we smoked last night," Anton asks, changing the subject completely.

As though on cue, my stomach rumbles loudly. "I guess there's your answer," I smile.

Twenty minutes later, my stomach is full and the nasty taste in my mouth gone, I look around the room for my clothes, suddenly feeling self-conscious. I can't believe I ate breakfast in my underwear, though Anton doesn't seem the least bit bothered by it.

"I hung them in the wardrobe," Anton says, somehow knowing what I'm looking for. He tips his head towards it, whilst gulping back another mouthful of tea.

"Thanks. I'll just get dressed then and start work I suppose. What time is it anyway?"

"It's ten-thirty," Anton says, getting up. He starts gathering the discarded plates and placing them on the tray. I'm pretty sure Ms Hadley would have a fit if she knew we were eating breakfast in bed, not that I give a shit what that witch thinks. Thoughts of her remind me that Anton unlocked the door to enter the room, and never explained why. She's a stickler for keeping the doors locked. I hope that isn't a sign she's back...

"Why was the door locked, Anton?" I ask.

"Erik came home last night... he refused to stay any longer."

"Shit, was that wise?"

"Not in the slightest. Ms Hadley begged him to stay at the hospital, but he wanted to get home."

"Doesn't he realise how dangerous it is to discharge himself before he's well enough to leave?"

Anton blows out a breath. "He's well aware, yes, but as I said, he wanted to come home."

"Why, was it because of the medical staff? I imagine it was difficult for him with the all the women..."

"No. He wanted to return home for... *you*."

"*Me?!*"

"You're surprised? Why? I told you, he never lets women touch him. There's something special about you, Rose. Ivan sees it, even though I'm betting he doesn't quite understand it yet. But, Erik, he *knows* it."

Anton tips his head to the side, the way he did when he was watching me in the studio yesterday. "There really is something so very enticing about you... Painting you is going to be addictive," he whispers, as though that's a bad thing.

"That's good though, right?" I ask. He makes it sound like it isn't. I'm not sure I understand given our arrangement.

Anton chews on his lip. "There's something about me you should know, Rose."

"What's that?"

He swipes a hand over his beard.

"Anton, what?"

"I have an obsessive personality. It affects everything I do," he blurts out.

"We're all a little obsessive. I'm a little OCD about cleaning," I say, shrugging off his concerns.

"No, you don't understand. I have an *unhealthy* obsession with my need to paint. Every single aspect of me needs to find the perfect shade, the perfect colour, the perfect... *muse*. I've searched my whole life to find her, to find the one person who can give me what I need. Who can help me to *see*..."

"Okay," I say, feeling a little nervous at his confession and the way his gaze cuts right through me. It's almost desperate, and desperate men are dangerous, I should know. A memory from a long time ago tries to claw its way into my mind, but I shove it away. Now is not the time.

"I've used drugs, Rose. I've tried every single one you can imagine, all of it in the pursuit to provide colour where there isn't any. I've cast aside numerous women in my absolute single-minded desire to obtain the impossible. I've been waiting for the right woman to bring colour into my life in every possible way. I've been searching for so fucking long..."

Anton reaches over and grasps my hand, his thumb trailing over my knuckles.

"I want you to know that if I really, truly, let you in," he says, tapping his chest. "I won't have the strength to let you go, *ever*. You see, Rose, if you turn out to be *the one*. The one who will truly help me to see, it isn't Ivan or Erik you need to fear. It's *me*," he says.

I almost expect him to laugh, to say 'just kidding', but he doesn't, and I'm left wondering what the fuck I've got myself into. Anton lets go of my hand and stands, gathering the tray stacked with our empty plates.

I don't know what to say to him.

The familiar pull of a dangerous man has my heart pounding and my demon gnashing to be set free. Why the hell do I find myself in these situations? Why do I attract these men? And why, oh why, do I want them so bad?

"If I were you, Rose, I would leave here and never return, because one day that door may just remain locked," he warns, before striding from the room, leaving me gaping after him. Eventually, after my pulse has calmed enough, I get dressed, pulling on my clothes absentmindedly. It only occurs to me once I've stepped out into the hallway that there isn't a spot of paint on any of them.

I DON'T HEED Anton's warning.

Despite my own doubts, I remain.

Returning to the office, I continue with the filing. Thoughts of Ivan, Anton and Erik filling my head all day. That's two men who've warned me personally how dangerous they are and another who I *know* is dangerous. Yet I'm still here.

I'm still damn here.

Curiosity killed the cat, Rose. That little voice in my head teases.

But it isn't just curiosity. I'm drawn to these men. Despite everything that happened in my past, I *can't* walk away.

I know I'm heading down a path that will only end in heartache, but I can't seem to fight the pull of the tide. All I can do is let it take me along and hope that I don't drown.

Pretty soon four o'clock ticks around and I head towards Anton's studio once more wanting answers, wanting to understand what the fuck I'm dealing with here.

This time there's no music to greet me, just a foreboding silence.

I knock on the door lightly, waiting for a response.

"Come in, Rose," Anton says, his voice low, deliberate.

Pushing open the door I step into his studio. Anton is standing in the centre of the room, behind him sitting on a chair is Erik, on the floor by his feet, his violin and bow.

"Hello," I say softly, trying to hide the surprise I feel at seeing Erik, trying to temper my sudden beating heart.

I catch Anton's eye and he nods his head, his expression unreadable.

"It's alright, Rose," he reassures me.

But I'm not sure it is.

I suddenly feel like a lamb to the slaughter.

Before me are two dangerous men. One who has told me as much, and the other who has shown me he is. Maybe now's the time to run, run and never return. I should lock down the demon in me. I should find another job. It wouldn't be hard to do.

"Are you going to join us?" Anton asks, and I know there's more to that question than appears on the surface. A tension fills the air as I decide what to do.

Stay or run.

Inexplicably, I ignore my instincts, and shut the door behind me. Anton visibly relaxes, whilst Erik tenses. Placing my coat and bag on the chair beside me, I wait.

No one moves.

I can feel both Anton and Erik's gaze, but I don't look at either of them directly, choosing instead to stare at a spot just to the left of them. Direct eye contact with Erik would be a mistake and Anton's gaze is making me feel simultaneously uneasy and excited. They both ooze danger, just like Ivan.

What the hell am I doing?

"Thank you for coming, Rose," Erik says, as though he was expecting me.

I'm almost startled by his voice, it's deeper than I remember with a wonderful rich baritone. For a brief moment I wonder if he's able to sing as well as play a musical instrument.

"How are you feeling, Erik?" I ask gently. I'm not sure why I feel the need to make polite small talk. I came here to get answers and instead I'm playing nice.

"Like I've been stabbed with a knife," he responds.

I wince at that. "Sorry, stupid question."

"No, it isn't. I apologise for my rudeness. Thank you for coming here, that's brave, given the way I acted."

"I didn't know you would be here this afternoon. I came to speak with Anton."

"I see," he responds quickly. I hear the sound of the chair scrape across the floor as he stands, and I can't help but snatch a look at him. He has a pained look on his face and I'm not sure whether it's because of his injury, or what I just said.

"I didn't mean it to come out that way. Seeing you *right now* is unexpected, but I agreed with Ivan and Anton that I'd be happy to see you, to *help*." And despite all common sense that's still true, I do want to help Erik.

I want to help them all.

No, Rose, you want to own them. These men call to the darkness in you. Don't fucking kid yourself.

Erik nods sharply, sitting back down. His hands are shaking, and though it's subtle, Anton moves to stand in front of him, shielding me from him I guess.

"You stayed, despite what I said?" Anton asks incredulously.

I don't answer Anton, not wanting to acknowledge suddenly what this means, what I'm choosing by shutting the door on my escape.

"Rose. There's still time..." Anton says once more.

But instead of frightening me off, my feet seem to move of their own accord and within a few steps I'm standing before Anton.

These men are dangerous.

I can feel it.

And yet I remain.

Erik stands, my closeness causing the whole of his body to shake violently. A sound releases from his mouth, a low rumbling growl, his own demon making itself known.

"Erik," Anton warns, holding his arm out.

But even wounded, I already know that Anton wouldn't be able to stop Erik if he wanted to attack me. He's a huge man, broad shouldered, *strong*.

Erik's hands are fisted, a sheen of sweat breaking out on his forehead. He's fighting himself with every breath and it only makes me want to help him more, *want* him more.

I know I'm playing with fire, and whilst the sensible part of me is well aware of what could happen if the wind whips up the flames in the wrong direction, the other part of me wants to be consumed by them.

Fucking let them devour me. All of them.

Ivan, Anton and Erik.

Three very different men, all utterly appealing. With Ivan, it's about the sex, yes, but it's also about the power he wishes to gain over another person, the need to devour a woman's soul until she's broken, ruined. Just like his wife Svetlana.

With these two, it's a different kind of danger.

Anton is obsessive, he's admitted as such. He's searching for the right colour, for the perfect image on a canvas, for a woman to fulfil the role as his muse. Something I've already agreed to without understanding what that means. Earlier he gave me the opportunity to leave, to run.

Yet I stayed.

He intrigues me, he gives me solace in allowing me the freedom to dance, yet he wants something from me, something that he's hinted at, but I can't quite put my finger on.

Then there's Erik, he represents a very real physical danger. Aggression and anger are thinly veiled by a vulnerability that attracts me to him. All of it, every aspect of him is so very alluring, dangerous.

"You should leave," Erik warns. "You're not safe here with any of us. We'll ruin you, Rose."

He's right, I *should* leave. I should run.

But I don't heed his warning, because I see something in these men, something I recognise.

"Only if you order me to," I respond.

Then I kneel on the floor, hoping I've read them right.

CHAPTER TWENTY-ONE

Ivan

"ANTON, where the fuck is Erik? Ms Hadley called and told me he checked himself out? I left London the moment she told me about his stupidity... I've been travelling all day!" I say, shoving open the door to his studio.

Erik and Anton make a startled noise as I enter the room, but it isn't them I see first, it's Rose.

"What the actual fuck?" I snarl, stopping in my tracks. I'm so shocked that I can only stand in the doorway staring at Rose kneeling before them. Her head is bowed.

Why the fuck is she on her knees for *them?*

"Someone tell me what the fuck is going on before I lose my shit!" I shout this time, unable to control the fucking rage I feel at seeing her submit like this to my two best friends, my *brothers*.

"It isn't what you think..." Anton begins, holding his hands up.

"Well, what the fuck is it? Because as far as I can tell, Rose isn't tying up your damn shoelaces!"

"This isn't the time for your temper, Ivan," Anton starts, his gaze flicking to Erik, but I cut him off.

"Don't fucking tell me how to behave, Ant."

Snapping into action, I stride over to Rose and grab her arm, pulling her to her feet roughly. "What the fuck are *you* doing, Rose?" I growl, forcing her to face me, to *answer* me. After everything we've gone through over the last few days, the back and forth, and she's on her knees for *them*. Why? Did that kiss mean fuck-all to her?

"Let go of me, Ivan," she warns. Her voice is calm, but I can feel her own anger through the tremor in her body and the steel in her eyes.

"No, I won't." And to prove a point, I squeeze harder.

"What the hell do you think you're doing?" She shouts now, yanking her arm free. "This is the last time you manhandle me, Ivan Sachov! Do you hear me?!"

"You're mine!" I roar back, not giving a fuck if this whole sorry episode is upsetting Erik.

Out of the corner of my eye, I can see his face turn pale as he looks at Rose with dangerous eyes.

"Ivan, for fuck's sake man, can't you see what you're doing to Erik?" Anton whispers in a rush.

"I don't give a fuck. She's mine!"

"I am *not* yours. I belong to nobody but myself. If I choose to kneel before these men then I goddamn will, Ivan," she seethes, her voice lowering to a dangerous level.

"You bow to me, and me alone!" I step forward, towering over her.

"NO. I. DON'T!" she shouts back, not backing down one inch. And fuck if I don't want her all the more for it.

"Leave her alone, Ivan," Anton warns.

"Fuck off! This has nothing to do with you!" I turn on him, pushing him roughly.

"That's where you're wrong. This has everything to do with me, with Erik too. Rose chose to be my muse, she chose to get on her knees before us just now. You don't own her like the others."

"YOUR FUCKING MUSE?!" I explode.

The anger that erupts is overwhelming. Even if I tried, I don't think I could contain it. In fact, I know I can't. Seeing red, I turn away from Rose and throw a punch at Anton. My fist meets his cheek with a loud smack, throwing his head back with the force of it. Anton stumbles, but he doesn't fight back. He never does, not with me and I fucking despise him for it.

"Tell me you fucking didn't?" I growl, grabbing his shirt in my hand and yanking him forward. My fist is clenched, pulled back ready to lay into him once more.

My best friend, my brother, looks me in the eye and I already know the answer before he utters a word.

"I've already painted Rose, Ivan. It's done," he says.

"You fucking prick! What have you done?! Do you understand what that means?" I rage.

This isn't good, this is a *fucking nightmare.*

Anton has painted her. He's stepped over the line he promised he'd never cross again and he's done it with Rose. What the fuck are we going to do now?

"She's the one, Ivan. You know it as well as I do. Stop trying to convince yourself Rose is like the rest, because she isn't."

We lock eyes, and I understand him well enough to know he really believes that's true. That in itself is dangerous. His *obsession* is dangerous.

"Look at Erik," he whispers, his gaze flicking over my shoulder.

I let go of him and spin around on my feet.

Fuck. In my rage I'd forgotten about him.

Rose is back on her knees, her head lowered, Erik standing before her. He towers over her, but she's still, *calm*, despite the commotion, despite the very real danger she's in.

Anton and I watch as Erik reaches forward and touches her on the top of her head. If he wanted too, he could slide his hands lower and snap her neck before I could even stop him.

"Look at me, Rose," Erik demands with a voice that belies the fear I know he feels.

Fear of himself, of *her*. I can see it in the way his hands shake, the tremble of his body, the grit of his jaw as he fights his own demons in her presence.

Rose looks up at him, her head lifting slowly. My fucking heart breaks at her courage, her strength. She's so brave, so strong, and in danger... because of all of us.

I swallow hard, my own breathing becoming shallow as I watch, trepidation creeps up my spine. Erik sucks in a breath as Rose finally meets his gaze. I understand what it feels like to be studied by her, feeling so insignificant and so fucking powerful at the same time.

"Are you worth the fight?" he asks her, his voice barely above a whisper.

"Are you worth the heartache?" she retorts, glancing at Anton and I briefly.

"I don't know," he answers honestly.

She nods her head and Erik's hand drops away. But still she remains on her knees.

"Stand up, Rose."

This time it's Anton who gives the order.

Rose gets to her feet with more grace than the most gifted prima ballerina. We all watch as she twists on her feet, walks slowly to the door and picks up her coat and bag before turning to face us.

"I have a lot to think about," she says, looking from Erik to Anton and then, finally, me.

"I need a few days to get my head straight. Don't call me. Don't come to my house. I will return to work on Monday. After that, we'll have to figure out what this is."

Then she walks out of the studio, shutting the door softly behind her.

That night none of us sleep.

Anton locks himself in his studio taking out his frustrations on a canvas. Erik spends the night pacing up and down in his room, and I spend mine sitting in the dance studio staring at the stain of Svetlana's blood, wondering whether this time Anton is right, and Rose really is *the one* that will save us from ourselves.

CHAPTER TWENTY-TWO

Rose

THE COLD WIND and sea spray from the waves lash against me, but the sting doesn't even register as I walk along the shore. I stop, turning to face the expanse of water, a heavy sigh leaving my lips.

The sea is as grey as I feel.

My stomach hasn't stopped churning since I left the men of Browlace Manor. Every minute, of every hour since, they're all I've thought about. Now it's Friday afternoon and I've had far too long to agonise over the consequences of my actions, of theirs.

Heading towards the derelict studio built beneath the promenade. I take in a shaky breath, filling my lungs with the fresh sea air, hoping somehow it will help to blow away the dark cloud that is beginning to linger around me.

The last time I visited this studio was five years ago on a rare visit back home when my mother was still alive. My old ballet teacher, Sylvia, had contacted me, explaining the studio was being closed. She'd begged me to return, and given I'd spent so much of my childhood here, I couldn't deny the opportunity to say goodbye to the one place I'd felt really at home. Then a year ago, just after I was fired from the Royal Ballet, I got a call from Sylvia's solicitor to say she had passed away and had left the studio to me in her will. I'd been too unwell with my own health issues to even contemplate coming down here to revisit the place I'd loved so much knowing it wouldn't be as I remembered it.

Today, inexplicably, this place has called me back and so, here I am.

Now, as I approach the studio, I can already see the damage caused by the wrath of the English Channel and with no one to take care of it, it's nothing more than a rundown building with boarded up windows and crumbling brickwork.

I certainly don't have the money to fix it up.

Peering through the gaps between the planks of wood covering the windows, I can see well enough into the open space. It's really just a room, with a tiny office at the back, but a space to dance, to express myself, was all that I ever really needed as a child.

And right now, I really, really need to dance.

This one room had given me freedom to be myself. It was a place I could let out all my emotions after everything that had happened with Roman.

It had helped me back then, I'm hoping it will help me now.

Reaching for my handbag, I feel inside for my ballet pointes, reassured by the softness of the frayed ribbon. My fingers delve further, and soon wrap around a key. Pulling it free, I look along the empty stretch of promenade then slide the key in the lock and turn. To my surprise the door unlocks without too much effort, despite the rusting hinges. I had thought, after all this time, someone would have tried to break in, but it would seem even the drug addicts that sometimes hang around the beach didn't think much of the empty space and so it's been left to the elements instead.

Pushing open the heavy wooden door, I peer inside. Streams of light filter through the wood covering the windows, and surprisingly, it isn't as dark as I expected it would be.

"Hello?" I call tentatively, knowing that there isn't anyone inside, but needing to check anyway.

Satisfied that I'm very much alone, I push the door closed and enter the studio. My first thought is to turn on the lights, but given this place hasn't been occupied for years I have no doubt the electricity has been switched off. But just in case, I flick the switch anyway.

No lights come on, not that it matters anyway, there's enough light filtering through the gaps in the wood for me to dance.

As I walk to the centre of the studio, I catch sight of my reflection in the mirrors opposite me. They are covered in a thick layer of dust and grime, giving me an aged look. I laugh a little at that. The girl I used to see in these mirrors, *Rosie*, has changed beyond recognition. That innocent girl turned into someone who sees the world a little differently, who has needs and desires that not everyone understands.

I lift my hand to my face, running my fingertips over my

cheeks, along my jaw and down my neck. They linger at my collarbone, remembering the hot kisses Ivan had trailed across my skin.

Shaking my head from thoughts of Ivan, I stare at the woman I am now. The woman I see is jaded, worn, physically very different, but mentally so much stronger.

Peeling off my coat, I walk over to the row of hooks that are still fixed to the back wall and hang my coat and bag on the one that was always reserved for me. Even now, after all these years, I can still just about make out my name written in black ink below it. At first, Sylvia had been angry at me for graffiting the walls, but as soon as she realised how good I was, that coat hook had been reserved for her *prima ballerina*, for me. She always had so much faith in me, which was way more than my parents ever had.

"Thanks for everything, Sylvia," I whisper to her ghost that I'm positive still lives on within the bricks and mortar of this very building. It's funny as I remove my shoes and slowly move across the dancefloor, I can almost feel her watching me from her spot in the corner of the room.

"That's it Rosie, point your toes. Beautiful arms, straight back. Remember that length of string pulling your spine straight..."

Drawing strength from the memory and not caring that the wooden floor is covered in a thick layer of dust and sand, I pull off my boots and put on my pointes shoes. The moment my feet slide into them, I feel a sense of peace. Just like I had in Anton's studio, just like I always do when I dance.

In some ways, I have him to thank for finally having the courage to return here. If I hadn't danced for Anton, I may never have felt the urge to revisit my childhood sanctuary. I'm grateful for that at least, even if thoughts of him, of Ivan and Erik has my guts churning and my thoughts roiling just like the turbulent waves that crash against the shore outside.

Despite the cold, the damp, and the musty smell of rot mixed with the distinct smell of the ocean, I'm happy to be here.

I've not felt happy in a very long time, and though I sense it might be fleeting, I hold onto it.

Taking hold of the barre, I turn towards the stream of sunlight pouring through the gaps of wood and turn my feet out into first position. Like a soothing mantra, I repeat the five positions until I am relaxed enough to dance. Today, the aches and pains that usually haunt me aren't so debilitating. Ever since I smoked that joint with Anton, I've felt marginally better. I've no idea what was in it, and I'm not sure I want to know, but today, I'm glad of it.

After more warm up exercises at the barre, I step into the middle of the studio ready to dance. Ready to feel. Ready to be me.

For just a moment I allow the sound of the waves crashing against the shore to wash over me, and then as I push off from my toes, kicking up clouds of dust and sand with my feet, I let my body move of its own accord. There are no rules in this space. No eyes watching me, assessing whether I'm good enough to dance. There is no judgement, or pressure, just freedom to move my body in any way I choose.

I twirl around the studio, pirouetting across the floor, moving freely between the balls of my feet onto my pointes and back again. As I dance, I leave everything I've ever learnt behind, moving to the beat of my own heart and soul. I think of my past and the man who twisted the girl I once was into something new. I think of the woman I became when I lost him, and the years of solitude after. I think of the handful of men that came into my life and left when they realised how damaged I was. Then, finally, I think of the men of Browlace Manor and the way they make me feel.

My heart pounds with the exertion as I dance, my skin covering in a layer of sweat, and despite the sharp pain I begin to feel in my knee and back, I don't stop.

I can't.

Distracted by the need to dance, to feel free, I don't hear the door swing open.

I don't hear the footsteps that enter the studio, the rolling sound of the waves nor the cawing of the seagulls.

I don't see Ivan enter until it's too late.

"Rose, we need to talk…"

The smooth command of his voice, and the edge of sadness beneath it cut through my escape and I come to a standstill. Beyond the dust motes that dance in the sunlight, stands Ivan and he looks as though he's seen a ghost.

"What are you doing here, Ivan?" I pant, my breath as ragged as my pulse.

I can't even pretend that it's solely due to exertion. We both know it's more than that. There's a dangerous chemistry between Ivan and I, a blazing desire that is no good for either of us. It's the kind that destroys, not heals. It's the kind that will eventually ruin us both if we can't find a way to control it.

"I followed you," he says, without apology.

Stepping into the room, Ivan's gaze trails over me. I'm

wearing my old ballet attire. The black leotard and leggings are a little tighter than I'd like, but they still fit, just.

"Why are you following me?"

"Because I have things I need to say, Rose. I need to fucking say them before I lose my damn mind."

"I'm not ready. I'm not ready to hear any of it. I came here to clear my head, to think. I asked you for space to do that. Why can't you just give me that?"

Ivan runs a hand through his hair.Dark circles ring his eyes, and he has a three day stubble that just makes him look even more handsome, not less.

"Ms Hadley said you were determined to take the job, and yet you ran. Why?"

"I didn't run, I asked for *time*. I said I would return on Monday and I meant it. Jesus, Ivan."

He steps forward, passing through the shards of light, getting ever closer.

"You can't kiss me like that, then expect me to sit on my hands and wait for your return. I've been going fucking crazy, Rose. You drive me fucking crazy."

"You kissed *me*, Ivan," I murmur as he steps closer.

"But you kissed me back..." he says, lifting his fingers to my cheek. "You infuriate me. I can't eat, I can't sleep, I can't think straight. What have you done to me?"

"I haven't done anything..."

"You danced for Erik, for Anton. I just watched you move like a fucking angel..."

An angel? Surely he must see the demon inside of me?

"You dance beautifully," he murmurs.

"I'm nothing compared to Svetlana."

"That's where you're wrong, Rose. You're so fucking wrong! But whether you like it or not, you belong to me now."

His fingertips feather over my cheek that is coloured a deep pink from the exertion, from the nearness of his body and the heat of his words. I can feel myself giving in, but I mustn't.

"You might have agreed to my terms, but I never agreed to yours, Ivan," I reply, twisting my head away from his touch.

Ivan reaches forward, cupping the back of my head in his hand, forcing me to face him.

"I told you. It doesn't matter, Rose. I won't let you run."

"What do you want from me?" my voice cracks, and I hate myself for it. He's caught me off guard in this place that means so much to me.

How ridiculous must I look? A broken woman, turfed out from the Royal Ballet dancing in a rundown building, dancing to run from her memories, dancing to protect herself from the man that stands before her now.

Ivan lets me go, but he doesn't move away, and despite all that I've just said, neither do I.

"*Tell me*, Ivan. What do you want?"

He swallows, the searing burn of his gaze making heat rush over my skin. Damn this body that betrays me.

"Everything, Rose. I want *everything*. Every moan of plea-sure, every cry of pain, every tear shed, every whispered words of love, devotion, submission. I want to rule you. I want to lose myself in the softness of your curves, and the tightness of your cunt. I want to plunder the depths of your heart, the bottomless ocean of your soul. I want everything I can get, and I won't stop until I get it, Rose. I will pursue you relentlessly until you break and give me all that I desire. Then when you've given it all, when I've gathered every last piece of you, I'll walk away satis-fied, whilst you shatter into a million pieces. That's the only truth I know. I'm not a good man, Rose. I won't pretend to be."

By the time he's finished my heart is pounding, my hands are shaking, and my pulse is racing. This is the man behind the locked door, this is the man I'm drawn to and he'll do everything in his power to break me, to own me entirely, to make me his. Just like Roman had.

He wants me to dominate me.

The question is should I let him?

I twist away from him and stride over to my coat and bag, then untie the ribbons and remove my ballet shoes, placing them back in my bag. I pull on my boots, my hands trembling. All the while Ivan is watching my every move.

"Do you have nothing to say?" he asks.

With my coat and bag in my hand, I turn to face him. "No, not here, not in this place that means so much to me. This empty, rotting building is all I have left. *Ballet* is all I have left, Ivan. It's the only thing that keeps me going."

"This place is yours?" he asks, frowning.

"Yes. My ballet teacher left it to me in her will. It's broken, damaged beyond repair, just like I am."

"We're all broken, Rose."

"Is that why you do what you do, because you're broken?" I ask him.

"Yes."

Sighing heavily, I press my fingers against my eyes and try to think. I already know that I can't run from him, from Anton and Erik. I know that on Monday I will return to Browlace Manor to face my fate, whatever that may be. I just need the time to get my head straight, to gather the strength I know I'll need to do what I must, because if there's one thing I know to be true, it's this; I can't stay away from Ivan, any more than he can stay away from me.

"Then you'll know that sometimes, no matter how much we wish it were true, broken things can't always be fixed," I say, then walk past Ivan and out into the cold air, leaving the keys to the studio on the step by the front door.

CHAPTER TWENTY-THREE

Ivan

MONDAY TOOK an eternity to come around.

The rest of the weekend ticked by agonisingly slowly. So much so that I had to stop myself from making up an excuse to drive to Rose's house demanding that she speak with me. Eventually, the hours without her had blurred into one long nightmare and Monday morning had arrived startlingly bright with a chill in the air.

Now, I sit in my office, watching the clock, waiting to see if she shows.

A minute after eight, the sound of a car pulling into the drive has me pushing back my chair and striding to the window. Even though she said she'd come, I'm still surprised to see Rose step out of the passenger seat. She leans through the open window and says something to the driver before waving him off.

Today, her limp is marked, pain evident in the lines around her eyes and the hard grit of her jaw. She danced and now she's paying for it. A slice of anger pushes through my chest. She needs to take better care of herself.

Why? A voice inside asks. *She hurts because she dances. You wanted this. Now you can have her.*

I laugh at that. Something tells me that Rose isn't going to make that easy. In fact, I know she's going to refuse me every step of the way despite the kiss we shared and what that had sparked between us, despite the desire I know she feels. I'm not averse to the chase, in fact I positively enjoy it, but one false move and I know I will lose her entirely, and that, I'm not willing to chance. It's the only reason I've left her in peace these last couple of days.

Seeing her dance had shaken me more than I'd care to admit. Her strength and fragility so powerful against the backdrop of that derelict dance studio. Watching her dance so freely had opened up every single cut I'd inflicted on myself over the past couple of years, but instead of scaring me off, it just makes me want her more.

If I own her, then I can control her. I just need to be patient.

The problem is, I'm not usually a patient man. In fact, I'm not patient full stop. I get what I want, and I want Rose. Yet, this time, even if it takes me the rest of my life to fucking claim her, I'll wait.

I lose sight of Rose as she enters the house. A minute later her footsteps sound outside the door. Not wanting her to know I've been watching her arrive, I return to my seat and pretend to be busy, my fingers typing a stream of nonsense.

"Morning, Ivan," Rose says as she enters.

I make it a point not to look up at her, knowing it will rile her but doing it anyway.

"You're late," I say, looking at my watch.

"It's only three minutes past eight. I had to take a cab..."

Out of the corner of my eye, I watch her remove her coat and hang it on the hook on the back of the door. She's wearing a tweed, knee length skirt and a cream shirt with flat black pumps and black tights. Her hair is drawn back in a simple bun at the base of her neck, a reminder of her past. A reminder of mine. I wonder briefly whether that was a conscious "fuck you" to me or simply an unconscious preference.

"Three minutes of my time. I expect punctuality, Rose," I say, not really giving a shit about her lateness, but making a point anyway.

"It won't happen again," she retorts, smiling sweetly.

It's a fake smile that angers me as much as it makes me respect her. She isn't weak, I like that about her. This time I watch her without hiding it. From the blush on her cheeks, I know she's aware of my attention, but chooses to ignore it instead.

"Where are Anton and Erik?"

"In their rooms, busy." I don't want to talk about them. Rose is with me now. That mess will have to be dealt with when I'm calm enough to do so.

She nods her head sharply, respecting my reluctance to talk about them further, then sits down and attempts to log in. After a minute she looks up at me.

"Have you changed the password?" she asks, frowning.

"I might've," I respond, trying not to laugh at the look she gives me.

"May I have it, or are you expecting me to guess?" she snaps.

"Well, that could be fun," I reply, leaning back in my seat, watching her.

"The password, Ivan."

"Three guesses." I grin, liking this game already.

Her cheeks flush a darker shade of pink, the angry shade I love so much, and for a brief moment I wonder if her pussy darkens the same way when she's turned on. My cock swells at the thought.

"You really want to do this?"

"Humour me."

Rose rolls her eyes, unimpressed, but takes her first guess anyway.

"Luka Petrin," she says, folding her arms across her chest, mirroring me. A smile plays around her mouth.

"No!" I retort, a little too angrily.

She smiles at that. Clearly enjoying pushing my buttons. "Hmm, so not as self-centred as I first thought. Let me see," she muses, her fingers tapping against her desk as she mulls it over.

"Browlace?"

She raises an eyebrow as I laugh at that.

"Come on Rose, you can do better than that. *Think*."

"I don't know, I give up," she says shrugging her shoulders and making a great impression of looking bored. Which really, really, pisses me off.

I'm a man who can command attention. I'm used to all eyes on *me*. When I say jump, people ask how fucking high, and yet Rose is pulling at a thread on her skirt as though it's the most interesting thing she's ever seen. Perhaps she's thinking about my brothers and how they make her feel?

She fucking knelt before them. A dark little voice says, poking the demon.

Well, *fuck that*, I want her attention on me and if it means riling her enough to get it, then so be it. Besides, I like angry Rose.

"I didn't think you were a woman who gave up easily. Perhaps I've got that wrong about you?" I ask, poking the demon.

"I'm not, but childish games are just that, childish. I've got work to do, Ivan. Please, would you just tell me the password?"

My fingers are itching to spank her. In just three strides I could have her pinned against the desk, that mumsy skirt pulled up over her ripe arse and her skin coloured a darker shade of pink that would rival her angry face. I stand up involuntarily and stalk towards her. A flicker of surprise ripples across her features and I find it interesting that she didn't expect me to make a pass at her so soon.

Honestly, until this moment, I didn't know I would either. I thought I'd at least last the day.

But now that I see the way her lips part on a rapid breath, how her fingers clench on her lap and her thighs press together as I move towards her, I can't seem to stop myself.

I fucking want her.

I *need* her, and I'm done waiting.

"Ivan, I'll guess again," she says quickly.

I laugh at that. As if that's going to stop me now.

"Red silk?" she blurts out.

"No."

Another step closer.

"Saville Row?"

I shake my head. "No, Rose, that isn't it," I murmur.

Another step closer.

"Brisé?" she whispers, her eyes darkening.

My step falters... how does she know about that?

"Say it again," I demand, as I move around to her side of the desk and sit down in front of her.

"Brisé" she whispers.

A growl escapes my throat before I can stop it. That word sounds so beautiful on her lips. Those fucking kissable lips.

Despite everything I've told myself, I want to kiss them again.

Damn her to fucking Hell.

Leaning forward, I invade her space. "No, not brisé," I say, tracing a finger over that cupid's bow mouth of hers.

She flinches, pushes her feet against the floor forcing her chair back, trying to put some space between us as she rolls away from me. The wheels squeak as they pass over the hardwood floor in her haste to get away.

"Where do you think you're going, Rose?" I ask gruffly, grasping the armrests and pulling her roughly back towards me.

"Ivan..." she warns, her hands flying out to stop her from crashing directly into me. They press against my chest, and she pulls them away quickly as though burnt.

"Now, now, Rose, no need to run away," I say, my voice lowering to a growl.

My thighs widen to accommodate her sitting between them. She pointedly looks at my face, even though my crotch is in her line of sight. If she were to look in that direction, she would see just how turned on I am.

And boy am I turned on.

Fuck Anton and Erik. She's alone in my office with *me* now and I can do what the fuck I want.

"I'm here to work, Ivan," she repeats.

"Working right now is the last thing on my mind, Rose."

"This," she says, waving her hand between us, "It won't work. Can't you see that?"

"But you're here, aren't you? You came today, despite everything. Why is that?"

"I need the money," she lies.

I know it's a lie. She's here because she can't stay away, because she wants me as much as I want her. I see it in the depths of her meadow-green eyes. I see it in the blush of her cheeks and the rapid rise and fall of her chest. I see it in the anger clamping her jaw tight and the whites of her knuckles as she holds onto the armrests.

"Stop lying to yourself."

"No, Ivan! You stop!" Rose says, standing suddenly. She shoves me backwards, knocking me off balance. It's enough for her to get out from behind the desk and move away from me.

"You really don't know me, if you think I will succumb so easily. The girl I used to be might've, but I'm not that girl anymore."

"But you knelt before *them*," I spit, unable to help myself. Unable to hide the jealousy.

"That was different."

"Why? Why am I any different?"

She backs towards the door refusing to answer, and for one horrifying moment I think she's going to cry. I can take a lot of things, but tears aren't one of them. They are like my fucking kryptonite. If Ms Hadley hadn't walked in on us when she had that night when we kissed, I would have devoured Rose there and then, licking up every last teardrop and maybe, just maybe causing some of my own.

"Rosie died a long time ago, and despite the kiss we shared, despite the wicked, sinful way you make me feel, I'll never, *ever*, let her out again with *you*. In this office I'm your assistant, nothing more, so I suggest you get used to the idea."

By the time she's finished her tirade she's panting and I'm fucking hard as hell. I've never felt more fucking turned on in my whole godforsaken life.

"Who are you?" I ask, not really expecting an answer. My whole body is shaking with lust and I'm so close to throwing myself at her mercy, be damned to the rules, be damned to the consequences.

She stares at me for one long moment before answering.

"I'm the girl who once upon a time submitted to a beast. I'm the girl who danced to forget, who danced to *survive*, and I'm the woman who is stronger than the demons of her past and the ones that live in her heart. Do not underestimate me, Ivan. Don't you fucking dare! I'm nothing like the women you've fucked before, so don't treat me like one."

And with that she walks out of the room leaving me trembling in her wake.

So much for patience.

CHAPTER TWENTY-FOUR

Rose

SOMEHOW IN MY RAGE, I end up finding myself by the large pond in the grounds of Browlace Manor. It's freezing, and I have to hug myself to keep the chill out. Across the pond a beautiful white swan lands, the tips of its expansive wings breaking the surface as it glides across the water. Out of the corner of my eye, I notice another swan, the male cob, glide towards her. Their heads bend towards each other as though in greeting.

"Did you know that swans mate for life?"

I tense, the smooth sound of Ivan's voice sending chills over my skin. He steps up beside me, his hands deep in his pockets, eyes fixed on the two swans as they circle one another. Small waves ripple outwards making bigger ones, disturbing the shore, changing it forever.

"Yes, I did."

His nearness makes my body flush with heat despite the cold. I consider stepping away from him, but realise it wouldn't make a difference, he'd pursue me anyway.

"Svetlana and I danced together in Swan Lake. She played Odette, I was Siegfried... Do you know the story?"

"I danced for over a decade, Ivan. I'm well aware of the story."

"Of course you are."

Out of the corner of my eye I see him breathe out slowly, clouds of white air billowing from his mouth. It's colder than the forecast predicted, a light frost lingers on the clipped grass and bushes. The weather has turned; it's going to be a cold autumn and an even colder winter if today is anything to go by.

"Both Odette and Siegfried died tragically, their love wasn't enough," I say eventually.

Ivan sighs. "You're right, it wasn't... *ours wasn't*," he murmurs.

Silence descends as I contemplate his admission. His Odette is dead, and yet he survives. I turn to look at him, taking in his profile as he watches the swans continue to circle each other. I hadn't noticed it until now, the pained look around his eyes. He hides it well under the arrogance and the sin.

"Do you miss her?" I ask.

He turns to face me, a host of emotions crossing his features. His eyes flick to the house, then back to me once more.

"Every single day."

I shake my head, not understanding this man. Anton was right, how can I possibly understand someone so complicated, so layered, so *lost in himself*. He loved Svetlana, I see that in the pain he tries to hide, and yet he admits to cheating on her repeatedly. That isn't love, or at least it isn't the kind of love I can understand.

"What do you want from me, Ivan?"

"I don't know."

"Yes, you do. Tell me what you want from me."

I hold his gaze and wait. I don't know why, but the answer to this question is important.

"I want to fuck you..."

"What do you really want, Ivan? This is your last opportunity to tell me the truth."

He scrapes a hand through his hair, but the dark strands fall back in his eyes the moment his hand passes through it. He contemplates lying to me. I see the indecision cross his face.

"I don't fucking know," he admits. "I don't know what it is that I feel. I don't know what I want. I'm so fucking confused, Rose, and it's tearing me up inside."

I nod my head. The truth at last, or at least as close to the truth as he's able to give me right now.

"Now will you answer me one question, Rose? Can you give me that at least?" Ivan asks.

I nod my head, my arms tightening around my body in defence. I ready myself for the inevitable question. They all ask it eventually. My past may hang over me like a dark cloud, but it may as well be a beacon. Every man that I've ever been with since Roman always asks the same damn thing. They know I'm broken, and they want to know the name of the man who caused such heartache. They want to know the name of the man who set the demon free.

"Yes."

"The demon you hold inside. Are you willing to show it to me?"

I stumble backwards. That wasn't the question I was expecting him to ask.

"Rose!" he reaches for me, cupping my elbow.

"You don't know what you're asking."

My heart pounds loudly as my vision blurs, not with tears but with the memories of my past...

ROMAN LIES *in a pool of blood, a strange gurgling noise leaking from his mouth as he tries to take in a breath.*

It's no use, he's dying.

"Roman, hold on, please," I beg, trying and failing to stem the flow of blood from the gunshot wound in his chest. It bubbles up beneath my fingers, leaking through the gaps as I desperately press my hands against him.

"You can't die. Please, stay with me."

"Rosie, leave the dirty bastard to die. You need to come with me now!"

I look up into my father's rage filled eyes and I hate him with a passion that no person should ever hold in her heart, let alone a child.

"I'm not going anywhere. I'm not leaving him to die."

My father rushes forward, yanking me backwards by my arm. I twist in his hold, screaming and thrashing. "Romaaaaannnnn!"

But my father's hold is strong as he wraps his arm around my waist and lifts me up.

"He deserved everything he got. That man is sick. You're just

a child, Rosie. Barely sixteen. You don't understand what he's taken."

"LET ME GO!" I kick backwards with all my might, my foot finding the soft spot between my father's legs. He drops me immediately, crying out in pain as he clutches his crotch. I run back to Roman's side, dropping to my knees in a pool of his blood. I frantically press against the wound once more, but it's no use.

He's dead.

Roman's dead.

Inside, a piece of me withers and dies whilst another more dangerous part roars to life.

"Rosie, come now. I can hear sirens, we need to leave," my father says as he walks awkwardly towards me.

I stand, turning in the slippery pool of Roman's blood.

"You killed him. You killed Roman," I say, darkness and rage blurring my vision.

In the corner of the room I see the gun my father used to shoot Roman, cast aside the moment he pulled the trigger. We both spot it at the same time, but I get to it quicker.

Lifting it, I turn on my father. "You fucking killed the man I love."

My father holds his gloved hands up, I notice that unlike me he isn't covered in blood, and I have the sudden need to change that.

"He was a predator, Rosie. You're too young to understand that. He wasn't a good man."

"He loved me!"

"No. That man didn't love you. He used you."

"That's a LIE! I wanted it. I wanted him. He made me feel

alive. He saw me, and he didn't run from it. You've taken him from me!" I scream, my lungs burning with agony.

"You don't know what you're saying. Rosie, please. I saved you."

"No! You've broken me."

My hands shake as my finger rests on the trigger.

"Put the gun down. Please, love," my father begs.

"Don't call me love. You don't know what love is. Roman showed me what love is. He showed me what it means to feel loved, to feel desired, craved, adored."

"You're too young, you don't know what you're saying. Stop this, Rosie."

"No. You killed him, and now, now I'm going to kill you."

I don't hear what my father says next. I don't hear anything other than the loud bang as I squeeze the trigger.

My father falls to the ground as the gun clatters to the floor. Behind him the window pane has shattered from the impact of the bullet. I'd missed him entirely, so why is he lying on the floor?

"Daddy?"

Stepping forward, I look down at him as he clutches his chest, his eyes widening as he gasps for breath. But all I can do is stand and watch as his heart gives out.

Roman may have stoked the demon within me, but that night my father had set it free and I've been running from it ever since...

I PULL my elbow from Ivan's grasp, a wave of sickness rising up my throat. It's been a long time since I've re-lived that memory and the utter belief my sixteen year old self had in Roman. Now, years later, I understand what Roman had done.

My father had been right, Roman had taken something precious from me. That night I'd lost more than my virginity, I'd lost my innocence, the man I'd loved, and my father. But I'd gained something too. Something that still lingers, waiting for the right man to unleash it on. The right *men*.

Ivan, Anton, Erik.

In each of them, lies my freedom, my way to tame the demon who's been hellbent on destroying me all these years.

Erik was abused and tortured by a woman. He lost his power and his ability to maintain control because of her, but I can give it back to him. I can submit completely to *him*, because I know he needs control more than anything. That without it, he will eventually destroy himself.

Anton is different. I believe, like me, he needs both. In his artistic life, he needs a muse to inspire him, to submit to him, and a woman to take control, to *see* for him. He's willing to move between the two states of mind in order to be happy. In him I see a man who can both dominate and submit. In him I see my mirror image. I agreed to our arrangement because in the brief conversation we had in my kitchen, I'd understood that, even if I'm only just acknowledging it now.

Finally, there's Ivan.

Standing here in front of me is the man who started all of this. Who, without even realising it, opened the door to a whole new possibility of living. I see how he teeters on the edge of understanding his whole heart, and whilst what he told me was the only truth he understands, it isn't the real truth of him.

Ivan has spent his life dominating women, ruling over them,

breaking them, but there's a part of him that wants to *be* dominated. I see it in him now. I see it in the way he casts his eyes downwards, I felt it in the way he kissed me and in the constant battle within him. He's so used to being the man who holds all the cards, who controls what happens to whom and when. But I also see that he's desperate to give it up, to let someone else take control. And I can do that for him.

I want to.

You see, the demon I harbour in my heart isn't dangerous because it wants to dominate, to switch, to submit. It's dangerous because it hasn't been allowed to.

And I'm done fighting.

In these men, I've found a place to belong, and with me they've found a way to be set free.

They just don't know it yet.

CHAPTER TWENTY-FIVE

Ivan

"GET ON YOUR KNEES," Rose demands.

It's such a sudden order, so out of left field that I can only stare at her in dumb shock, my brain trying to figure out what the fuck she's asking of me.

"I said, get on your knees, Ivan."

Something in her voice registers in my brain. A tiny part of me subdued for so long begins to burn bright. Despite everything I've ever known, ever understood, I react instinctively, falling to my knees. She stares at me for a long moment, the dampness of the ground seeping up through my trousers as I wait.

"I will never submit to *you*. That isn't how it's going to work for us. From this moment on you are mine, Ivan. The only orders I will take from you will be to do with work and the running of Browlace Manor. Anything outside of that, I'm in control. Do you understand?"

I nod my head, then cast my gaze downwards, already falling into the role of Sub. Knowing Rose has control over me in the only place it counts, lifts a burden I didn't know I was carrying. A heavy fucking weight that has been intent on destroying me for years now.

"Good." Rose steps close to me, reaching down to grasp my chin in her hand and bringing my gaze to hers. "What's the password, Ivan?" she asks as her thumb pulls gently on my lower lip. I want to lick it, but she hasn't given me permission to do so, so I don't.

"Speak," she adds.

"Domination," I respond, the word falling thick and heavy in the air around us.

When I'd changed the password, I had every intention of dominating Rose. It was my way of trying to creep into her psyche, of breaking her down. And yet, the opposite has happened. Somehow, she's crept into mine.

A smile pulls up her lips.

"In a moment we shall go back to the office. You will tell me what I need to do for the day and we will remain professional. No touching, no hot stares or snatched glances. From eight until four, we work. At lunch we shall remain friendly, civil, but that's it."

"Yes," I respond, relief flooding through me. The turmoil I'd felt every second around her slowly falls away and in its place a sense of peace, contentment even.

"And tonight, I will return at eight. You will show me the room behind the locked door. You will invite one of your women and you will show me how you dominate her. Then once you've got it out of your system, I will show you how to submit to me. From that moment on, there will be no other women. Is that understood?"

"Yes."

My whole body begins to relax at the soft cadence of her voice, the firmness of her fingers grasping my chin and the warmth of her body heat as she moves her hand to cup my cheek. "Now all we need is a safe word, Ivan. This time, you get to choose."

I know immediately what it will be. Wetting my lip with my tongue I smile at the gift she's given me. "Red," I say.

"Then Red it shall be."

Rose lets go of my face and moves a step backwards. "Let us get back to work."

On shaky legs, I stand. Rose waits for me to get a hold of myself. It takes me a good few minutes to calm my racing heart and to fully comprehend just what has taken place, but once I do, I feel a peace unlike any other. Years of turmoil and self-control fall away as I walk in step beside her.

In a matter of days, Rose has managed to do something no woman before has ever succeeded in doing. She's tamed the demon within and we haven't even started yet.

FOUR O'CLOCK COMES AROUND QUICKLY. Rose and I have worked together peacefully now the boundaries have been set. She spent the morning filing away the rest of my mess and after a pleasant lunch where we talked about my business dealings, I dictated a couple of letters to some associates of mine and a lengthy email to the Freed brothers following up on our meeting in London a few days ago.

All in all, between us we got a lot of work done.

It's funny, now that I'm free to view her as an employee, a friend, rather than just an object of possession, I see Rose in a new light and I know that she's going to become an integral part of my business... and my life. Hopefully.

"It's four o'clock, Rose. Do you need to call a cab home?"

"Almost four," she says looking at the watch on her wrist. She sits perfectly still, her eyes downcast. A few seconds later she looks up. "Now it's four."

As she stands and walks towards me, the change in her whole countenance is astonishing. Her spine snaps straight, her nipples pebble beneath the thin silk of her shirt, and her cheeks tint with a sexy pink hue. Instinctively, I cast my gaze down.

When she reaches for the middle drawer of my desk, I know immediately what she's about to do and despite myself I let out a low moan, my cock already straining against my trousers.

With my head bowed, I can see Rose grasp the length of silk and pull it out of the drawer before she shuts it once more.

"You've washed it," she says, and even though I can't see her face, I know she has the length of silk bunched in her hand and is smelling it.

I don't answer. She hasn't given me permission to. But she's correct, I have washed it. I washed it the moment I knew she'd found it. Even then, subconsciously, I'd wanted to wash away the women who'd been in my life before Rose.

"Good. From this moment on, the only person you'll smell on this piece of silk is me."

Rose pushes firmly against my thigh as she urges me to give her space. I roll the seat backwards just enough so that she can take her position between my parted thighs. I'm acutely aware of the power play here, the fact that Rose is mimicking what I'd done earlier, and despite everything I've ever known, I give up control easily.

I welcome the release.

"You can look at me now, Ivan," she says, her voice firm, demanding, but still beautiful to hear. My eyes roam slowly upwards from her tweed covered thighs to the dip of her waistband and the silk covered peaks of her breasts before finally trailing up the delicate skin of her décolletage until I finally meet her gaze.

"Take it all in, because this evening, once you've finally let go of your need to dominate, I will show you just how freeing it is to submit completely to *me*."

I watch, barely able to breathe as Rose slides her hands over her hips, her fingers curling up under the hem of her skirt. She lifts the material so that it bunches at her waist. Underneath she's wearing stockings and garters. The creamy white of her thigh stark against the black of her suspender belt and stockings; lace black panties cover the mound of her sex.

In such close proximity to Rose, I can smell the heady scent of her desire and my lips part on an involuntary moan. God, how I want to bury myself in her sex. I crave it.

I crave *her*.

Rose holds out the length of silk to me, dropping it into my hand.

"I want you to take that, and I want you to mark my scent upon it," Rose says, resting her backside on the desk and leaning back on her elbows. Her legs come up either side of me, her feet propped up on the armrests.

"You're free to speak, Ivan," she murmurs this time, her eyes never leaving mine.

I nod my head, not trusting myself to say the right thing. I'm not sure I even have the words to describe how fucking turned on I am.

"What are you waiting for?" she asks, a smile pulling up her lips.

I slide forward in my seat and, with shaking hands, pincer the end of the length of silk in my finger and thumb. With the back of my hand, I press the very top of the silk against her lace covered pussy. A little sigh of pleasure escapes Rose's mouth at that simple touch. That sound alone has my balls twitching and precum beading on my cock.

If this can make me almost come, fuck knows what tonight is going to bring.

"You need to cover the whole length with my scent, Ivan, because every time you get the urge to use this on another woman, it's me I want you to remember."

"Yes..." I reply.

"Yes what?"

"Yes, Mistress?"

"No, not Mistress. I'm not your bit on the side, Ivan. Choose something else, something fitting."

My hand shakes as I hold the length of silk in place as I think of what to call Rose. Then it comes to me on a rasping breath.

"Yes, Domina," I reply, the title perfectly fitting for the woman who owns me now.

Rose nods her head, before allowing it to fall back. I take that as permission to finish what I'd started.

Holding the back of my hand firmly against her sex, I pull the length of silk upwards until every inch of it has passed over her molten core. The sound that releases from Rose's lips is intoxicating and even though the old me would have buried my head in her pussy, the one that's under her rule refuses to do anything without her instruction.

When the final inch of silk has been released, I drop it onto the desk beside her leaving my hand in place.

Then I wait.

I see Rose's chest rise and fall rapidly as the warmth of her core heats the back of my hand. She slides her hips closer, so that her pussy is just mere inches from my face. My hand is still in place as she begins to rock her hips up and down.

"I want you to fuck me with your fingers, Ivan. I want you to slide my panties to the side and I want you to make me come," she pants, the cadence of her voice dropping lower as she uses me for her own pleasure.

"Yes, Domina," I murmur, barely able to speak.

"Do not disappoint me. If I don't come, you'll be punished later. Do you understand?"

"Yes, Domina," I repeat.

I've no intention of leaving her wanting. Rose has given me a gift today, and I intend on fulfilling her demands completely.

Flipping my hand over I cup her pussy, allowing Rose to gyrate her hips against the palm of my hand. I can feel the smoothness of her skin beneath the lace, and a thin strip of clipped hair that leads to the bud nestled between her folds. With my forefinger, I slide her panties to the side, exposing her to me.

She's as beautiful as I imagined she'd be. The plump outer lips, the same colour as her creamy skin. Within the folds, her skin darkens from a lush pink to a berry red right at her opening. I trace the edges of her lips, my fingers committing to memory the feel of her as much as my sight is committing this moment to memory. Even if she were able to keep her moans under check, the slickness and heat of her beautiful cunt tells me how turned on she is.

With two fingers, I find the tiny nub that has the ability to give her indescribable pleasure and press against it gently, circling my fingers in a gentle motion and with just the right amount of pressure. After a minute of gentle caresses, her back arches forcing me to adjust my hold as she cries out in bliss. She hasn't come, not yet, but she's close enough to reveal her pleasure with the melody of her cries.

It's a beautiful sound, one I want to hear over and over again.

Using the moment to move with her, I slide my fingers to her opening turning my palm so it's facing upwards then push gently into her wet heat. Her back slams onto the table, her hips rocking upwards as my other hand holds her in place, the pad of my thumb finding her sensitive nub.

With one hand resting on the lowest part of her belly, my thumb pressing more firmly against her clit, I pick up the pace of my fingers moving inside of her. As those two fingers slide in and out in a steady motion, my thumb circles her nub, alternating the pressure between feather touches and firm strokes. Around my fingers I feel her muscles tightening, her body telling me that she is close to release. Pushing further inside her molten core, I seek out the delicate spot of tissue that, caressed in just the right way, will make her come long and hard.

Just as Rose's pants become quicker, her cries louder, I find the spot I've been searching for and press against it firmly, one finger remaining still whilst the other moves back and forth quickly. And then, like a damn bursting its banks, a groan releases from her throat, her internal muscles clamping around my fingers as she rides the wave of her orgasm.

I wait until Rose's orgasm has ebbed away before gently removing my fingers from her and adjusting her panties back in place. My first instinct is to raise my fingers to my lips and taste the essence of her, but Rose hasn't given me her permission, so instead I sit back in my chair, rest my hands in my lap and wait.

Eventually, Rose sits up, her feet falling away from the chair as she rests them back on the floor. Two bright spots of pink sit high on her cheekbones and her eyes have that post-orgasm haze about them as she focuses on me once more.

Standing she adjusts her skirt, pulling it back over her hips and sliding it into place, then reaches over to grab the length of silk I'd placed on the desk earlier. She hands it to me once more.

"This is yours. Tonight, you will keep it on your person, but you won't use it on the woman you choose to invite. When the time comes, I intend to use that on you, and when I do you'd better be ready to give up control and submit to me completely. Will you do that, Ivan?"

I gaze up at her, my eyes locking with hers. The heady scent of desire thick in the air around us. She only needs to look at me to know the answer, but I reassure her anyway.

"Yes, Domina, completely and utterly, I will submit to you," I murmur, knowing with every part of my being that this is the one truth I can give freely.

CHAPTER TWENTY-SIX

Rose

A THREAD of excitement scatters over my skin as I sit in the back of the cab. It's almost eight o'clock. Twenty-four hours ago, like Ivan, I had been in turmoil, not knowing how to control my desires, not understanding what I needed in order to be free. Now, as the car rolls up the driveway, I know exactly who I am, and what I want; the men of Browlace Manor.

As I step out of the car, acceptance settles over my skin. Tonight, I am Domina, tonight I shall own Ivan, as much as he will own me. I shall see him at his most dominant and then I will see him at his most submissive, the place where he'll finally find freedom, peace.

Whether Ivan is aware of it or not, there is a power in his submission. To give yourself over to someone so completely, trusting them implicitly is a gift. To me, to himself.

I intend to honour that gift tonight.

"Have a good evening, Miss," the driver calls as I walk towards the door.

"I intend too," I murmur under my breath, heat infusing my cheeks at the thought of Ivan serving my every whim whilst I free him from the shackles that have bound him for so long.

As I enter the house, the cab driver pulls away, the sound of the car's tyres crunching over the gravel drive as he leaves. The house is quiet when I enter, the only sound is the ticking of the grandfather clock as I walk across the floor.

"Evening, Rose."

I stop, twisting on my feet at the sound of his voice. "Good evening, *Anton*," I respond, lifting my gaze to meet his.

I expected to see him tonight. He hadn't turned up at all during the day, but I knew he wouldn't be able to stay away for long.

"You're here to see Ivan, aren't you?" he asks, pushing off the wall and padding over to me silently. His bare feet barely making a sound as he approaches. He holds a paintbrush between his finger and thumb, spots of bright colour scattered over his hands and trousers. At least this time he's wearing a t-shirt. I'm not sure I could cope with seeing him topless given what I'm about to do with Ivan. Anton bare chested and beautiful would be one distraction too many and tonight I owe all my attention to Ivan.

Tonight is for Ivan, and Ivan alone.

"Yes," I respond. My eyes trail up the thick, corded muscle of his arms covered in the same tawny hair that is pulled up in a loose bun on his head.

"But he has company..." Anton's voice trails off as he realises the potential harm his words could cause me. A few days ago, they might've, but not tonight.

"I know that. I asked him to invite her."

I don't know who the woman is, and I don't want to know. This isn't about including another woman in our relationship. Tonight is about Ivan letting go of who he once was and becoming who he's always meant to be. This woman, whoever she may be, is just a tool to do that.

Anton cocks his head, a strand of hair falling over his face. "You did?"

He seems surprised by that.

"Yes. Ivan and I have come to an understanding, one that will be beneficial to us both, I believe."

"An understanding? You make it sound like a business trans-action," Anton replies, a shade of anger in his voice and an undercurrent of desire that is more than a little enticing.

"No, you misunderstand. It isn't like that. Ivan and I need something from each other. We're both willing to see where this goes. I won't hurt him," I add, needing Anton to understand that.

In private, I will only take this as far as Ivan is able to. I understand what's at stake only too well. That's why we have a safe word, once uttered everything stops. That's the one rule that's never broken, no matter what. Tonight, I will learn where his boundaries lie, where mine do. Over the coming weeks and months, I intend to test those boundaries with each of the men.

"And you're certain he won't hurt you?"

"I'm not certain of anything, but I have to trust my own judgement this time. The same applies to you. I'm taking a risk with you too."

"I know that," Anton sighs.

Ivan may have been dominant for all his adult life, yet the fact he submitted so easily, so *willingly*, tells me that this is his true self, the one he's been running from. Anton has his own demons, though they're not as obvious as Ivan's or Erik's, but I can sense them nevertheless.

"And what about Erik? Have you forgotten about him? He's been asking after you."

"Of course I haven't forgotten about him. How could I?"

"He was afraid you wouldn't show today. He thought we'd driven you away, but I knew you'd return."

"You did?"

"Yes. You see the devastation that surrounds us, you sense the dangerous nature in each of us, yet you don't run," he says, looking at me with his bottomless brown eyes. "Why?"

"You know why, Anton," I respond softly. "Because I'm not so very different from you all."

I cast my own gaze downwards. There's a part of me that wants to submit to the dominance I feel in his gaze. I want to succumb to his scrutiny, but I can't.

Not yet.

Not until Ivan and Erik agree to it first.

I refuse to be the person Ivan had been to the wife he betrayed. Because even though I'm drawn to all three men, their acceptance and agreement of me being with each of them is the *only* way I can move forward. If they can't agree to that, I will have to walk away and never return. Just the thought makes my throat constrict in fear.

"You're not afraid of him, are you?" Anton asks.

"No. I'm not afraid of any of *you*... I'm afraid of who I'll be without you all," I say before I can stop myself.

Anton steps closer. Even though I have heels on, he's still a good head taller than me.

"And what would that Rose be like, without us?" he asks, gentler this time.

"Someone who would break in this life eventually. Someone who's afraid of living."

"Then I'm glad you've found us, Rose. I'm glad we've found you. Whatever happens between you and Ivan tonight, know that I'm okay with it."

I cast my gaze downwards, somehow not able to confront the sudden ache in my chest at the thought that I may screw this all up. What if I'm doing the wrong thing? What if this won't work, *can't*? There are so many factors that could ruin it. Me being a huge one, the three men not agreeing to share, another.

Anton lifts my chin with his finger. "I see you doubting yourself, don't. Don't do that, Rose."

"Why do *you* trust me?"

Even I realise what a strange question that seems. Anton doesn't know about my past, neither does Ivan or Erik. They may suspect something has happened, but they don't know about Roman or about my father and how I'd watched him die without even trying to help. They don't know about the secrets my own childhood was filled with and the impact that's had on me. A therapist might suggest that's why I fell for Roman, and perhaps they'd be right. All I know is, secrets have a habit of carving open a person and ruining them eventually.

Anton regards me a moment. "*Because* you're like us. Because you carry secrets too. Because within you I see myself.

Because you're here now about to walk into the room Ivan locks himself in with the intention of setting him free."

"You know what happens in there?"

Anton smiles a little at that. "I've lived here with Ivan since Svetlana, of course I do. I understand the demon he holds inside, the *guilt* that's been eating him alive for far too long. It's time he let it go. I'm glad you're the one who can do that for him. I'm hopeful you can ease the pain for Erik too."

"You love them both very much, don't you?" I ask.

"They're my brothers in every way bar blood. So, yes. Yes, I do. Are you still willing to help Erik?"

"I will do *whatever* it takes." *I will submit to him wholly*, but I don't say that part out loud.

Anton nods his head sharply, his finger falling away.

"And me, do we still hold our agreement?" he asks gently.

Now it's his turn to cast his gaze away.

"I will do everything I promised..." *and more.*

Anton opens his mouth, words trembling on his lips.

"What is it?"

"Nothing that can't wait. Have a good evening, Rose," he says, then spins on his feet and walks back towards the door he appeared from. With one last assessing stare he pushes it open and disappears, the sound of the key turning in the lock, shutting me out for now.

CHAPTER TWENTY-SEVEN

Ivan

IN THE CORNER of the room sits the same nameless woman I'd invited to the house the first day I met Rose. That night I'd wanted to fuck her to get Rose out of my system, but it was only thoughts of Rose that had got me off.

She's all I've thought about since.

In a couple of weeks, Rose has crawled under my skin and settled in my bones as though she was always meant to be there. In different circumstances I would be cautious. In business, I would never move so fast. There would be weeks of consideration, talks, contracts sent back and forward between the two parties. Yet, with Rose, none of that has happened.

I've dived in without thought. I've acted on *instinct*.

Pure instinct.

And for the first time in my life, I'm not afraid of trusting it.

I look at the woman before me, really look. She isn't unattractive, but the usual excitement I feel isn't there. I don't want her.

I want Rose. Inexplicably, I want *her*.

My hand goes to the length of silk tucked into the back pocket of my jeans. I've carried it on me since she left earlier today, and I've been rock hard from that moment. I've had countless opportunities in the few hours she's been gone to relieve myself, I could've already done so with this woman.

But I can't do that. I won't.

Rose is my Domina now and I've handed all control over to her. I almost laugh at how easily, how willingly I've given up that control. I've no desire to touch this woman. None. Yet she's here because Rose wished it so.

She doesn't even compare to Rose. Where Rose makes my pulse race every time I look at her, this woman barely raises it above normal. I just don't feel the same about her, about any of the women I've fucked before. Those experiences pale into insignificance when it comes to Rose and the handful of times I've been in her company.

Despite all of that, I invited this woman anyway. When I looked through my book of names earlier it seemed fitting, somehow, that this woman would be the one I invited back. A small part of me feels guilty about the way I'd left her so unfulfilled the last time. The Ivan before Rose wouldn't have given a shit.

But I'm not him anymore. I'm not even Luka.

I'm beginning to feel like somebody new.

Anne shifts in her chair, she's been sitting waiting for almost an hour now. When I invited her personally, I made the point of asking her name. The question had concerned her enough to not respond immediately. She knows the rules well enough to understand that giving her name was probably the end to our meetings. But she told me eventually, and here she is now.

Anne is dressed as though in mourning, her knee length black skirt and matching shirt stark against her blond hair. She's already grieving for what she's about to lose. I can see that in the slump of her shoulders and the way her mouth turns down in sadness.

She's another woman I've broken, not through the Dom-Sub relationship, but through how I've treated her.

Me, Ivan.

"Fuck," I say, the sound of my voice breaking the heavy anticipation in the room.

Anne's head snaps up, her eyes resting on me. The sharp sound of my voice breaking through her submissive nature. I allow her to look at me, it's the least I can do.

"You understand that this is the last time I will ever allow you into my home, yet you came anyway, why? Speak freely," I add.

"Because you asked me to, Sir," she replies.

She tips her head, a silent question on her lips. Despite understanding the finality of this evening, she doesn't break the rules and ask the question I know she's desperate to.

She wants to know *why* it's the end, and as soon as Rose arrives, she's going to find out.

Anne shifts again in her chair, a nervous kind of sigh releasing from her lips. She understands tonight is different, that the goalposts have shifted. That nervousness bleeds into the room, and into me as we both wait for something to happen.

She waits for release, I wait for freedom.

"Are you uncomfortable?" I ask. It's a benign question, of course she isn't comfortable. Nothing about this evening will be comfortable for her.

Her head remains lowered, she doesn't answer. She won't until I tell her, specifically, that she can. Such a good Sub. Normally that kind of behaviour would be rewarded, but the thought of touching her makes me feel numb.

My hands reach for the items in the back pocket of my jeans once more, to the length of red silk and the flick blade I always bring with me into this room.

Both are a source of comfort.

Holding up the length of silk to my face, I breathe in deeply, the alluring scent of Rose making my heart hammer loudly and my cock lengthen painfully. I hang the silk around my neck needing the constant reminder of her, not because I need it to distract me from fucking Anne, but because it soothes me. How ironic given that only a few days ago Rose's presence in my company was far from soothing. I'd been driven mad with desire, with the need to claim her in the only way I knew how.

Now that's all been upended, and whilst I still want Rose the same way, I don't have to destroy me or her to get it. Pulling up my shirt sleeve, I look down at my arm, running my fingers over the old white scars, and the newer, more pinkish ones. All of them are there to remind me for all eternity what I did to my wife, what I've done to all the women I've fucked in this room since that fateful day. My eyes flick to the centre of the room and to the stained floor. Svetlana's blood, her essence, forever captured in the dark wood of this house.

I'm not sure I'll ever be free of the memory...

. . .

"SVETLANA, I'M HOME," *I call from the entrance hall.*

I've been away for a few days to audition for a new part, or at least that's what I told Svetlana. It's not a complete lie, I was auditioning, but I also spent my evenings fucking a nameless woman I met in the hotel bar the first night back in London.

Placing my weekend suitcase on the floor, I tuck away the guilt and push the memories of that woman deep down into the pits of my soul.

I love my wife. I do.

But I can't fight the need I have. I've never been able to.

"Svetlana, where are you?"

Music filters from the open doorway leading to our studio, so I follow the sound, removing my jacket as I walk along the hallway. Reaching the door, I lay my jacket across the side table in the hall and loosen my tie. It's red, made of the finest silk money can buy. For the briefest of moments, I imagine it tied around Svetlana's wrists, her body bare and open for me. But that isn't her. It never will be. I shred those thoughts as I push open the door.

"Svetlana, Ms Hadley told me you've been in here all day. It's past midnight..."

The room is shrouded in darkness and as my eyes adjust to the feint moonlight that filters in from the high windows above, I see a figure curled up in the middle of the dancefloor.

"Svetlana?"

She doesn't respond.

"Svetlana?!" I shout, running towards her.

I reach her side in seconds, my heart beating loudly in my ears. She doesn't move as I kneel behind her curved back. She's in the foetal position, her legs drawn up against her chest, her arms wrapped loosely around her body.

"Svetlana?" I whisper, understanding on a deeper level that something is terribly, desperately, wrong.

A low murmur releases from her lips and it's all I need to fire me into action. I pull her body towards me, something clattering loudly to the floor as I do.

A flick-knife. My flick-knife.

The sharp end of the knife is covered in liquid... It's covered in blood.

"Svetlana, what have you done?" I whisper, pulling her into my arms.

Her head lolls backwards, her jaw slack. I feel a wetness as I hold her, and I pull back my hand finding that it's covered in blood too, just like her white dress. Red leaches into the white like a rose blooming in the snow.

Then I notice her wrist, the deep cut carved across the flesh and the blood that weeps from it still.

"No, no, no, no, no," I cry, my hand closing over the wound.

I manoeuvre her body, trying to see if she's cut the other wrist, relieved to see that she hasn't. But it doesn't matter, the floor is slick with her blood, I see it now in the dim light. There's too much of it. How long has she been like this?

Laying her back on the floor, I pull my tie free and wrap it around her wrist tightly. I don't want to leave her, but I need to get help. She needs help.

Getting up, I run blindly from the room and collide with Ms Hadley, almost knocking her over.

"Luka? What is it? What's wrong?" she asks.

"It's Svetlana... she's, she's," I choke out, before throwing up the contents of my stomach.

Ms Hadley pushes past me and strides into the room. I hear the surprise in her voice, then the loud click of her heels as she rushes to help. I reach for my jacket, remembering I left my mobile phone in the pocket. With trembling hands, I attempt to call for help, but I'm shaking so much my fingers won't do what my brain is asking it to.

"Shit, shit, shit!" I exclaim, trying to force myself to calm down.

Trying and failing.

My wife is dying. Dying! And I can't even call for help.

Before me, Ms Hadley is leaning over Svetlana, her ear close to her parted mouth. She looks up at me and shakes her head.

"What? What?" My legs buckle beneath me, as the truth of Ms Hadley's gaze trickles through my consciousness. I fall hard to the floor, my knees cracking on the wood.

"No. No! Do something! You have to do something, please," I beg.

"I'm so sorry, Luka. She's gone." I watch as she leans over Svetlana and presses a kiss on her cheek. She's saying goodbye, but I can't seem to move from my spot on the floor as it tips on its axis, my brain trying to comprehend the truth before me.

"Why?" I cry, tears scoring hot tracks down my cheeks, mimicking the cuts being made in my heart.

It's a futile question because I already know the answer.

She did it because of me.

"I'm sorry Svetlana. I'm sorry for everything."

The moonlight from the window dances in front of my eyes as a pain unlike any other tears through my chest. I slam my fist *into the wood floor over and over as a roar releases from my mouth. I hear the agony of it reverberate around the room as though it belongs to someone else...*

MY EYES REFOCUS on the stain, the only reminder now of what happened that night. Every memory between that moment and Svetlana's funeral is nothing but a haze of broken glimpses my mind still can't quite put together. I'm not sure I'll ever be able to.

I do remember stumbling from the room barely able to hold myself upright. I remember running out onto the gravel drive and screaming until my voice was hoarse and my lungs were burning. Then I remember waking up in bed a few days later, Anton and Erik by my side. I remember the funeral and the months of emptiness that followed.

But what I remember most clearly was the vow I'd made that night, the vow to never dance again. I cut all ties to the person I once was. I left the room as Luka. Six months later I returned as Ivan.

Now, as I stand here remembering my wife's last moments, I wait to see the man I will become.

CHAPTER TWENTY-EIGHT

Rose

IVAN TURNS SLOWLY on his feet as I enter the dimly lit room. He moves gracefully, the slide of his left foot kissing the floor as he faces me. I can see the echoes of his past in the way he holds himself. No matter how much he tries to rid himself of the dancer that lives within his soul, it will always linger in the movements of his body despite his efforts to distinguish it.

One day, I hope he will dance again. If not for me, then at least for himself.

Today is not that day.

"Good evening, Ivan." I smile gently, moving into the room and closing the door behind me. Opposite, a row of mirrors line the wall, a wooden barre running along their length. This is the same room that Anton had sketched, this is where Ivan and Svetlana must have danced together. I can imagine it now, their bodies moulded together, Ivan's strong arms lifting Svetlana in the air, her body arched, her toes pointed.

They were beautiful dancers separately, together they were astonishing.

A thread of insecurity runs through me. I will never be like her; perfect, flawless, untouchable.

"Rose," he says softly, his accent more pronounced this evening.

His eyes graze over me, at the floaty red dress I'm wearing beneath my floor length coat. It seemed fitting that red would be the colour I wear this evening.

I can hear the nervousness he feels, and I'm surprised by it given this is his territory, his domain. I imagined he would be his usual arrogant self, predatory even. Right now, he's neither. Right now, he's just a man who's baring the deepest, darkest parts of his soul. This is where he danced with his wife and this is where he brings the women he fucks. I can't even begin to unravel that.

Ivan looks over his shoulder at the woman sitting perfectly still a few metres to his left. Her head is lowered, her hands are clasped together in her lap. She's subdued, quiet.

"Who is this, Ivan?" I ask.

"Her name is Anne," he responds, watching me as I remove my coat.

Even though the sound of my voice gives her cause to stiffen, she doesn't lift her head, trusting Ivan implicitly.

I learn something valuable about Ivan in that moment. Despite what he's told me about how he hurts women, within the confines of these four walls he treats them with the utmost care and the respect they deserve. She wouldn't return otherwise. It makes me wonder then, why this room is the place his demon comes alive. I guess I'm about to find out.

Placing my coat over the seat of a chair next to me, I walk towards Ivan. As soon as our eyes meet, he drops his gaze.

"In this room, be as you always were, Ivan," I say.

"Are you certain, Rose?"

"Yes. We need to see this through."

He nods, understanding.

Beneath his tight fitting top, Ivan's muscles tense with apprehension. Then slowly, as he raises his head, his dark hair falling into his eyes, I see the man whose past haunts him still. As we look at each other, the arrogance returns in his gaze and the darkness creeps into his soul.

I see the demon emerge.

This, this is the man I've been battling, unable to control himself around me without strict rules in place, and now I've given him permission to be the dominant man he's always been in this space. Was that a mistake?

I guess I'm about to find out.

"I need to see, Ivan. You need to show me what happens in here." I'm fully aware that I've tilted the scales of power, that we're walking a precarious tightrope.

"Once I start, I won't be able to stop," he responds tightly, still holding onto the threads of his control.

I understand his fear, I do. But I'm not afraid of him and I don't fear the demon he holds inside either. He needs to see this through if we're going to move forward. We both do.

"Show me what happens, Ivan," I repeat.

He looks at me for a long time, and for a minute I think he's going to back out on our arrangement. Then he nods his head and reaches for something in his back pocket, pulling out a flick knife.

I watch in a kind of sick fascination as he pulls the blade free, the sharp point glinting in the low light of the room. Somehow, I manage to keep my face neutral, even though inside my heart is hammering and my demon is roaring. Ivan has often referred to himself as a *bad man*, but I know he isn't a murderer or a sadist. This blade is used for something else.

"She used this knife to end her life, right here in this room. The stain of her blood remains here still," he says, pointing to a darker section of wood in the middle of the floor.

I turn to look at where he's pointing, understanding dawning... *suicide.* Not knowing what to say, not being able to find the words, I let him continue.

"I use it to remind myself that I was the reason Svetlana died. Every time I bring a woman in here, I add my blood to hers. A small offering to the sacrifice she made because I couldn't love her the way she needed to be loved," Ivan says, as he pulls up the sleeve of his top.

On his arm I see a multitude of scars, some old, some new. They crisscross his skin, his guilt and pain etched forever into his flesh, a constant reminder of the damage he caused to Svetlana, to these women, to himself. I have the same kind of scars, but none of mine are visible. Mine are wrapped inside a heart that broke the day my father murdered Roman.

"And the women?" I ask, wanting to understand why he brings them here of all places.

"I fuck these women in this room because I need to rid myself of the memory, of the pain her death caused. When I find release, I find peace, and for just a moment I'm able to convince myself Svetlana has given me her blessing."

"But it doesn't last," I say.

"No."

I nod my head, understanding the complicated man that he is. His guilt, his pleasure, his pain, his *need*, it's all wrapped up in the death of his wife.

But what he wants and what he needs are two very different things.

In this room they become twisted and I need to help him unravel them. I need to show him the difference, because today, for a few hours, he did find peace when he submitted to me. I want him to find that again, more permanently this time.

"This is me, Rose. This is the man who's responsible for his wife's death. This is the man that takes more than he should, so he can feel something other than the monster who ruins the women he uses. I can't be saved. For a moment today, I thought I could, but the minute you gave me permission to be the man I've always been I realised that I *can't* be anything else. I'm not strong enough."

Ivan drops his gaze and without flinching runs the tip of the knife over his arm. The wound is about an inch long and deep enough for his blood to run freely. A very large part of me wants to go to him, to wrap my hand around his wound and comfort him, but to do that now would be dangerous for both of us. So, instead, I watch as his blood slides from the wound and runs down his arm, dripping from his fingers onto the floor below.

"Svetlana didn't understand what I needed, she was too pure, so I searched for it elsewhere. In the end, I broke her. I may as well have cut her wrist myself," his voice breaks on the admission.

Behind him Anne draws in a frightened breath and as her fear takes hold, as the atmosphere turns a darker shade of black, I make a decision. Call me stupid, foolhardy even, but so help me I'm going to save this man from himself and I don't need a stranger to help me to do that.

"You should leave," I say to Anne.

But still she remains.

"You shouldn't be here. This stops now."

Anne doesn't move. I know she's frightened, but her loyalty to Ivan remains. She'll only go if he tells her to. "Ivan, she needs to go."

Ivan clenches his fists, his body shaking with anxiety, lust, fear, pain. All of it swirls around him in a dangerous storm that needs to break before he does.

"If Anne goes there'll be only us, Rose," he warns.

"I know what I'm doing," I respond, stepping closer, not further away.

"Rose, I'm telling you. I won't be able to stop. I will just take. Do you understand?"

"Yes. I understand *you*. Do it, Ivan. Tell her to go."

"Anne, leave. Don't fucking come back," Ivan barks out.

He doesn't even look at her. Ivan stares at me, with lust, with fear, with fucking agony.

Anne stands abruptly, relief evident on her face. She picks up her shoes and rushes towards the door. As she draws level with me I grab hold of her arm.

"What you've heard in here remains between us. I will

come for you if any of this gets out, do you understand me?" I warn.

Anne nods her head and with one last look at Ivan, runs from the room.

Now it's just me, Ivan, and his demons.

"Why did you send her away?"

"Because you don't need her anymore."

"You've no idea what you've done, Rose. You've unlocked the door and now my demon wants release, and he'll take it any way he can," Ivan growls.

"I know exactly what I've done," I respond, taking a step towards him.

Ivan's hand shoots out and he grasps me on the arm, pulling me roughly towards his body. His other arm wraps around my back as he crushes me against him. Lowering his head, he whispers in my ear.

"I have you now, Rose, and this time you won't get away."

Leaning back, I twist my head to face him. "This time I'm not leaving. You don't need to run from who you are anymore and neither do I."

For a beat we just stare into the heart of each other, then Ivan lifts me into his arms hauling me against him. He strides over to the wall of mirrors, drops me to my feet and turns me around roughly.

"I'm not fucking running, Rose," he growls.

I watch him in the mirror as his hands reach for the opening of my shirtdress. His fingers curl around my collar and with one quick tug he pulls apart the material, red buttons scattering across the floor like drops of blood, my own offering to the woman who took her life in this room.

I watch us both in the mirror as his hands cup my lace covered breasts. He squeezes them hard, and I feel a warm slickness as his weeping wound leaves a trail of blood over my skin.

"I can't stop, Rose. I will devour you," he grinds out, his gaze catching mine in the reflection.

"Tell me to stop."

But I don't.

I need to feel the full force of his demon, I need to stare it in the eye and then I need to rule it. It's the only way.

Ivan's hand lowers to my panties and his fingers seek out the warmth between my legs. He isn't gentle, he doesn't explore me the same way he had when I was spread wide for him on his desk earlier today. No, his fingers plunder and pillage, they spear my hot centre searching for power over me and though my insides turn to molten lava at his touch, on the outside I remain impassive, still.

It infuriates him.

"I won't be gentle, Rose. I won't be kind," he bites out, yanking my torn dress from my body.

"I know that, Ivan," I respond as my dress spills to the floor, a red puddle at my feet.

Ivan's face darkens further as he steps away from me. I see the last reserves of self-control leaching from him. He's trying to take it back by separating himself physically from me.

But he needs to see this through. It's the only way.

Turning on my feet, with my back to the mirror, I face Ivan.

"Don't be afraid. Take what you need, Ivan," I say.

I'm offering myself up to the most dangerous parts of him. I'm giving him permission to take from me in the knowledge that he won't break me, because I'm stronger than the demon that bares its teeth now.

I'm stronger than Svetlana who took her life in this room.

I'm stronger than the women he's dominated in here before.

You see, in the second it takes for Ivan to rise to my bait, one truth becomes clear.

I already own him.

He's already submitted to me, and even if he doesn't realise it, he's submitting to me now.

"Do it!"

Ivan throws his head back and roars. The sound is pained, animalistic. The veins on his neck protrude with the emotion, the anger, the absolute agony he feels.

I know what he's trying to do, but he won't frighten me into submission.

I've stared into the eyes of a beast once before, and Ivan is nothing like that man. I had loved Roman, yes, but he was all shades of wrong. If I can survive him. I can survive this.

Ivan prowls up and down. Like a caged animal, he watches me, trying to decide whether to pounce or stalk me further. Either way, it doesn't matter.

I'm ready for him.

"Get on your knees, Rose," he snarls, taking a step forward.

I remain still. "No."

"Get on your fucking knees!"

He's trying to assert his power, to dominate, because that's all he's ever known until recently. But underneath it all I understand the heart of him even if he still doesn't quite understand that himself, and because of that I allow him this last act of dominance.

"I'm going to fuck you into oblivion, Rose," he says, ripping his t-shirt from his body.

The red length of silk I'd given him falls to the ground with his top, a splash of bright colour against the white.

"I will own you," he continues, stalking towards me.

The tautness of his muscles and the dark smattering of chest hair has my body reacting to him. My nipples tighten, and my breath quickens, but even though the sheer manliness of Ivan has my heart beating faster, and my core clenching, I remain impassive, waiting. Even if my body betrays me, I must not submit.

I need to see this through.

"I will crawl into your soul and shred it with my own. You will never find peace with me, Rose," he says, yanking his trousers down, the long hard length of his cock springing free from the confines.

"You don't scare me, Ivan," I say, with a calm self-control.

"No?"

"No."

Ivan rushes forward, and in less than three strides he has me wrapped in his arms and pressed up against the cold mirror, my arse perched on the wooden barre. His mouth closes over my nipple, sucking hard through the thin lace of my bra. A rumble rises up his throat as my nails curl into his shoulders, but still I refuse to make a sound. Ivan's fingers seek out the clasp behind my back and in less than a second, he's released my breasts from the material. He moves backwards snatching the bra from my skin, then his searing hot tongue and mouth is clamped over my nipple once more.

Inside I'm a roaring wildfire, snapping and crackling with desire and need. On the outside my resolve is strong.

I will not submit.

So he tries harder.

"You will let go," he growls, lifting me off the barre and back on my feet. He spins me around, yanks my hips back towards him and places a hand between my shoulder blades forcing me to bend forward. Instinctively, I reach for the barre, holding on.

"You are going to scream for me, Rose," he snarls, raising his hand and slapping me hard on the arse.

I swallow the scream he's so desperate to hear, refusing to give in.

Between my legs heat erupts as the sting fades and his fingers feather over the sensitive skin of my arse. Ivan rips my panties from my body, then drops to his knees behind me. The elastic of the waistband snaps, leaving a pink welt over my hip. That sharp pain is taken over by another as Ivan bites the round globe of my arse, then kisses the same spot, his tongue lapping at my skin.

A hard slap, followed by a light touch, followed by a bite, followed by a searing kiss.

All of it winds me up into a whirling vortex of feeling, poking my own demon. I can feel her respond in the heat of my skin and the twitch of my clit. She wants nothing more than to unleash on Ivan, but I have to see this through.

Not now, not yet.

Ivan slides his tongue up my slit in one steady motion. Then he raises his hand and slaps me again on my other arse cheek.

"You *will* call my name, Rose. You will kneel for me," he says, his fingers lightly tracing over the sting.

I clamp my mouth shut on the moan that he elicits, my hands tightening around the wood as I hold on for dear life. Trying to find an anchor, to centre myself.

I will not submit.

Ivan is relentless in his pursuit to dominate, in his need to hear my cries. But I won't give him what he wants. Not like this.

"You will scream for me, Rose," he snarls, before forcing my legs apart and sliding between them.

Beneath me, Ivan sits on the floor facing my glistening pussy, his hands slide up the back or my legs, drawing a trail of fire from ankle to hip.

I'm so wet, so turned on, but still I make no sound. He leans back slightly, looking up at me.

"You're strong, I'll give you that, Rose," he chuckles darkly before grabbing my breasts that dangle over him.

A wickedness glints in his eyes as he tugs on them, twisting my nipples. The sudden sharp pain is swallowed by intense pleasure as he suckles on them. Lightning bolts of pleasure rush to my core, but still I remain silent.

He lets go of my breast, his mouth popping open as he looks back up at me.

"So fucking beautiful, Rose. So responsive. I know you want this. I can see it in your eyes, but if you think I'll back down, you don't know me very well. I *always* get what I want, and I want your cries of pleasure, I want your tears. I want your fucking soul."

I stare back at him, biting down on the moan desperate to release from my lips. I don't respond, knowing if I were to open my mouth now, no words would come, just the pent up pleasure that's desperate to release.

Ivan's lips curl up in a smile.

"You won't win this game, Rose," he says, before closing his mouth over my other breast, sucking and licking with sheer determination to get what he wants from me.

But, I refuse to make a sound, and suddenly my silence becomes a commodity valued like no other. Ivan will work my body until he gets what he wants, but I refuse to give it to him.

He must break first, only then can I build him back up and set him free.

CHAPTER TWENTY-NINE

Ivan

THE NEED TO own her rushes beneath my skin.

The need to carve open her chest and devour her heart burns inside my soul.

With every slap, with every lick and every touch of her velvety skin I pluck away at the petals protecting her heart.

I know she's enjoying it. I see it in the pink flush of her skin, the clamp of her jaw, the smell of her desire and the slickness between her legs.

Yet, she battles me with her silence.

Sliding between her legs, I pull on her breasts, twisting her nipples into hard points. She clamps her lips closed, biting down on the cries of pleasure I know are bubbling in her chest.

"This isn't a battle you can win, Rose," I say, then bury my head in her pussy.

Her hips pull back in her need to escape, but my hands grip onto them forcing her wet heat against my mouth.

Still she remains silent.

Stubborn, beautiful, fierce. I want to own her. I need to own her. I need release. It's like a drug I can't satiate.

I spear her opening with my tongue, lapping at her juices. I suck on her folds, graze my teeth against her nub. I devour her, sliding my tongue up and down her length. I feast on her like she's a meal fit for a king.

"You *will* scream my name, Rose," I taunt, my fingers delving into her slick heat.

Her whole body stiffens as I spread her juices up towards the puckered hole of her arse, circling my finger over the rim, then as my mouth slides against her wetness once more she relaxes and my finger eases into the tightness, moving gently within as my mouth and tongue eat her out.

Still not a whimper.

But me, I'm so fucking turned on, so damn hard that I groan and growl as I lap and tease, lick and nibble. I want nothing more than her sweet heat encasing my cock. I'm so damn hard it's almost painful.

Not yet. Not until she cries out my name and gives herself to me.

So I continue to fuck her with my mouth, my fingers.

And as she takes everything I can give, as she rocks against me something niggles in the back of my head. Some small part of me wants more than her cries of pleasure, more than the tears she will weep when I break her.

And the closer I come to letting go, the stronger it gets.

The demon in my chest snarls and forces me back to the

moment. I find Rose's clit and suck hard. She arches her back, pressing herself against me and just at that moment, I slap her on the arse once more. The sound cracks in the air, but it's the only sound that does.

Rose loses more petals, but still she remains silent.

And it angers me like nothing else.

She's fucking with me.

She's baiting the demon.

Without warning, I pull her downwards, and in one quick motion impale her on my cock. She throws her head back, her nails scoring marks over my shoulders as she holds onto the silent cry that parts her lips.

Her chest heaves, her beautiful, lush breasts tantalisingly close to my parted mouth. The dark pink of her nipples like two rose buds blush against her creamy skin.

I fill her completely. I *feel* her muscles tightening around my cock.

And yet not a sound escapes her mouth.

"Submit to me, Rose!" I growl, grabbing her chin and forcing her to meet my gaze.

I can barely see the meadow-green of her eyes, her pupils are so large, filled with lust and a desire so white hot it almost consumes me. It licks over my skin, it taunts me with its power to swallow me whole until I'm nothing but dust.

"Submit to me, Rose," I repeat through gritted teeth.

Then she smiles, before shaking her head.

It's enough to set off a bomb within me. A fucking explosion that rips out my heart.

Grabbing Rose around the back, I twist my body so that she's pinned against the hardwood of the floor.

I'm angry. I'm fucking furious.

She has a will of steel.

She's the strongest woman I know.

But I *will* break her.

With a ferocity that I've never felt before I pound into her, hard and fast.

I use my cock as a weapon, sliding into her with determined ferocity. Needing her to break so that I can finally let go, so I can *come* and find blissful release.

Yet, she refuses. She bites her lip hard enough to draw blood, but still she remains silent.

"LET GO!" I shout, rutting into her.

Rutting hard.

Pounding deep into her wetness.

Fucking her like I've never fucked any woman before.

This feeling I have, it's primal, angry. I'm angry at Svetlana, at all the women I've fucked. I'm angry at Rose for refusing to break.

"LET GO!"

NO! her eyes tell me, even when her mouth remains shut.

I reach up and yank her hair, pulling her head to the side, not caring that it must hurt. The tight clench of her pussy and the sharp pinch of her nails against my back tell me she's enjoying every second even if she refuses to voice her pleasure.

Unlike me.

I pant and snarl.

I groan, I moan, I fucking *roar*.

The demon in me is taking over and there's nothing I can do to stop it.

We slide across the floor, my thrusts moving us over the

hard surface but still she remains stubbornly quiet. My cock hardens further at the thought of her back bruised by the force of our fucking. A tiny slither of me feels guilt at hurting her, but a bigger more powerful part can't stop, doesn't want to.

I *need* to devour her. I *need* her cries of pain, of pleasure.

I *want* her fucking tears.

Rose tightens her legs around my waist, and her nails claw at my back for more.

More. *More.*

And so I give it to her, I allow the demon free reign.

My hand blindly reaches for her throat, my thumb pressing against the pulse that beats in her neck, the only thing stopping me from cutting off her air supply is my need to make her cry out. I want her to give in. I want her to give herself up to me like all the other women who've passed through these doors.

But she won't.

She fucking won't.

And I can't stop.

The sensation building in my balls has me panicking. I'm so close to coming, so close to tipping over into the blissful euphoria that I seek, but I still haven't got what I want.

I still haven't won.

Then Rose does something that changes everything.

She brings her hand up high and slaps my arse as hard as she possibly can. The pain breaks through every damn wall I've ever built. It bulldozes through the darkness like a shooting star ripping through the night sky.

"Now you can come," she says, and behind my eyes the universe explodes.

· · ·

EVENTUALLY THE DARKNESS clears like the mist over the moors.

My forehead is pressed against the crook of Rose's neck. My whole body is trembling. Sweat rolls off my skin, my hair plastered to my head. I must have passed out.

Moving my head to the side has stars blurring my vision. I feel as though I've run a marathon. I feel as though I've been ripped to shreds, as though I've cut myself more than the one time I remember.

Every single part of me hurts. I fucking hurt like nothing else. But beneath the pain is something more. Within me, where the demon once lived is a swirling void of nothingness. It's gaping and raw, but it's *empty* and that gives me hope. Hope, that with Rose's help I will begin to close the wound, I will begin to heal, eventually.

Slowly, I lift onto my forearms, my gaze refocusing on Rose beneath me.

The smile she gives me shatters my heart, and I know in that moment she's the one I've been searching for. She's the one who can give me peace. Give *us* peace.

Anton was right, she is *the one.*

And whilst I know what that means for me, I don't know what that means for Anton, for Erik, for Rose. I've never had to share before, never needed to, never wanted to.

I don't want to now. Right now, in this room, she's mine as much as I am hers.

Everything else will have to be worked out later.

I pull Rose to her feet, and then, as though I can do nothing else, I lift her up and spin us both around. The moment her feet touch the floor, she twirls away from me. But I capture her hand, pulling her back against my chest. Rose folds into me, her leg hooking over my hip as I slide my hand beneath her thigh, the other supporting her back. We sway together like this, our bodies moulding against one another and for the first time in my life I finally feel as though I've found the one person who truly *fits.*

She owns me, completely.

On a deeper level, past all the sex and the desire, the lust and the heat, I understand that Rose has stolen something precious, but I don't even care.

I want her to have it.

I want her to rule me. I want her to dominate me and in return I will give her anything, *everything* she wants.

Rose presses a kiss against my chest, bringing me out of my thoughts.

"Let me go, Ivan," she says softly.

I do as she asks, willingly. My hands fall away, and she drops her leg, twirling out of my arms. I watch as she pirouettes away from me, stopping on the other side of the room.

Naked. Bare. Beautiful.

Fucking powerful.

"Dance for me, Ivan," she murmurs, holding her hand out. It isn't a request, even though it sounds like one.

Can I do that? Can I dance for Rose now?

My gaze falls to the stain of Svetlana's blood, to Rose's red dress that I tore from her body, and to my own arm streaked the same colour.

"Ivan? Dance for me," she repeats.

Looking down at the reminder of my wife's death one last time, I make the only choice I can.

Turning my feet and arms out into first position, I push off from my toes and step towards a future that is as bright and as startling as the woman waiting for me.

And for the first time in my adult life, I feel *free*.

When I reach Rose, I drop to my knees ready to do anything she asks. I don't think there is anything I wouldn't do.

Rose grasps my chin, urging me to look up at her.

"Rose?" I murmur. I want to know if she's okay. I want to know if she can accept this man that's still hard for her, growing ever harder as she stares at me without fear, but with acceptance. I want to know that she won't ever fucking leave me, *us*.

She smiles gently, urging me to my feet. "Kiss me, Ivan," she whispers.

And so, I do.

And as we kiss, I give in to the courage of her heart, the strength of her body and the dominance of her will.

This time I have no urge to rule her, command her, dominate her.

This time I submit, knowing from this moment on I'll only ever find peace in her arms.

My Domina.

My Rose.

My Muse.

EPILOGUE

Anton

PEELING BACK the sheet that covers the painting of Rose, I study my work.

It's far from perfect.

There's so much more I need to add to bring it to life, bring Rose to life.

In the flesh she is so much *more* than what I see before me.

She is a rare beauty on the outside, a goddess, yes. But there's more to her than that, and I need to capture it.

I *must* capture it.

I need to *understand* the inner workings of her mind in order to replicate it on canvas. I need to reach inside Rose and drag out her secrets. I need to see beyond the everyday, the mundane and peel back the layers that make up the person she is. I need to pull her apart and stare into the very heart of her.

I need to see into her soul.

And then, I must capture it for all eternity.

Scraping a hand through my hair, I let out a frustrated sigh. The need to immortalise Rose on canvas is eating away at me. It has kept me up for days. No drug has softened the hard edge of my obsession; weed, cocaine, heroin even. Nothing has tempered the need in me.

Ivan and Erik may need Rose to set them free from the demons they hold inside, but I need her for so much more than that.

I need her to *see*.

I need *her*.

And I will stop at nothing to rid myself of the monochrome greys and blacks of my sight until they bleed brightly with the colour of Rose's essence.

Even if that means destroying her in the process.

Picking up my art pad and pencil, I walk towards the large canvas leaning against the wall and push it aside. Behind it is a door which leads into a darkened corridor. Stepping into the musty space, I allow my eyes to adjust to the dim light, then head towards a room at the other end, smiling in the knowledge that very soon Rose will be locked within its four walls with no means of escape.

Find out what happens in book two - Strokes, available now to read

STROKES
FINDING THEIR MUSE - BOOK TWO

AN EXCERPT

PROLOGUE

Anton

If I told you that I've never seen the bright golds and yellows of a sunrise, the dusky pink blossom of a cherry tree, the stark red of blood blooming from a wound, what would you think?

Like most people, you'd believe I was blind. That I see nothing.

The thing is, I see *everything*.

But I don't see colour.

You could tell me how the ocean off the coast of Land's End is a deep midnight blue, how green the meadows that surround the manor look on a bright spring day. You could even tell me that my eyes are a rich chocolate brown with flecks of gold.

But I won't understand what that means.

I never will.

During the day, my life is lived in shades of grey. The light might break up the darkness so that I can distinguish one object from another, but at night I live in a black void, a pit so deep, so dark, that no light can penetrate it.

If in the daytime I'm barely alive, then at night I'm a fucking ghost.

I'm a ghost who walks amongst the living.

Every night, whilst the world sleeps, dreams filled with kaleidoscopic colour, I wade through the inky darkness trying to find a way back to the living.

Tonight, it's no different.

Along the silent hallways of Browlace Manor, I roam. I'm an apparition, as pale and as colourless as the world around me.

But I'm not the only ghost that treads the wooden boards beneath my bare feet.

This home is filled with them.

Mine, Ivan's, Erik's.

Each of us have demons that taunt us, memories that haunt us daily. Our hearts may beat, we may breathe the dust-filled air of this old, creaking house, but none of us really *live*.

We hide behind locked doors. Closed off from one another, trapped in our own versions of hell.

Ivan bleeds for the woman he destroyed, fucking women in the studio where his wife slit her wrists. He craves that one moment of blissful release because it's the only way he can find peace from the guilt he'll never be able to outrun.

Erik is a prisoner to his own memories, the west wing of the manor his personal jail. It wouldn't matter if Ms Hadley left the doors unlocked because he's never been able to escape the night-mares of his past. There's no freedom in being free, not for him.

And me? I crave the impossible. I search for something I'll never be able to have. I search for colour, any shade other than the faded monochrome that surrounds me. I use drugs, willing to chase the dragon just for a glimpse of its fiery breath, and as a result insomnia plagues me. Not that it matters, there is no comfort in the arms of sleep, only more torture, more anguish, more pain, more fucking *grey*.

It's a thankless colour. A colour that's bland, dull, lifeless, drab. It's the colour of nothingness, of the space between day and night, light and dark. It's the colour of punishment, of a father's disappointment. It's the brittle cold mist that hangs over Browlace Manor in the middle of winter. It's the colour of aging, of paper thin flesh over brittle bones, of ash and dust, of smoke. Of everything that happens *after* life. It's Svetlana's gravestone that sits nestled amongst the wood she once loved to roam in.

Grey is the remains of dreams, of whispers painted along the edge of sanity.

And the one thing, the *only* thing that keeps me from losing my mind entirely are my pencils, paintbrushes and the possibilities of an empty canvas. The small shard of hope, that one day I might finally be able to breathe colour into my life through art.

Pushing open the door to my studio I turn on the light switch, objects take shape, forming slowly as my eyes adjust to the sudden change. This room is my sanctuary. It's the only place where I feel a little less ghostlike and a little more alive.

In the far corner of the room a large canvas leans against the wall, a painting of the woman I've been trying to recreate for the past two years. Even from where I stand, I know it hasn't captured her. It pales into insignificance.

How can I capture someone so pure, so free, so innocent, so full of colour, *life*?

For months, following my arrival at Browlace Manor, she'd been my muse. She'd posed for me in my studio here.

She'd come willingly at first.

She'd laid bare so that I could draw every contour of her body; the sharp point of her jaw, the curve of her breasts and hips, the thatch of hair between her legs, the dip of her waist under a ribcage that expanded with anticipation and exhaled with desire. She was young, only twenty-two and had the soft plumpness that comes with being so youthful.

She'd been in love with me.

I knew that, and I used it to my advantage with the sole purpose to get what I wanted.

Her name was Amber. A name that taunted me with another colour that I've never been able to see. She'd told me once that her hair was the same colour as her name, it was why her parents chose it for her. She'd even told me that if she stood in the sunlight just right, that her hair would become a halo above her head, conjuring images of angels and magical creatures that I had no right to capture on canvas, let alone anywhere else.

Unknowingly, she taunted me with her words and it sent my obsession to seek *her* colours into the realms of insanity.

Mine, hers.

Neither of us got out without irrevocable damage.

By the time I'd finished with her, she'd lost the innocence she'd started with, her passion for life dwindled to the point of non-existence and I'd lost another piece of my soul.

I'm responsible for her slow spiral into madness and though she lives still, it's not a life I wish on anyone.

I *ruined* her.

I took and took and took until all her colour bled onto the floor of my studio and seeped into the cracks between the wooden boards never to be seen again, not one ounce of it captured on the canvas that still lies unfinished to this day.

She's as grey as me now. A ghost just like I am.

I'm a monster.

I seek the impossible and I will do whatever it takes to get it...

I destroy people, and I'm about to do the same thing again.

CHAPTER ONE

Rose

Above me grey clouds billow with the threat of rain as I make my way up the drive towards Browlace Manor. Ivan's insistence on sending a car to pick me up every morning for work is a kind one, but on this bitterly cold Friday morning I turned the offer of a lift down, sending Patrick, the head gardener slash impromptu chauffeur, away.

Despite the aches I will suffer later, I need the fresh air and time to think.

Tomorrow evening, Ivan leaves for Moscow for a couple of weeks to meet with a potential new client. He's looking into opening a new hotel in the centre of the city and he's asked me to go with him as his personal assistant... as his Domina.

And even though the thought of being away with Ivan thrills me, I have a reason to stay.

Two actually.

Anton and Erik.

Sighing, I tuck my mitten-covered hands deep into the pockets of my wool coat. It's been almost two weeks since I became Ivan's Domina. Every day has been filled with a new found happiness as Ivan and I work besides one another. Every night filled with mind-blowing sex.

Ivan has submitted to me entirely, giving me his body and handing over his control willingly and though a huge part of me wants to go with him to Moscow, another part wants to stay, wants to explore the newly forming friendships with Anton and Erik. But more than that, I want to understand the dangerous attraction bubbling between us. Dangerous because unlike Ivan, their demons are still untamed.

Erik is volatile, the threat of physical harm in his presence a very real one.

Anton is a mystery, someone I've not really been able to work out. He's layered, much more so than Ivan, and probably Erik too.

Though Ivan still has days when he struggles with his past, he is secure in the knowledge that I am his Domina, that with me he can submit and let go of all the pain of his past, all of the guilt, the control.

I believe he's healing a little day by day, and to know I've somehow had a hand in that makes me feel a little better about myself. It eases some of the hurt of my own past, and the memories of a man who broke my heart when I was just a child.

Erik's demons lie in his past too, but in a very different way. His anger and violence are wrapped up in the memories of the torture he was subjected to. I don't know all the details, but in the brief moments when I've been around him it's clear to see that out of the three men his demon is the closest to the surface.

But at least with Erik I can see exactly what I'm dealing with.

It's like standing in front of a lion in a circus. It might be tamed to a certain extent by rules and training, but it still has the ability to gut you with one well-placed claw. It's still a wild animal beneath all the conditioning.

With Anton, his demons are buried so deep, hidden so well, that I suspect he'll be the hardest to uncover. Just like his paintings he's layered, each colour painted over the other, hiding the first sketch, the heart of who he is.

Something about the way Anton's been acting over the last week or so has me concerned for him. That's another reason why I can't go with Ivan.

I've always been attracted to broken men, and Anton is more broken than most.

Stopping at the top of the driveway I look at the looming sight of Browlace Manor. It's a beautiful home, built entirely with Cornish stone. Ivy trails up the left side growing over the windows of the west wing of the manor and crawling across the grey slate roof. The gravel drive has a central grass island, and in the middle sits a cherry blossom tree which is nothing more than barren twigs given it's practically winter, or at least it feels like it on this freezing October day.

Beyond the thick stone and inside the manor there are still areas that are off limits to me, Erik's wing being one of them. I haven't had a chance to spend time with him since Ivan and I fought for dominance that night in Svetlana's dance studio. He's kept his distance whilst recovering from his stab wound. His mother, Ms Hadley, is taking *'care'* of him.

I laugh out loud at that, white plumes of breath leaving my mouth. My demon coming alive from the inside out.

That woman makes my skin crawl. Since the night I warned her not to fuck with me, she's stayed away. But that doesn't mean to say her threat to ruin me has lessened any. She's biding her time.

I know that, because so am I.

I will get to the bottom of her role in their lives. It's more than mother, housekeeper, ex-nanny. Much, much more.

If anyone holds secrets, it's her.

And I intend to find out what they are.

Entering our office, I find Ivan sitting at his desk drinking a cup of coffee. He looks up when I enter, a smile lighting his blue-grey eyes even if the rest of his face remains impassive. It's as though he still can't quite give in to the happiness he feels. Even though his guilt has lessened, and his demon vanquished, he still can't allow himself that gift.

Perhaps one day that will change. We just need to take it one step at a time.

"Morning, Rose. Did you clear the cobwebs?" he asks.

"Something like that."

I close the door, hanging my coat on the hook, before settling behind my desk. He watches me thoughtfully. I know what he's itching to ask, but I'm not ready to tell him just yet.

Ivan waits for me to log onto the computer before broaching the subject without asking me outright what I've decided. Gone are the days where he would demand an answer, trying to bully me into responding. That man who needed to control, to rule, he's no longer here.

"I've just been going over the itinerary. It's going to be a busy couple of weeks," he says.

Opening up the file on the computer that holds the details of his trip, I glance over the information. "Is there anything left I need to do? Would you like me to call the hotel and check everything is in order?"

"There's no need. You put this itinerary together, Rose. It's foolproof. You're very good at your job. I'm a lucky man."

I raise my eyebrow at that.

"I mean it."

Ivan stands, his movements far more graceful than they were the first time we laid eyes on each other in this office. Whilst each day he becomes a little less stiff, I fight to remain subtle. My medical condition worsening with every passing day, despite my efforts to stop it from ruling me. I'm well aware of the swelling surrounding more of my finger joints. They're ugly. I feel ashamed of them.

As Ivan approaches, I hide my hands beneath the table. I don't want him to see them. Which is entirely crazy given he's sucked every single one of my fingers and never complained.

"You don't believe I'm lucky?" he asks, approaching me.

I shrug, not willing to answer that question.

"Rose, I know I'm not the type of man to express how he feels with words..."

"Unless he's in a rage," I mutter, with a half-smile.

"I'm not particularly articulate then either," he responds with a rueful laugh as he perches on the corner of my desk "The point is I *feel* lucky. I'm grateful for you, Rose. You've changed everything."

Although I can tell he wants to, Ivan doesn't try to touch me. In this room we work. It must be that way otherwise we'd never get anything done. In this room it's just Rose and Ivan, not dominant and submissive. We can be free to talk, behave naturally, but there is absolutely no sex. None.

Being intimate now happens in the privacy of Ivan's bedroom. We haven't entered the dance studio together since that night he submitted to me. I won't dominate him in the same room his wife committed suicide. He doesn't need a reminder of that kind of guilt and frankly neither do I.

After what happened that night, I took the decision out of his hands and made sure that whenever we come together it would be anywhere other than Svetlana's studio. Besides, there's something about that space. The handful of times I've gone there, I feel as though I'm being watched. That I'm not alone somehow.

Svetlana's ghost lingers in that room, just as much as the stain of her blood. That room belongs to her, to Ivan's past. Not his future.

"Rose, are you listening? You've changed everything."

"Not everything," I reply before I'm able to stop myself.

I haven't changed Anton, Erik. I haven't set *them* free, and something deep within me really wants to do that. My need to *save* them is becoming an obsession of my own. Perhaps it was because I couldn't save Roman, perhaps it's just because broken men are the ones I'm most drawn to. Either way, it's becoming a very real need in me.

"Rose..." he starts, a frown pulling his dark eyebrows together.

But he doesn't get to finish his sentence, not when the door to the office slams open and Ms Hadley comes rushing in.

Both Ivan and I stand abruptly. Ms Hadley wouldn't be here unless it's an emergency. Ivan made it quite clear that's the *only* reason she could ever come to our office uninvited. The fact she's still allowed to be in the building makes me uncomfortable, but currently I have no reason to persuade Ivan to change that... yet.

"What is it, Ms Hadley?" Ivan asks.

Her face is pale, her mouth pinched. She glances between us both.

"Is it Erik?" Ivan bites out, his muscles tensing under his white shirt.

Ms Hadley's gaze flicks to mine, and for the briefest of moments I swear I can see triumph in them before it disappears and is replaced with fear.

"No, not Erik. It's Anton. I can't wake him."

CHAPTER TWO

Anton

Darkness looms, the black gulf of its gaping maw ready to devour me.

I don't fall into the darkness peacefully.

I fight. My arms flail, my legs kicking as I fall...

Then nothing.

No sound. No images. No light.

No. Fucking. Colour.

I can drink myself into a stupor. I can smoke weed in the hope that, somehow, it'll allow me to see.

And yet I'm left with...

Nothing.

I'm floating in a void of *nothingness*.

And even though I can no longer feel my body, it isn't a peaceful weightlessness.

It isn't *anything*.

There's no pain, no happiness. No relief.

I lift my head trying to see a shape, *anything* that I can grab hold of, something to anchor me. Something to keep me from floating away into space, from dispersing into the air.

But I realise there's no anchoring a soul that can't find peace in its own body. How can you anchor something that has no substance?

You can't.

There's no helping me.

No matter how much I want to fill the pain that lives inside. No matter how much I crave colour to make me whole, it's useless.

It's fucking useless.

My mind wanders to the girl I ruined.

She lives half a life because of what I did to her, because of the way I used her for my own gain. I'm not proud of myself, I hate that I hurt her.

But I'll do it again if I have too.

Because without colour, I'm nothing.

Without colour I'm a swathe of smoke; weightless and insubstantial.

Dangerous.

I'm a secret assassin. I creep into the cracks of people's hearts, seep into their lungs and steal their breath, consuming them slowly over time. I suffocate and destroy.

But the thing is, whilst I destroy others, I destroy myself too. I've been doing it for a very long time...

Time.

It ticks away endlessly as I float in the darkness.

Darkness that consumes me, that threatens to break up the

molecules that barely bind me together. One strong wind and I will disperse, with no strength to remain whole.

Then slowly... grey filters into the black, absorbing it so that it isn't so bottomless.

The void fills with smoke, it billows around me.

It *is* me.

I take form, the tendrils of my soul feathering outwards.

The colour grey might be who I am, it might allow me to see.

But it reminds me of everything I'm not.

It reminds me of what I desire.

Colour.

My muse.

Rose.

CHAPTER THREE

Rose

We all rush from the room, following Ms Hadley to Anton's studio. As soon as we enter, I can smell the stale stench of weed, alcohol and vomit. In the corner of the room by his easel, is Anton. He's lying naked on his side in a pile of his own sick.

"Fuck's sake, Anton," Ivan growls, leaning over him, checking for a pulse. "How long has he been like this?"

"I don't know, I just came to bring him some breakfast," Ms Hadley says, pointing to a tray on his art table. "And this is how I found him."

Her voice cracks as her hand flies to cover her mouth, and a small part of me wonders whether I've got her wrong. Right now, she seems genuinely concerned.

"He's breathing, Ms Hadley. Anton's just passed out. Luckily for him, he's puked up the contents of his stomach.

Hopefully, whatever shit he's taken will be out of his system now and he can sleep it off."

"Shouldn't we take him to the hospital? Get him checked over just in case?" I ask, dropping besides Ivan.

I run my fingertips over the cool skin of Anton's thigh, unable to stop myself from touching him. It's then that I notice the tiny red pinpricks peppering the crook of his arm. They aren't fresh marks, definitely more than a couple of weeks old, but they're concerning enough.

"Ivan...?" I murmur, catching his eye.

"No! No hospital. We've done this before. He'll sleep for the day, then wake up with a fucking hangover from hell. I'll speak to him then, but for now we need to get him to his room," Ivan says, before turning his attention to Ms Hadley. "I'm going to need Erik's help, go get him."

"But what about..." she says, flicking her eyes to me.

"I can't lift him on my own. Get Erik!" Ivan snaps.

Ms Hadley nods sharply and rushes from the room, but not before giving me a wicked look. Frankly, I couldn't care less what she thinks of me. I'm glad she's been sent away, even if it is only for a moment.

"Ivan, the marks on Anton's arm. Is that what I think it is?"

Ivan sighs. "I thought he'd got it under control. He *did* have it under control. He's been clean for months. FUCK! How could I miss this?"

"Hey, don't do that. No guilt," I command, lowering my voice to the familiar tenor that is Domina. Ivan nods, his guilt leaving him in one long breath. I envy him that, because inside I feel guilt constricting my own lungs.

"Does this happen often?" I ask.

"Often enough for me to worry about the stupid bastard." Ivan confesses.

"Talk to me, Ivan. Don't carry this burden alone. What's going on here?"

Ivan considers me a moment, conflicted.

"Ivan," I prompt him.

"Over the years Anton falls into bouts of..." He swallows hard, unable to continue.

"Depression?" I ask gently.

He flicks his gaze to me, scraping a hand through his dark hair. "Yes, partly that, but mostly psychosis. Ant loses himself for a time. He takes drugs, which makes it worse. He doesn't sleep, barely eats. Anton locks himself in this room, he withdraws from everyone except the one person he shouldn't be around because of how obsessive he becomes."

"What do you mean, the one person he shouldn't be around?"

"His muse, Rose. *You.* He chose you. I should've warned you, I should've seen this coming. This is just the start. He can't control his obsession. When he said you're the one, I thought he meant something different. But it's happening again."

"The one?"

Ivan gives me a pained look, one that tells me he's holding back from telling me the whole truth. Everything about this moment is worrying. Anton's drug abuse, the threat of his obsession that has been brought up by both Ivan and Anton on more than one occasion, and lastly the truth being held back from me.

"I thought he meant you'd be the one to help him get over his need to see colour. I thought he meant you'd be *enough.* Now I know I'm mistaken and that puts you in danger, Rose."

"Why?"

"When he's like this, he's dangerous."

"How so?" I look from Ivan to Anton. To me, he just looks vulnerable.

"Because he's capable of anything. He will hurt you."

"Not in this state he won't. He's comatose," I retort.

"I don't mean physically, Rose..."

"No one has the capability to hurt me that way anymore, Ivan. It's impossible."

Ivan looks at me with troubled eyes. "He'll find a way. Don't underestimate him, Rose."

He falls silent, unspoken words hanging in the air between us.

"Will you ever tell me about your past, Rose?" he finally asks me.

The vulnerability he shows me in that one question almost floors me. For a man who until recently kept everyone at arm's length, it's a show of emotion that's perfect in its nakedness.

"I don't know," I respond honestly.

Ivan gives me a lingering look, then nods his head turning his attention back to Anton.

"I should've kept a closer eye on him."

"Stop that now. He's a grown man, Ivan. The decisions he makes are his alone. You didn't roll those joints," I say, pointing to the overflowing ashtray. "You didn't pour that bottle of whiskey down his throat either, and you certainly didn't inject heroin into his arm. You aren't responsible, and you can't prevent this kind of self-destruction. Believe me, I know that better than anyone."

Memories of Roman pull at the corner of my consciousness,

but I push them away, slamming the door on them. I won't be reminded of that time. Not now. Not when I feel so afraid, because despite my words of comfort for Ivan, inside I feel my guts churn at the thought Anton is suffering like this and that *I* might be responsible.

"You don't get it... There's more to being his muse than you think, Rose."

"Let's try and sit him up so that it's easier for you and Erik to lift him," I say, trying to be practical and, more importantly, avoiding the conversation for now.

Ivan sighs, but doesn't push further. Between us we manage to get Anton into a seated position. His head rolls forward, the long strands of his hair falling over his face.

"This is the last fucking time I do this," Ivan snarls as he hauls Anton against his chest, guilt replaced with anger now.

AUTHOR'S NOTE

First and foremost, this book really wouldn't have happened without Courtney and Janet's support. Your encouragement and belief in me got me through the days when I lacked the belief I could actually continue to write, let alone write *this* story. I will be forever grateful to you both for truly believing in me. Thank you from the bottom of heart.

Thank you to my readers who've supported me all this time. Who've read and enjoyed my other books and who keep me company in my reader group Queen Bea's Hive when I'm feeling a lonely or just happy to hang out, you guys rock!

Know that every story I write is for you all.

And finally, special thanks to Sergei Polunin who may never even read this book, but who inspired this story and deserves a mention nethertheless. Having stumbled across the video of Sergei dancing to *Take Me to Church* by Hozier, directed by David LaChapelle, I was immediately inspired to put pen to paper and within a few hours an idea for Steps was formed. Truthfully, I was mesmerised, enthralled and utterly spellbound by Sergei. I think I may have even fallen in love a little!

So, thank you Sergei Polunin, for being *my* muse.

Much love, Bea xxx

ABOUT BEA PAIGE

Bea Paige lives a very secretive life in London... She likes red wine and Haribo sweets (preferably together) and occasionally swings around poles when the mood takes her.

Bea loves to write about love and all the different facets of such a powerful emotion. When she's not writing about love and passion, you'll find her reading about it and ugly crying.

Bea is always writing, and new ideas seem to appear at the most unlikely time, like in the shower or when driving her car.

She has lots more books planned, so be sure to subscribe to her newsletter:

beapaige.co.uk/newsletter-sign-up

ALSO BY BEA PAIGE

The Deana-Dhe Duet

#1 Debts & Diamonds

#2 Curses & Cures

Grim & Beast's Duet

#1 Tales You Win

#2 Heads You Lose

Their Obsession Duet (dark reverse harem)

#1 The Dancer and The Masks

#2 The Masks and The Dancer

Academy of Stardom

(friends-to-enemies-lovers reverse harem)

#1 Freestyle

#2 Lyrical

#3 Breakers

#4 Finale

Academy of Misfits

(bully/academy reverse harem)

#1 Delinquent

#2 Reject

#3 Family

Finding Their Muse

(dark contemporary reverse harem)

#1 Steps

#2 Strokes

#3 Strings

#4 Symphony

#5 Finding Their Muse boxset

The Brothers Freed Series

(contemporary reverse harem)

#1 Avalanche of Desire

#2 Storm of Seduction

#3 Dawn of Love

#4 Brothers Freed Boxset

Contemporary Standalone

Beyond the Horizon

For all up to date book releases please visit

www.beapaige.co.uk

Printed in Great Britain
by Amazon

30099869R00174